ARLO FINCH

IN THE LAKE OF THE MOON

Also by John August

Arlo Finch in the Valley of Fire

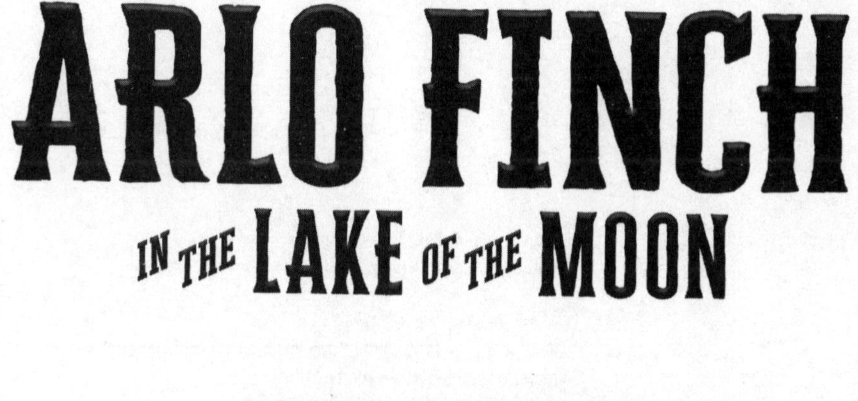

JOHN AUGUST

ROARING BROOK PRESS
New York

Published by Roaring Brook Press
Roaring Brook Press is a division of Holtzbrinck Publishing Holdings Limited Partnership
175 Fifth Avenue, New York, NY 10010

mackids.com

Library of Congress Control Number: 2018944868

ISBN: 978-1-62672-816-5

Our books may be purchased in bulk for promotional, educational, or business use. Please contact your local bookseller or the Macmillan Corporate and Premium Sales Department at (800) 221-7945 ext. 5442 or by e-mail at MacmillanSpecialMarkets@macmillan.com.

First edition, 2019
Book design by Elizabeth H. Clark
Printed in the United States of America by
LSC Communications, Harrisonburg, Virginia.

1 3 5 7 9 10 8 6 4 2

1
THE BROKEN BRIDGE

THEY WEREN'T COMING.

He didn't blame them. It sounded crazy, and he hadn't made much sense on the phone. *You just have to hurry!*

But why? What had he found?

Arlo Finch couldn't really explain. That's why he needed them. That's why he was standing atop Signal Rock on a hot Sunday in June, watching the canyon road far below. There was only one way up to Arlo's house on Green Pass Road, so if his friends were coming, he'd spot them.

He adjusted the focus on the binoculars. His hands were shaking a bit, and the vibration was making him dizzy. He exhaled, trying to control his breath. That helped. His thoughts steadied as well.

Arlo would show his friends what he'd found. Wu would have a wild theory. Indra would have a reasonable explanation. They would argue it out. Eventually, together, they would arrive at a third idea that was more or less correct.

But only if they came.

None of them had their own phones, so Arlo had used the old one in the kitchen. He'd called Indra first. She was practicing piano; he had heard it in the background when her father answered. Even though Indra said she would come right away, her parents probably made her finish her lesson. Plus she had an aunt visiting from Boston. Odds were they wouldn't let her leave.

Wu had seemed hesitant to come at all. For the past few months, he had been playing *Galactic Havoc 2* nonstop, competing in virtual sci-fi battles with a league of strangers from around the world. Arlo had watched over his shoulder, but didn't really understand the game. Arlo's family still didn't have internet at the house, so he couldn't play with Wu anyway.

Arlo knew it took fourteen minutes to bike here from town. It had already been twenty. They weren't coming.

He lowered the binoculars, wiping the sweat out of his eyes. He had to make a decision.

He could go back and investigate by himself. It might not be that dangerous. After all, Arlo had been exploring the edges of the magical Long Woods by himself for the past few months without incident. Usually, he would just cross in deep enough to feel that shift where normal directions no longer applied, where north and south became meaningless. After a brief visit, he would make his way back to the normal world, using his Ranger's compass to find a path out.

But this afternoon, just after lunch, his curiosity had taken him down a new trail, one leading deeper into the Woods.

That's where he'd found it. That's where he'd found *them.*

The clock was ticking. If Wu and Indra weren't coming, Arlo would have to go back and do the best he could by himself. It might be smart to write down what he'd seen first, in case he didn't return.

He had just made the decision to go alone when he saw something. Movement.

He raised the binoculars so fast they banged his nose. There, on the road. One bicycle. No, two. It was Indra and Wu, riding side by side, pedaling furiously.

His friends were coming.

Wu and Indra ditched their bikes on the gravel road.

When they got to Arlo, both were breathing too heavily to speak; the last quarter mile was steep. Wu hunched over his knees, dizzy. Indra held an elastic in her mouth while she wrestled her hair back into submission.

Arlo handed them his water bottle. "We have to hurry. I'll explain when we get there."

Nodding, they followed him across the tall, dry grass, where tiny insects flitted in the bright sun. As they approached the edge of the trees, Arlo could smell the pine sap in the air. Unseen birds were singing in the forest, the sound interspersed with bursts of woodpecker hammering.

In the six months since the Alpine Derby, Arlo had discovered five different paths into the Long Woods. He suspected there were dozens more around Pine Mountain, each route leading into and out of some distinct part of the Woods.

Of course, the trails were never straight or obvious. They couldn't be mapped, because they invariably required doubling back, or crawling under a fallen tree, or circling a specific boulder counterclockwise.

Sometimes the paths disappeared altogether. Arlo had spent weeks trying to find a way back to the Valley of Fire, with no luck. He wasn't certain the canyon even existed anymore. Maybe it had died along with the hag, the forest witch who had lured them there back in the winter.

"Stay close," he said, leading Indra and Wu down into a gulch just taller than their heads. A thin trickle of spring water ran along the bottom. In the wet dirt, he could still make out his footprints from an hour earlier.

Arlo led his friends forward no more than thirty feet until he felt his compass vibrate. This was the spot.

To the left, the bare roots of a tree reached into the ditch. Arlo grabbed hold and pulled. The roots shifted in the dirt, but held firm. A few pale beetles scurried out, alarmed.

Something was wrong. This wasn't how it had worked before.

"Maybe we all have to do it together," Arlo said.

Wu and Indra didn't question why. They each grabbed a section of root and tugged along with Arlo.

This time, the roots didn't budge at all. Instead, the world around them seemed to swing, as if the roots were the handle to a very heavy door. The sun slid across the sky, strobing as it ducked behind branches.

Wu gasped. "Whoa!"

Water rose up over their sneakers. The stream was suddenly much more substantial—and ice cold.

"Sorry," said Arlo. "I should have warned you." He let go of the root and they continued along the path of the burbling creek.

Ahead, iridescent moths fluttered in a shaft of light, forming elaborate patterns as they chased each other. As always, Arlo wished he could take a photo or video, but the strange magic of the Wonder made that impossible.

Indra was fascinated. She reached out her hand. A moth landed on her finger, shimmering dust falling from its wings. "Is this why you called us?"

"No." Arlo pushed through the moths as if they were curtains. Wu and Indra followed him.

The gulch opened to a clearing, yellow grass swaying in a gentle breeze at the border of an ancient pine forest. It wasn't the landscape that made this place remarkable, but rather a building.

An immense stone tower stood at the edge of a cliff. From its base, a truncated arch reached for a matching tower on the far side of a great chasm.

"What is that?" asked Indra.

"It's a bridge," answered Wu. "At least it was." It was easy to envision the intact structure, its heavy stone arms connecting the span. What was harder to imagine was how it got there, and who had built it.

Everything they'd encountered in the Long Woods so far had been natural—or, in the case of the hag's hut, primitive and handmade. But this ancient tower, this bridge, was a massive feat of engineering. The huge stones appeared to have been carved to precise specifications and somehow placed into position. There was artistry and planning behind this structure. It had a purpose, a history and a maker.

"This is what you wanted to show us," said Wu.

"No," said Arlo. "Over there." He pointed to the far side of the chasm, where a group of four kids stood beside the matching tower. They were all wearing Ranger uniforms with blue neckerchiefs. One girl with wild, curly hair waved to them.

Arlo handed Indra the binoculars.

"Who is that?" asked Wu, confused.

Arlo waited for Indra to answer. She slowly lowered the binoculars, perplexed and intrigued.

"It's *us*," she said. "Blue Patrol. *That's us over there.*"

2
HIDDEN LIGHT

WU TOOK THE BINOCULARS to see for himself. And to see *himself.*

Henry Wu and Indra Srinivasaraghavan-Jones were, quite impossibly, standing on both sides of the canyon simultaneously.

It wasn't a mirror. The Wu and Indra standing next to Arlo were wearing everyday clothes, while Other Wu and Other Indra were in their Ranger uniforms, as were twins Jonas and Julie Delgado.

Somehow, these four members of Blue Patrol were on the far side of the canyon, staring back at them. All that stood between the two groups was a broken bridge, a vast chasm and a thousand unanswered questions.

"Is that really us?" asked Indra.

"How can we be there and here at the same time?" asked Wu.

"I don't know," said Arlo. "When I called you, I wasn't sure you'd answer. I figured maybe you and Jonas and Julie had ended up in the Long Woods for some reason."

"How?" asked Indra. "You're the only one who can find your way in or out."

"And why would Jonas and Julie be with us?" asked Wu. "We don't hang out with them." It was true; other than Ranger meetings and monthly camping trips, none of them socialized with the twins.

Indra took back the binoculars. "Maybe it's an illusion, some sort of trick. Like with the hag." In the Valley of Fire, the hag had been able to make herself appear as a beautiful woman. Indra studied the group on the far side, who were busy conferring with one another. "I mean, I don't even look like that."

"You do," said Wu.

"He's right," said Arlo.

Indra was aghast. "No, I don't! That girl's hair is crazy. And she's so slouchy and gross. It's not me!" Arlo didn't know what to say. For better or worse, the girl on the far side of the canyon looked and acted exactly like Indra.

"I think it could be a parallel dimension," said Arlo. "Like in comic books. Maybe the Long Woods connect to another Pine Mountain, and that's the Blue Patrol in their world."

Wu sparked to that idea. "Maybe they're evil. Maybe the Rangers in their universe commit crimes and rob banks."

"Why would they rob banks?" asked Indra.

"Because of the Anti-Ranger's Vow. It's a whole thing."

"I don't think they're evil," said Arlo, raising the binoculars.

He watched as Other Indra and Other Wu had a whispered disagreement. Jonas shook his head and rolled his eyes. Julie stood a few feet away, lost in thought. "I mean, they seem totally normal."

"Guys," said Wu. "Where's Connor? They're all in uniform, so it's something to do with Rangers. But why would they be out here without their patrol leader?"

"And where's Arlo?" asked Indra. "It's weird that both Arlo and Connor are gone."

"Maybe they're dead," said Wu. Indra glared at him. "I mean, in their universe. I'm just saying that if you and I are there and Arlo isn't, something is deeply messed up."

"Well, obviously. But you don't need to say it while Arlo's right here."

"It's okay," said Arlo. "When I saw them earlier, it seemed like they were waiting for me. Like they knew I was going to come. They were trying to tell me something, but I couldn't understand it. That's why I needed you guys."

"What do you mean, 'tell you something'?" asked Indra.

Arlo pointed across the canyon, where Julie was readying two sticks with neckerchiefs tied on the ends: improvised semaphore flags. She slowly raised and lowered them to indicate she was about to send a message.

"I still haven't really learned semaphore," said Arlo. Between knots and first aid and supernatural zoology, he hadn't had time to memorize the semaphore alphabet. But he was sure Indra had it down. It was required for the Owl rank, which she'd already earned.

"We have to send back an *R*," said Indra. "'Ready to receive.'" She held her arms out to her sides at ninety degrees. Arlo and Wu followed her example.

Julie began signaling individual letters, positioning the flags at specific angles. As she did, Indra and Wu called it out character by character:

B-E—

The next letter stumped them. "Is that a *P*?" asked Wu. Indra shrugged—she didn't recognize it, either. Julie kept going.

U-I-E-T

"It was a *Q*. 'Be quiet,'" said Indra.

"Why?" asked Wu.

"I don't know! Ask her."

Wu held his arms up overhead in a *Y*.

"That's *U*," said Indra, pulling his left arm down to ninety degrees.

"Are you sure?"

The truth is, while both Indra and Wu could read semaphore, neither of them were particularly adept at sending it. The patrol had always relied on the twins, who were remarkably fast and accurate.

Arlo watched through the binoculars as Julie turned to the others for guidance. Other Indra said something, which Julie relayed with the flags: *D-A-N-G-E—*

"Danger," said Indra.

Julie held the flags on the final *R*, indicating that was all she was going to send.

Arlo felt his pulse quickening. Should they have been talking at all? Had they already made too much noise? He looked back at the dark trees behind them. Anything could be out in the forest, watching them.

"They're moving," whispered Wu.

Indeed, the four members of Blue Patrol were headed towards the giant tower on their side of the canyon. Using the flags, Julie pointed at the matching tower on Arlo's side.

"They want us to follow them," said Arlo. He led the way, with Indra and Wu close behind.

According to page 223 of the Ranger Field Book, one could use trees and angles to accurately estimate distances outdoors. Yet despite the simple-looking illustrations, Arlo had never gotten the hang of it.

The world wasn't a triangle, and trees seemed to come in lots of sizes. Like semaphore, it was a skill he hadn't yet mastered.

So as Arlo made his way along the rim of the canyon, he had no means to calculate its width. He figured it was greater than the length of a soccer field, but a perfectly thrown Frisbee might make it across.

Arlo could, however, estimate the canyon's depth: it was endless.

"Holy cow," said Wu, getting his first real look over the edge.

Even in bright sunlight, there seemed to be no bottom to it. It never stopped, never narrowed. It just went on forever, until it finally went dark. This canyon was a fracture in the Long Woods, an unlikely feature of an impossible place.

Wu slowed, then stopped. He looked around, unsettled. "Wait. Something's weird."

"What do you mean?" asked Arlo.

"Look at their tower. See how the bridge is broken off? There are chunks missing." Arlo and Indra followed Wu's pointing finger as he indicated the notches and gaps.

"So?" asked Indra.

"The exact same things are missing on our side," said Wu. "And look at the stuff on the ground. See the big rocks? They're in the same place on both sides. Everything lines up: tree, tree, rock, rock. It's symmetrical. Their side is the mirror image of ours."

Arlo had a hard time picturing it until he imagined a bird's-eye view looking down on the scene. The left side and the right side of the canyon were exactly the same: matching towers, matching cliffs, matching stones.

The only difference was who was on each side.

Indra pointed to the other patrol, where Julie was slowly raising and lowering the flags to get their attention. "They're signaling something." Indra put her arms out to form an *R*.

Julie held her flags low. On a clock, she would have been pointing to 6:35.

"That's *A*," said Indra. "But *A* what?"

On the far side of the canyon, Other Wu and Other Indra were emphatically gesturing at a pile of rubble next to their tower.

Lowering the binoculars, Arlo turned to find an equivalent pile beside their tower. Many of the stones were square on the edges, apparently broken-off pieces of the missing bridge.

"I think they want us to look for an *A*," said Arlo. He started climbing through the rocks, searching for one with the right shape. Indra and Wu joined him, each taking a section.

The fallen stones had evidently been on the ground for quite a long time. They were covered in moss and lichen, which made it harder to discern their edges. Arlo picked up a promising rock only to find a stickbug clinging to the underside. The frightened insect trilled and snapped itself into two pieces, each scurrying in different directions.

"Over here!" called Indra in a whisper-shout. As Arlo and Wu joined her, she pointed to a chunk of granite roughly the size of a school desk.

A faint *A* was scratched into the lichen.

"What are we supposed to do with it?" asked Wu. The trio looked back at the patrol on the far side of the canyon, where everyone was miming a lifting motion.

"There must be something underneath," suggested Arlo.

Indra was dubious. "It's too heavy. We could never lift it."

"Maybe we can tip it," said Wu. "If we all push on one side, we can get it on its edge."

Standing shoulder to shoulder, the trio each found a spot on the massive block. On a silent three-count, they started heaving with all their might. The massive stone finally moved, one edge lifting off the ground almost six inches.

"Can you hold it?" asked Arlo.

"No!" said Wu and Indra in loud whispers. But Arlo suspected they probably could, if only for a few seconds.

"Just try!" Arlo took his right hand off the block, feeling blindly under the granite. The dirt was wet and cold. He touched something he assumed was a worm. It wriggled away.

Indra suddenly gasped, her hands slipping a bit. "Hurry!"

Arlo reached deeper under the stone, sweeping with his whole arm. If his friends lost their grip, he'd be pinned or worse. But he was certain there had to be something hidden here.

Indra and Wu were straining. He could see it in their faces, their knuckles going white. They braced their bodies against the block, desperate to keep it up.

"Arlo, get your hand out!" whispered Indra. "We can't hold it!"

Arlo kept reaching, now all the way up to his shoulder.

Wu grimaced, the stone sliding through his hands. "It's gonna drop!"

Just then, Arlo felt it. Something metal. Something that shouldn't be there. He grabbed it.

The massive stone suddenly crashed down. "Arlo!" gasped Indra.

Arlo rolled back onto his butt. He had just gotten clear. His right arm was still attached and unsquished.

He smiled. "I got it."

He held up a metal flashlight. It was standard-issue, the kind that took two D batteries. Originally silver, it was now completely rusted. Even the lens was cloudy, the bulb barely visible through the glass.

"Does it work?" asked Wu, helping Arlo to his feet.

Arlo tried the switch. It took the strength of both thumbs to slide it. Once it finally scraped into position, he checked the bulb. Nothing.

"Batteries only last a few years," said Indra. "It's probably rusted inside, too."

Arlo held the flashlight over his head, showing it to the patrol across the canyon. Their reaction was immediate: jumping and high fives. He hadn't seen that kind of enthusiasm since the Alpine Derby.

"Why are they so excited?" asked Indra. "It's just an old flashlight."

"Maybe it's actually a light saber," said Wu. He took it from Arlo, holding it like the hilt of a sword. He shook it, trying to get it to activate. But nothing happened. "It might need a code word."

"Or maybe it really is a flashlight," said Indra.

"There could be something inside it," said Arlo. "Like a map or something." Wu tried twisting it open. It was badly rusted.

Indra stopped him. "Wait! They don't want you doing that." Indeed, on the far side of the canyon, the four Blue Patrol members were waving their hands frantically and shaking their heads.

"Maybe it's a grenade or something," said Arlo. Wu handed Indra the flashlight like a hot potato.

"They're moving again," said Arlo. He watched through the

binoculars as the other patrol headed for their tower. They disappeared behind it, then emerged from an entrance onto the broken bridge itself.

Other Wu gestured directly to Arlo—*C'mon!*

That's when Arlo spotted it—something he didn't tell Wu or Indra.

On the left shoulder of Other Wu's uniform was a patch with two red bars. Arlo knew exactly what it represented—not a rank, but a position: *patrol leader.*

Maybe that explained why Connor was missing from the other Blue Patrol.

On that side of the canyon, Wu was in charge.

3
THE CATCH

AN ARCHED PASSAGE ran through the center of each tower, the worn granite slabs of the floor extending to become what was left of the fallen bridge.

To Arlo, it resembled an open mouth with its tongue sticking out. Across the canyon, the other tower was poking out its tongue as well. They were like two bratty siblings petrified in childish bickering.

"Who do you think built this?" asked Wu as they made their way through the arch. "The Eldritch?"

That was Arlo's guess as well. He knew almost nothing about the civilization that lived on the far side of the Long Woods—in the Realm—but something felt familiarly odd about this place, from the oversized proportions to the ornate metalwork of the gates dangling from their hinges. It was all grander than it needed to be, more artistic.

"Whoever they were," said Indra, "they were hauling something." She pointed to the deep grooves in the stone, presumably worn down by wheels.

What were they transporting? wondered Arlo. *And where were they taking it?*

The trio emerged from the tower to find themselves on the bridge itself. The remaining spur extended roughly a quarter of the way across the canyon before abruptly ending. Arlo noted that there was no railing. Stepping just five feet left or five feet right would send one falling over the edge into the bottomless chasm.

As they moved forward, Arlo chose to stay smack in the center, between the two grooves.

The four Rangers on the far side of the canyon had come to the end of their bridge segment. Other Wu motioned for them to circle up to discuss something. *Just like a patrol leader would do,* thought Arlo.

Wu had always been one to blurt out whatever he was thinking, a contrarian rather than a consensus builder. But Other Wu seemed to be listening to the patrol's opinions, nodding along.

A decision was reached. As the huddle broke up, Jonas approached the broken edge of the bridge. He waved to Arlo across the gap, then made a beckoning motion. He held both his hands out, ready to catch.

"What's he doing?" whispered Indra.

"I think he wants us to throw him the flashlight," said Arlo.

"No," said Wu. "He wants *you* to throw it to him."

Indeed, Jonas was pointing emphatically at Arlo. When Arlo gestured handing off the flashlight to Wu, Jonas waved his hands no.

It was time for their own huddle.

"We can't just give it to them," said Wu, glancing back at the patrol. "We don't know who they are."

"They're us," said Arlo. "Well, *you*. They're Blue Patrol."

Wu corrected him: "They *look like* us . . ."

"I don't look like that," said Indra.

Wu rolled his eyes. "Fine. The point is, they could be impostors. Or Eldritch! Maybe they can't even speak English, and that's why they're not talking. Or maybe they're holograms!"

Indra scoffed. "Why would they be holograms? You're being ridiculous."

Wu said nothing, quietly seething. Arlo had seen this happen more and more often over the past few months: Indra brusquely dismissing Wu's ideas. She seemed to be unaware of how much it stung, or why Wu had stopped inviting her over to pan for gold in the creek behind his house. *Are they even friends?* he wondered. *Or are they both just friends with me?*

Arlo tried to refocus the discussion. "Why would they impersonate you guys but not me?"

"Maybe because you trust us more than you trust yourself," said Indra. "I mean, if you saw another Arlo Finch over there, you'd be wondering who he really was. But because they look like me and Wu, you're probably going to do whatever they tell you."

Arlo was a little offended, but had to admit she was right. His instinct was to trust his friends.

"Well, what do you think we should do?" As he said it, Arlo realized he was proving her point. He was always relying on Indra and Wu's advice. He had a hard time making decisions on his own.

Wu shrugged. "You're going to do whatever Indra tells you to do. You'll side with her. Because that's what always happens."

Arlo was stunned. "No, it's not," he said—though he couldn't think of any examples to prove his point. He didn't like being in the middle of this.

Indra turned on Wu: "Why are you being weird?"

"Because I don't know why I'm here," snapped Wu. "Or there." He pointed across the canyon. "You're the super Ranger know-it-all. Arlo is the one with mystical-destiny stuff. I'm just the other guy."

You're patrol leader, thought Arlo. *At least on the other side of the canyon.*

Indra looked at Arlo. "You found the flashlight. It's your decision."

Arlo peered across the canyon at Blue Patrol. Maybe his friends were right: he was a follower rather than a leader. Part of that was because he'd moved three times in the last three years; he was always the new kid trying to learn names. But part of it was just his personality. Some kids loved the spotlight. Arlo loved standing a few feet away, where it wasn't so bright.

Still, watching from the sidelines helped Arlo spot things other people might miss. He recognized the way Other Julie looked at her brother, a mix of sisterly concern and annoyance. He saw Other Jonas's physical confidence, his focus. He observed how Other Indra nervously twisted her hair, always scanning for new threats. He saw Other Wu biting his lip as his head bobbed up and down, as if willing the future to work a specific way.

The choice was obvious.

"They're not impostors," he said. "I don't know why they need this flashlight, but they do. So I'm going to give it to them."

Arlo carefully approached the edge of the bridge, willing himself to not look down. The final few stones sloped a bit, not fully supported. He inched forward as far as he dared. A cold breeze dried the sweat on his forehead.

The other patrol had picked Jonas as their receiver. He held out his hands, ready to catch, but Arlo wondered if he could even throw it that far. Together, the two sections of bridge spanned approximately half the canyon. But that still left quite a distance. Even under perfect conditions, with no crosswind and no bottomless chasm, Arlo wasn't sure he could make it.

He needed to test it out first.

Tucking the flashlight into his waistband, he picked up a crumbled fragment from the bridge. It was the wrong shape, but roughly the same weight as the flashlight.

Jonas recognized what he was doing and gave a thumbs-up.

Arlo silently debated between overhand and underhand, settling on the latter. He lobbed the rock at Jonas. It traced a gentle arc in the air. Jonas reached up and snagged it with both hands.

A perfect toss and a perfect catch. Easy. Rangers on both sides of the canyon silently cheered.

Now it was time for the real thing. The rusty flashlight felt gritty in his hand. It was also a bit heavier than he had expected. He was suddenly less confident about his throw. Even if he repeated the last toss exactly, it might not make it. But if he tried to throw even ten percent harder, he might overshoot. Since the bridge had no railing, it could easily bounce over the edge.

But was the flashlight really any heavier than the rock? He began second-guessing his second-guessing.

Shaking off his doubts, he locked eyes with Jonas. They were both ready. They only had one chance.

Arlo threw the flashlight.

The moment it left his hand, he knew he'd messed up. Some drop of stray adrenaline had goosed his arm, causing him to throw too hard. Plus he'd given it an extra flick of the wrist. The flashlight was now tumbling end over end. All he could do was watch as it sailed across the endless void, off course and uncatchable.

Jonas knew it was doomed. It was going to fly over his head, and maybe over the edge of the bridge. He turned to the rest of the patrol.

Other Indra stretched up her arms, but she wasn't anywhere close to it. Julie squeezed her eyes shut. Only Other Wu was in the vicinity.

The flashlight clanged on the bridge just left of center, ten feet from the nearest Ranger. It skidded and scraped before finally coming to a rest.

Arlo breathed a sigh of relief. At least it hadn't gone over.

Except that momentum kept the flashlight rolling towards the edge. It was a foot away. Six inches. Three. Two. One . . .

Other Wu dived for it. Arlo expected to see the flashlight dropping into the chasm below.

But it didn't.

After a few seconds, Other Wu rolled over onto his back, holding up the rusted flashlight like an Olympic torch. He'd done it. He'd saved it.

The patrol huddled around him, silently celebrating. Other Wu seemed scraped up, but otherwise unhurt.

Arlo stepped back from the edge. He resumed breathing, smiling with relief.

Indra was watching the other side through the binoculars. She seemed puzzled. "They're opening it."

"What do you mean?" said Arlo.

"The flashlight. They're unscrewing it."

Arlo took the binoculars. The other patrol kept moving around, so it was hard to focus on exactly what they were doing. But he saw the flashlight in two pieces, and then an object being slid out. It was wrapped in blue cloth. All he knew was, "It wasn't batteries inside. It was something else."

"We shouldn't have given it to them," said Wu.

"Can you see what it is?" asked Indra. "What was in it?"

Arlo adjusted the focus on the binoculars, but couldn't get a clear image of the bundle.

Other Indra turned back to look directly at Arlo. She could see him watching through the binoculars.

She held a finger to her lips: *silence*. Then she nodded with a smile, heading off with her patrol towards the tower arch. They seemed to be in a hurry.

"Wait, they're leaving?" asked Wu.

Arlo watched as Jonas discarded the rusted flashlight. It rolled off the edge of the bridge, falling into the bottomless chasm. The flashlight was just the container; they had only wanted what was inside.

And Arlo would never know what it was.

He felt something rising inside him. It was more than curiosity. More than a question. It was anger. Betrayal. Whatever was hidden in the flashlight, he had found it for them.

He had risked his arm and his friends to retrieve it.

He had a right to know.

Arlo Finch shouted at the top of his voice: "TELL ME WHAT IT IS!"

After so many minutes of whispering, it was jarring to feel his whole body shaking with the words. But it felt good, too. A release.

On the far bridge, the patrol turned to face him, stunned and panicked. Jonas and Julie were backing away.

Other Wu and Other Indra traded a look. They yelled at the same time: "Run!"

Then they took their own advice, racing to catch up with the twins. The whole patrol disappeared into the mouth of the tower. For just a moment, Arlo thought he saw a fifth person in the passage.

Arlo turned back to face Indra and Wu. All three were confused.

Then they heard the sound.

Technically, it was a howl. But had Arlo encountered it out of context, he might have thought it was a fork scraping across a steel drum, or a peal of thunder slowed down and distorted. It made his bones vibrate. He could feel it in his teeth and jaw.

"There!" shouted Indra, pointing to the far tower. A massive arm was reaching over the top of the bridge from the chasm below. Finding a handhold, a mottled green creature began pulling itself up.

His hands shaking, Arlo lifted the binoculars.

A second arm grabbed hold of the bridge. The creature's skin was dried and cracked, with tufts of hair sprouting in random places. Finally, the monster's head rose up over the edge. Its yellow eyes were set far apart, its face smushed like discarded clay.

Arlo, Wu and Indra were so busy staring across the canyon, they failed to notice an identical beast rising right behind them.

And then it howled.

The trio spun around to face it. Arlo dropped the binoculars. He heard them smash.

The creature climbed all the way up onto their bridge. It sat back on its haunches like a baboon, yet it was easily fifteen feet tall. It took up the entire width of the bridge, blocking the entrance to the tower.

And it smelled as bad as it looked: a combination of rotten garbage, dead skunk and a backed-up toilet. The stench was so strong that Arlo's eyes watered.

"I think it's a troll," said Indra. She tried to back away, but there were only a few feet of bridge left. Three more steps and they'd be falling into the bottomless chasm.

Wu looked at her. "How do we . . ."

"I don't know."

Arlo had stopped carrying a salt shaker in his pocket, but this didn't feel like the kind of creature it would work on anyway. Salt dispelled summoned creatures; this was the troll's lair. They were the trespassers.

The troll was slowly approaching, its clawed hands gripping the sides of the bridge. Its mouth opened in a smile of broken teeth.

Wu grabbed Arlo's arm. "Use a snaplight. Like the hag."

Months before, during the Alpine Derby, Arlo had managed his first-ever snaplight. It erupted from his fingers with such force that it knocked the forest witch down. But ever since, Arlo's snaplights had been completely unremarkable, no better or different than any other Ranger's.

Still, they had nothing to lose. Arlo cocked his arm back, rubbing his fingers to generate the familiar tingle. Then he snapped his hand forward, sending a glowing ball of light streaking at the troll.

The snaplight hit the beast square in the face. And did nothing—it was just an ordinary snaplight. The troll barely registered that it had happened.

It kept approaching. Indra and Wu grabbed Arlo's arm. They took another step back. Arlo's gaze drifted over the edge of the broken bridge. He felt a wave of vertigo.

The troll reached for them. Its claws were black and splintered, like charred wood from a dead campfire.

Then, from the far side of the canyon, came another unearthly howl.

The troll looked past them, its attention suddenly drawn to the other tower. Arlo risked a look back.

The troll on the far bridge had evidently stopped pursuing Blue Patrol. Now it was focused on them—or more precisely, on the creature that was about to eat them. It leaned forward, bellowing again.

The troll on their side howled back, standing taller. These were identical monsters, right down to the scars. But at this moment, they were two predators fighting over a meal, or territory.

Wu was the first to recognize the opportunity this presented. "C'mon!"

He led the way, charging straight at the troll. He ducked between its legs and kept going. Arlo and Indra were a few feet behind him. They didn't dare look back.

The arch of the tower was just ahead.

A new howl, one of frustration. Then claws. The troll was following them.

Wu didn't stop running until he'd made it through the tower. Only then did he turn back. Arlo and Indra crashed into him, all three falling in the yellow grass.

The troll was too big for the tower arch. It stared at them through the passage and howled in frustration.

Arlo and his friends got to their feet. For the moment, they were safe.

The troll climbed away—Arlo couldn't tell where it went.

"Can you get us out of here?" asked Wu.

Arlo pulled the Ranger's compass from his pocket. His hands were shaking so much he wasn't sure he'd be able to feel the subtle vibrations. He took a deep breath, trying to quiet himself.

"Do you hear that?" asked Indra.

He did: scraping. It was coming from the canyon. But where, exactly?

Then he saw it. The troll was climbing around the outside of the tower, its claws digging into the stone. It was going to get to them, one way or another.

Wu ran for the forest, headed for the ravine that had brought them there.

"No," shouted Arlo. "This way!"

He led them down a different path. There wasn't time to consult the compass. He was working off a combination of instinct and memory. Over that log, behind that tree, around that rock.

The troll was following them, but the forest was slowing it

down. They could duck and scramble; the huge beast could only smash its way through the trees and brush.

His heart pounding, Arlo led them into an aspen grove. The straight white tree trunks were dizzying, and closely spaced. The troll would have a hard time following them here.

But something was wrong. Arlo stopped short.

"What is it?" asked Indra.

"I took a wrong turn. This isn't the way."

"Well, find a new way," said Wu. "Any way!"

Arlo consulted his compass, slowly turning in a circle. Out of the corner of his eye, he could see the troll coming. Its massive arms knocked entire trees out of its path.

"Hurry," said Wu.

"Don't rush him!" snapped Indra.

Arlo wanted to yell for both of them to shut up. In the months he'd been practicing finding his way in and out of the Long Woods, he had learned he had to be still, so quiet he could hear the leaves quaking in the breeze. He had to retreat inside himself while simultaneously imagining himself distant.

In order to find a path, he needed to be tiny and vast.

The compass vibrated. He'd found something. "This way!"

The new path led deeper into the aspen grove, across a burbling stream. Straight ahead lay a massive boulder, cleaved straight down the middle. Arlo took them right into the gap, wedging his shoulder in to scoot sideways.

It was a very tight fit, but he made good progress. He looked back to see Indra and Wu behind him. By the time the troll arrived, they had moved beyond the reach of its claws.

The beast howled, then seemed to smile as it got a new idea. It headed left, out of sight.

"It's just going to be waiting for us on the far side," said Wu.

Arlo was confident: "No, it's not."

A few shimmies later, Arlo emerged from the gap to find himself in a new forest. The light was different. So were the bird songs.

They weren't in the Long Woods anymore.

He waited for Indra and Wu, catching his breath. He could still feel his pulse beating in his ears.

Ahead, the forest opened up. Together, they stepped out of the trees to find themselves on the shoulder of a two-lane asphalt road. Arlo had never been so glad to see blacktop.

"Where are we?" asked Indra.

Wu dug something out of his pocket. "Hold on."

He pulled out a phone.

It wasn't the latest model, but its mere existence was remarkable. None of the sixth graders in Pine Mountain had a phone. They weren't allowed in school, or on Rangers campouts. Yet Wu had one. *Why didn't he tell me?* Arlo wondered. *And why don't I have his number?*

Wu was checking the maps app. He whistled, surprised, then showed them the screen.

"There's Pine Mountain. And that dot, that's us. We're twenty miles away."

4

A RIDE HOME

"COULD BE KETCHUP, could be blood," said Uncle Wade, examining the dark red splotch on the seat belt latch. "I've had my share of french fries and roadkill in that seat there, so I'd say the odds are about even. Either way, it's dry, so it's not gonna bite you."

Indra reluctantly took the seat belt back from Wade and snapped it into the buckle.

Wade rarely had passengers in his pickup truck. Arlo suspected that he and Wu were the first to use the narrow jump seats in the back. They had to sit sideways with their feet resting on a heap of scrap pine, copper wire and industrial trash bags.

After considerable discussion, they had decided that Arlo's uncle was the best choice to pick them up at the edge of the highway. He would ask the fewest questions, and was unlikely to tell any of their parents that the three of them had wandered twenty miles out of town.

During the phone call, Wade had grumbled, complaining that he had way too much work to finish. But with Arlo's mother and sister both gone for the day, Wade was ostensibly responsible for his nephew's safety.

"So, what, did you guys get lost out there?" he asked, pulling back onto the highway.

"We sort of got turned around," said Arlo. It wasn't a lie, exactly.

Wade caught his eye in the rearview mirror. "If a person was to ask, like your mother or one of these kids' parents, might be good not to be too specific about how far out of town you ended up. Because that might raise some questions about exactly what you were doing." He paused. "If you understand what I'm saying, a nod might be appropriate."

All three kids nodded.

"Then we'll say no more."

Back in the winter, Wade had helped Arlo dispel the ferocious Night Mare that had smashed its way through the house. Together, they had cleaned up the mess, and never spoke of it again.

Uncle Wade seemed good at keeping secrets.

As they came around a bend, Wade slowed the truck, studying a lump of fur at the edge of the road up ahead. Arlo knew he was deciding whether it was worth stopping to collect it.

Wade declined, shaking his head. "Folks drive too fast on these roads. Anything above forty, and squish. There's nothing left to salvage. No one wants to buy tire tracks, trust me."

Uncle Wade knew a lot about the market for dead animals.

His taxidermy business had suddenly taken off. He had begrudgingly allowed his friend Nacho to build a website showcasing a few of his best works. Wade distrusted the internet and people who used it, so he didn't bother pointing out that there was a typo in the address: *bellmantaxidery.com*, missing the second *m*. But then the calls started coming. Those pieces in the photos, were they for sale? What else did he have? Could he ship to Japan?

Then a ski lodge in Jackson Hole had offered Wade a major commission. ("That's when rich people tell you what art is," Wade had explained.) He had spent six months working on a new series depicting a dark kingdom of raccoon lords and goose warriors. Now he was three weeks late, and needed to deliver by Friday or risk being sued. He had taken to napping on a cot in his workshop, a few hours here and there.

Indra and Wu had always been intrigued by Arlo's uncle, but had never actually spoken to him. This was their chance.

"Did you ever stuff a jackalope?" asked Wu.

"Most jackalopes you see, that's just antlers glued on a rabbit," said Wade. "'Frankensteins,' we call them in the trade. No artistry in that."

He hadn't actually answered Wu's question, a pattern Arlo had come to expect. No matter what the topic, Wade seemed impervious to direct inquiry.

"You were in Rangers, weren't you?" asked Indra.

Wade didn't look over. "Most boys were, back in the day." It was strange to think of Wade ever being young.

"Which patrol were you in?"

"Green, mostly."

"What do you mean, 'mostly'?" she asked.

"I mean Green."

"Not Yellow?"

"There is no Yellow Patrol." Arlo noticed Wade shifting tenses as well as his grip on the steering wheel. "There weren't girls in Rangers back then, either. It was a different time. People used to smoke cigarettes, even though it was pretty well known that they would kill you."

Indra wasn't ready to switch topics. "Arlo had a yellow neckerchief. He said it was yours." She was referring to the scarf they had later discovered hidden in the hag's hut, the one apparently used to train the wisps to track Arlo's scent.

"I'm sure other companies have Yellow patrols."

"This one had a Pine Mountain logo on it."

Wade shrugged. "Could have been a mistake. Maybe they made one by accident. Do you know what's one of the most valuable stamps in the world? It's called the Inverted Jenny. A red-and-blue stamp with a plane on it—only the plane is printed upside down. Originally a twenty-four-cent stamp. But do you know how much it goes for?"

"A million dollars?" asked Wu.

"One point three, at least." Wade looked at Indra. "And you know why it's worth that much?"

"Because it's unique?"

"No, because it's authentic. You can glue antlers on a rabbit and call it a jackalope, but that doesn't make it one." Wade gestured idly. "Way I look at it, we're surrounded by frauds, counterfeiters, impostors. People deceive us. We deceive ourselves. So when something's real, that's worth something. The Inverted Jenny—that stamp was an accident, but it's honest. It is exactly what it purports to be, and that's rare these days."

With that, Wade turned on the radio. He'd be taking no follow-up questions.

Back at the house, they had just gotten out of Wade's truck when Arlo spotted his mom's station wagon turning off the road.

Wu squinted, making sure he was seeing clearly. "Wait, your sister can drive?"

"Not well," said Arlo.

Jaycee had recently gotten her learner's permit, so she was at the wheel, with Arlo's mom in the passenger seat. It seemed impossible that Jaycee was allowed to pilot a deadly machine on roads crowded with innocent civilians, even if she had somehow passed her written exam.

Wu and Indra quickly moved their bikes out of the way, just in case.

Jaycee pulled the station wagon over beside the pickup truck. It lurched and stalled. Still, Arlo noticed no bloodstains or new dents, so the trip had evidently gone better than he had expected.

"How was your day?" asked their mom, pulling some bags from the back seat.

"Fine!" said Arlo, a little too enthusiastically. "We were just hanging out."

Indra pointed to the shopping bags. "Did you go to Cross Creek?" Cross Creek was the nearest mall, a ninety-minute drive away.

"We did. Jaycee's headed to China on Tuesday to see her dad, so she needed some things for her trip. And Arlo needed a new poncho for camp."

She tossed him a square bundle—the folded-up poncho. It was heavier than expected, and smelled like sugary plastic.

"Thanks," he said.

His mom gestured to Wu and Indra. "You guys want to stay for dinner?"

Indra demurred. "I should be heading back."

"Me too," said Wu, climbing on his bike. He nodded to Arlo. "We can go over stuff at school tomorrow."

"Can you believe it's your last day before summer vacation?" asked Arlo's mom. "The year went by so fast."

As his friends pedaled away and his family went inside, Arlo spotted a shape emerging from the forest. It was Cooper. The ghostly dog was on patrol, pacing up the driveway.

Arlo had seen Cooper on his first day in Pine Mountain, before meeting Wu and Indra, before learning about Rangers and snaplights and the Long Woods. So much in Arlo's life had changed, but Cooper was exactly the same.

It was the identical routine every day—rain, snow or shine. Cooper would take seventeen steps to reach the tree stump. Once there, he would sniff it, digging futilely at the dirt with a spectral paw. Three scratches, then the dog would suddenly cock his head, hearing something.

Except there was no sound. Cooper was living in a memory, endlessly repeating a day from the past.

Arlo was the only one who could see Cooper. He'd gotten in the habit of telling the dog things he didn't dare tell anyone else.

"I saw a troll today. At least I think it was a troll." He kneeled down beside the ghost dog, scratching the air behind its translucent ear. "Also, Wu was the patrol leader. Isn't that weird? You'd sort of think Indra would be, but . . ." He trailed off, not sure where the thought was taking him. "I guess they seemed fine without me."

Cooper began silently barking, his attention focused on a spot near the road. The dog took off running, chasing the same nonexistent threat he did every day.

He was a ghost chasing ghosts.

Arlo stood, watching as Cooper vanished into the woods. There was something reassuring about watching the cycle play out. You always knew what was coming.

Something is coming. Arlo felt certain about that. Whatever had actually happened at the Broken Bridge, whatever was hidden in the flashlight, it marked the start of something new.

For months, he'd been in a kind of holding pattern—waiting, wondering when the next thing would happen. Like an athlete in the off-season, Arlo had practiced his fundamentals: knots, knaughts and the Ranger's compass. His quick visits into and out of the Long Woods were a way of testing himself, to prepare for what was coming.

And he knew something was coming.

In the winter, a pointy-mustached man named Fox had introduced himself in the parking lot of the church. It was a cold night, just after the Ranger's Court of Honor in which Arlo had received his Squirrel rank.

Fox hadn't said much—he had a way of talking in circles—but he clearly knew about the Valley of Fire and the hag and the Eldritch forces who had sent her. Before Fox suddenly vanished, Arlo had asked what the Eldritch wanted. *Something hidden. Something you may be able to find. But that's for another season. I'll come back when it's warmer.*

Now it was summer—another season, and warmer. Maybe Fox was coming back.

Maybe Arlo would finally get his answers.

5
STRAY MARKS

THE NEXT MORNING AT SCHOOL, Arlo spotted a girl he didn't recognize locking up her bike at the racks. She had long, dark hair that fell across her face as she bent down to fasten the chain.

It seemed strange that a new kid would enroll on the last day of class. Stranger still, this girl had Indra's bike. Was she a relative? A previously unmentioned cousin? Finished with her lock, the girl looked up at Arlo. She tucked her hair behind her ears. "What are you staring at?" the girl asked. Suddenly, it all clicked: *This was Indra.*

"What happened to your hair?" He didn't mean it as an insult. He was honestly perplexed: her hair was impossibly straight and shiny. "Did you forget to curl it or something?"

"You think I curl my hair?"

"I don't know! I don't know how girls' hair works."

"My hair is naturally curly. I just ironed it out."

"Why?"

"Just because. It's no big deal."

But it felt like a big deal. Indra had altered one of her fundamental characteristics, and the timing felt like too much of a coincidence. "Is this because of the bridge, and the other Indra?" asked Arlo.

"No!" she said, a little too insistently. "Don't be crazy."

As the bell rang, Arlo walked alongside her into school. He couldn't help but feel she was an impostor somehow. This wasn't the Indra he knew.

Arlo Finch was going to miss sixth grade. Not that he'd ever admit it.

Given all the dramatic events of the past year—the move to Pine Mountain, joining Rangers, the various attempts on his life by otherworldly creatures under the direction of still-unknown forces—school had been comfortably predictable. Spelling was spelling. Fractions were fractions.

Sixth grade was the most normal thing in Arlo's life. He felt a little unsettled to realize this was the last day.

That said, he certainly wasn't going to miss waking up early, combing his hair or remembering to put his homework back in his bag. He had no fondness for his squeaky chair, or the drinking fountain that barely burbled, forcing you to lean in so close you could smell the spit and wet metal.

Nor would he miss his teacher's habit of standing beside her desk, keeping watch over her students while they worked. That's what Mrs. Mayes was doing right at this moment, idly twisting the beads of her wooden necklace while the class went through their textbooks page by page.

"Remember, you need to erase anything that wasn't already printed in the book," she said. "Think of the students who will use them next year."

"Poor fools," cracked Wu. The class tittered. Mrs. Mayes glared at Wu, but everyone knew there would be no consequences.

Arlo dutifully flipped through his world studies reader page by page, searching for stray marks.

It occurred to him that the last day of school was devoted to erasing any trace that students had been in the school. They had scrubbed the desks, emptied the closets and taken everything off the bulletin board. Everything had to be reset to zero. Wiped clean.

He thought about the *A* scratched into the rock at the Broken Bridge. Someone had deliberately made a mark for others to find—presumably the same person who had hidden the flashlight underneath it. But why? If there was something valuable hidden inside it, why stow it under a rock deep in the Long Woods?

As he kept flipping pages, Arlo found himself in a new section of the book filled with maps and photos of Asia. They hadn't reached the last few chapters that year. Based on how crisp the paper felt, he doubted any sixth-grade class had ever reached them.

On a map of China, he located the city of Guangzhou along the southern coast. That's where his father was living. Tomorrow, Jaycee would be flying there to visit him. There was only enough money to buy one ticket, and everyone had agreed that Jaycee should go. Of the two kids, she needed him more. Arlo could wait.

He had flipped the page when his classmate Merilee Myers leaned over to whisper: "Who is Celeste?"

Arlo had no idea why Merilee was asking. "That's my mom's name," he whispered back. "Why?"

"I heard someone talking about her. And you. So I figured you must know who she is." She smiled coyly. "I thought she might be your girlfriend."

Arlo didn't know how to respond. Over the past few months, Arlo had often noticed Merilee watching him, as if there was something fascinating about him, when of course there wasn't.

She had also taken to wearing high-heeled boots and bright red lipstick, which often ended up on her front teeth.

Arlo needed to say something to make it less weird. "Who was talking about my mom?"

"The wind," said Merilee.

Arlo assumed he must have misheard her. "Did you say 'the wind'?"

She nodded. "The wind behind my house. It talks sometimes.

It likes when I put my head like this." Grabbing the edge of her desk, Merilee tipped her head down, letting her long hair fall forward. It nearly reached the floor. "The wind loves blowing through it. You can touch it if you want."

"That's okay."

Arlo noticed Indra watching them from across the room, curious why Merilee was leaning across her desk to show off her hair. Arlo shrugged, equally perplexed. Why had today become all about girls' hair?

At the front of the room, Mrs. Mayes was busy logging in textbooks. She wasn't paying much attention to the class.

Merilee snapped her head back up. "Wait—how old is your mom?"

"Forty, I think. Or almost."

"No, then. It's not her. The wind was talking about a girl. That's why I assumed she was your girlfriend."

Arlo wasn't sure what to say. Finally, a question came to him: "What did the wind say about me?"

Merilee smiled. "It said you were a hero."

With that, Merilee got up from her desk and carried her world studies book up to Mrs. Mayes. Arlo sat in his seat, flummoxed.

"Merilee is crazy," said Wu. "In second grade, she insisted shoelaces were made of spiderwebs."

Arlo was waiting with Indra and Wu at the library desk while Mrs. Fitzrandolph finished a phone call.

Indra disagreed. "Merilee's not crazy. The whole thing's an act. She's just trying to get attention."

"Like when you two would dress up as princesses and throw glitter," said Wu. Indra shot him a deathly stare. Wu turned to Arlo. "Indra used to be friends with Merilee until she joined Rangers."

Indra snapped back, "You used to play together all the time!"

"Only because she lived across the street!"

It was weird for Arlo to think of his friends before he'd come to Pine Mountain. He had originally assumed that Wu and Indra had been lifelong friends, but over the past few months he had realized that they hadn't hung out together much until he'd arrived. But it was such a small town that they had been in class together since kindergarten.

"How would Merilee know my mom's name, though?" he asked.

"Your mom works at the diner," said Indra. "Everyone goes there, and her name tag says 'Celeste.'"

Mrs. Fitzrandolph hung up the phone. "Let me guess. You want to see the book."

They smiled sheepishly. They had been asking to look through *Culman's Bestiary of Notable Creatures* nearly every week all year long. Mrs. Fitzrandolph sighed, sorting through her ring of keys to find the one that unlocked the book's special drawer.

"Is there any chance we could check it out for the summer?" asked Indra in her sweetest voice.

Mrs. Fitzrandolph smiled. "Honey, if I let any child bring this book home, I'd hear no end of it. Parents would take one look at it and say it was gruesome and inappropriate. They'd be right, at least for some children. The job of a school librarian requires both courage and discretion."

Mrs. Fitzrandolph slid the book across the desk.

"You don't think any of this is real?" asked Arlo.

"Of course not! But I believe a vivid imagination is the mark of a curious mind. And the world needs more of those."

Arlo was continually surprised by how most residents of Pine Mountain seemed completely unaware that they lived at the edge of the Long Woods. Just beyond the trees was a different world with impossible geography and remarkable creatures, many of them documented in *Culman's Bestiary*. Yet the magic of the Wonder kept them from encountering it—or made the memories fade away.

A few adults did acknowledge the strange happenings. Uncle Wade knew about the creatures, and had helped Arlo dispel the Night Mare. Some of the Wardens from Ranger events were able to perform feats of spectacular firecraeft. But they didn't talk about it as anything special. *They forget what's extraordinary,* Arlo thought.

Maybe that was the Wonder. Or maybe that was just being a grownup.

"Five minutes," said the librarian, tapping her watch. She then packed up the Scottie dog figurine from the counter and headed back into her office.

Alone with the book, the trio went straight to the entry for *Troll.*

There was no illustration, but the description seemed to match closely the creature they had encountered, singling out its "unfathomably noxious odor."

"I can still smell it," said Arlo. "It's like it's stuck in my nose."

According to *Culman's*, trolls were exclusively found near bridges, swamps and sea caves. The entry noted that there didn't seem to be any such thing as a young troll; trolls didn't mate or rear young. One possible explanation was that trolls were generated by the location itself.

"Wait, so somehow the bridge *created* the troll?" asked Wu.

Indra shrugged. "That's what it seems to be saying."

Arlo slid the book closer, noticing something in the margin of the page. A single word had been written in pencil:

FINCH

They were simple letters, not cursive. If Arlo had had to guess, he would have said it was written by a student rather than an adult. But it certainly hadn't been one of the three of them.

"Why would someone write your name?" asked Wu.

Arlo was stumped.

Indra had a thought: "What if it's not Arlo? This book could have been in the library for forty years. Maybe fifty. It could be a different Finch."

"Like your uncle," said Wu. "Or your mom."

Arlo shook his head. "Their last name is Bellman. My mom only became a Finch when she married my dad. And I don't think he's ever been to Pine Mountain."

They stared at the word for nearly a minute, no better theory to explain it. Finally, Arlo took a pencil from the desk and began erasing his name.

"What are you doing?" asked Wu.

"It's the last day of school. It's what you do."

He blew off the tiny scraps of shredded eraser. The pencil marks were gone, but he could still make out a faint impression of *FINCH* in the paper. His name would be part of this book forever.

6
IN-BETWEEN DAYS

ARLO HADN'T INTENDED to hug his sister.

By mutual and unspoken agreement, they hadn't touched each other in years: no pats on the back, no fist bumps, no mussing of hair. Even on long car trips, they were careful to maintain at least a three-inch gap so their legs didn't brush against each other. Given this history, Arlo had assumed Jaycee would head off on her trip to China with nothing more than a nod and a mild insult.

But here they were, hugging. Arlo could feel her ribs under her marching band T-shirt. Her deodorant smelled like baby powder. "Take care of Mom," she whispered. "Don't let her get all sad."

"I won't," he promised. "Say hi to Dad."

It was six A.M. They were standing on the gravel driveway beside the pickup truck. Uncle Wade was at the wheel, impatient to go. He had agreed to drive Jaycee to the airport in Denver before heading north to install his artwork at the resort in

Jackson Hole. Arlo had helped him load the boxes into the back of the truck, using taut-line hitches to tie down the tarps.

"If we don't head out, we're going to hit traffic," grumbled Wade, cracking open his second energy drink.

Their mom pulled Jaycee in for one last hug. "Promise me you'll keep your phone charged. And don't ride on any motorcycles."

"Okay!" Jaycee extricated herself and climbed into the truck beside Wade. She checked her passport one last time, then shut the door.

Their mom rested her hands on the open window. "Call me when you're through security, and again from San Francisco."

"I will," said Jaycee, buckling her seat belt. "It's going to be fine. You don't need to worry about me."

Wade started the engine. Their mom reluctantly released her grip on the truck.

"Try not to burn down the house while I'm gone," said Wade.

"I was seven," said their mom. "And that was as much your fault as mine."

Wade shrugged. Arlo couldn't tell if they were joking.

The truck drove off, a cloud of dust rising behind it. Arlo wondered how Wade and Jaycee would fare on their long drive. In all their months in Pine Mountain, he couldn't remember his uncle and sister speaking more than twenty words to each other. They were like strangers who happened to live in the same house.

Arlo looked over just as his mom wiped tears out of her eyes. He had already broken his promise to not let her get sad.

"She'll be fine," he said.

His mom smiled. "I know. I'm not even that worried about her, really. She's tough."

Arlo could think of other adjectives to describe Jaycee—gruff, moody, bossy—but he kept them to himself.

"It's just that sometimes when I squint, I can still see the little version of her," she said. "Like when she was first learning to walk, pushing this toy stroller, and no one better get in her way. She's still the same person, just bigger."

"Am I the same?"

"Absolutely. Even if someone hadn't seen you for years, they would know it's you."

"Because of my eyes." Arlo had one green eye and one brown eye. Even in baby photos, he could see they were mismatched.

"It's much more than that. Personality-wise, you're cautious, but brave. You're sweet. And sometimes when you're tired I still see that baby with fat little cheeks."

"I'm twelve," Arlo protested. "Almost thirteen."

"And I'm almost forty. But honestly, deep down, I'm still the same girl I always was. People don't really change. They just get more like themselves."

The next four days were unlike any other, and unexpectedly fun.

Indra had gone with her family to her older sister's fencing competition in Tucson. Wu was practicing for a *Galactic Havoc 2* tournament, and noncommittal about hanging out. ("I mean, I'm going to see you for two weeks straight at camp.")

That left Arlo to hang out with his mom.

Every morning, Arlo went with her to the Gold Pan diner. He read fantasy novels and his Field Book while she waitressed. He learned how to operate the cash register, the compactor and the french-fry slicer. He helped her refill the ketchup bottles and salt shakers, and wiped down all the menus.

The manager didn't seem to mind how often Arlo refilled his soda. By three o'clock, Arlo was buzzing from too much caffeine, so he ran from the diner to the elementary school and back, timing himself. By Friday, he'd shaved a whole minute off his time.

At around five each day, Arlo and his mom walked down to the Pine Mountain Garage to pick up receipts and invoices. His mom did most of the bookkeeping back at the house, but orders and inventory needed to be handled in person.

Mitch, the mechanic, showed Arlo how to change oil and patch a leaky tire. "That's eighty percent of car maintenance, by the way. If everyone knew how do them, I'd be out of business." Mitch could perform both tasks one-handed; he had broken his left arm in a motorcycle accident a few weeks earlier.

Something had changed between Mitch and Arlo's mom. Back in the winter, they would laugh and tease each other about things they'd done in high school. Now there were fewer jokes. They were still friendly, but they didn't linger in conversation the way they had before. And Mitch hadn't been to the house since Easter.

Arlo's favorite part of the day was dinner.

Jaycee and Wade were both picky eaters, so Arlo and his mom took advantage of their absence. Every night, they tried a new recipe: sausage and sauerkraut, tofu with black bean sauce, Yorkshire pudding, spaghetti with clams. Some dishes were good, some were terrible. But it was exciting to try them out.

Afterwards, they had ice cream at the coffee table, watching old VHS videotapes of movies Wade had recorded off TV as a teenager. The films were good, but the commercials were better. Arlo couldn't believe how goofy the clothes had been: bright neon colors and cutoff sweatshirts.

"Don't laugh," said his mom. "I would have killed for that kind of fashion in Pine Mountain. I used to beg my parents to take me to the mall."

His mom let him stay up until ten thirty. Then he'd spend another hour in bed with a book, until he couldn't keep his eyes open any longer.

He would have been happy to keep repeating the same day all summer. But then a stranger came to town.

7
THE MAN IN THE DINER

THE ROAD TO PINE MOUNTAIN was long and winding, and didn't lead anywhere else, so anyone who came to town wasn't merely passing through. Visitors always had a purpose.

For a few weeks each autumn, tourists arrived to see the aspen trees change color, vast mountainsides covered in gold. After the aspen-watchers came the hunters with their orange camouflage and pickup trucks. Then came the snow. In the winter, almost no one showed up in Pine Mountain. The ski areas were too far away, and the plows struggled to keep the road clear to Havlick.

In spring and summer, most visitors arrived with the intention of investigating the ruins of Old Pine Mountain, the original town site that had been washed away by a flash flood more than a century before. With maps printed from websites, they explored the crumbled foundations of destroyed buildings and marveled at the wagon still suspended in a massive tree. Camping wasn't allowed, but people did it anyway, hoping to encounter one of the ghosts or tommyknockers said to haunt the former mining site.

It was summer and the leaves were still green. So when Arlo first saw the stranger seated alone at a booth by the window, he assumed he was there for the ruins.

The man looked to be Uncle Wade's age. He had graying blond hair and weathered skin, and wore a hunting knife on his belt. Arlo's mom brought him an iced tea while he looked at the menu. He ordered a hamburger and fries, offering a friendly smile.

Arlo's mom went back into the kitchen to start working on his food. It was three in the afternoon, and the cook had run home to give his basset hound his eye drops, so she needed to work the grill.

The man exchanged glances with Arlo, who was looking up from his Ranger Field Book at the counter. They were alone.

"What rank are you?" asked the man, pointing to the book.

"Squirrel," said Arlo. "Still have a few more patches before I can get my Owl."

The man nodded but didn't say anything more. He drank most of his iced tea in a single chug, evidently parched. Then he set the glass down and sat silently, looking out the window.

Arlo reached over the counter and took the iced tea pitcher. After some negotiation, his mom had agreed to let him refill customers' drinks as long as he was careful.

The man slid his glass over with a smile. Arlo filled it to just below the rim.

"Thanks," said the man. He had a pale scar that ran along his left eye. Around his neck, he wore a smoky crystal hanging from a thin cord.

"Are you here to see the old town?" asked Arlo.

"I didn't know there was an old town."

"It's down along the river. People say it's haunted, but it's not, really."

"You don't believe in spirits?"

"I do," said Arlo. "Just not like that."

"So what do you believe?"

"I don't know."

"Feels you should believe in something, right? Isn't that what they're teaching you? *Loyal, brave, kind and true . . .*"

"Were you in Rangers?"

"I was. That's actually why I'm here. To see an old friend from camp."

Arlo noticed the man had a coin in his right hand. It was rolling back and forth across his knuckles. It was simple sleight of hand—Arlo had seen magicians on TV doing similar feats—but he had never seen it so close up. The coin seemed to be dancing.

"You have two different color eyes."

"I know." Arlo hated it when people pointed out something so obvious.

"In Peru, that's considered good luck. *Tocado por espíritus.* 'Touched by spirits.'"

"You've been to Peru?"

"Oh, I've been everywhere."

The man held up the coin so Arlo could see it clearly.

"It's Spanish, sixteenth century. Made from Mayan gold. And perfectly balanced. Watch." The man set the coin on its edge, then flicked it with a finger. It spun on the table, glinting in the sunlight.

Arlo was transfixed. With each flash of light, he felt himself zooming in on it. Falling towards it. His arms were getting heavy.

But he wasn't frightened. He didn't want the coin to stop spinning. He didn't want anything. It was like floating in the last moments of a dream.

The man was talking, but Arlo couldn't hear what he was saying.

Arlo was speaking as well. He could feel the vibration in his throat. But he had no idea what words were coming out.

The only thing he could focus on was the spinning coin. He could hear it on the table, a heavy whir that seemed to climb in pitch endlessly.

And he could taste it. *Why can I taste it?* he wondered. The coin was on the table, but he could feel the metal in his mouth. And in his bones. And muscles.

I am the metal, he thought. *I'm the coin and the light and the air and the table and the trees and the pyramid and the sky and the gold and the mine and the darkness and the ax and the ice and the flame and the bell . . .*

"Arlo!"

It was his mom. She had her hands on his shoulders. She seemed panicked.

His shoes were wet. He stared at them, and the ice cubes at his feet. The plastic iced tea pitcher was on the floor. He'd evidently dropped it.

"I'm sorry," he said.

She wasn't upset about the pitcher. "What was that man talking to you about?"

Arlo looked to the booth by the window. The man was gone. So was the coin.

"Nothing," said Arlo. "Just Rangers and stuff."

His mom ran to the door of the diner. Arlo wanted to follow her, but his feet still felt heavy. So instead he watched through the window as his mother chased after a pickup truck with a camper shell. It was pulling out of the parking lot and onto Main Street.

His mom was shouting at the driver. Arlo couldn't hear the words, but he was pretty sure they were ones she wouldn't let him or Jaycee use in the house.

Eventually, the truck was out of sight.

His mom returned to the diner, winded and frustrated. By this point, Arlo's feet had decided they could move again. He felt sluggish and disoriented, but otherwise okay.

"What was . . ."

His mom held up a finger. She was writing something down on her notepad. "Okay, sorry," she said as she finished. "I needed to get his license plate number."

"Why? Did he not pay?"

"It's not that," she said. "I wish it were that." She paused for a moment to collect her thoughts. Arlo suspected she was deciding how much to tell him. "That man was probably FBI, or some other kind of government agent. They're not supposed to come near us. We had an agreement."

She thinks he was after Dad, Arlo realized.

She took Arlo's face in her hands. They were warm and soft and smelled like the grill. "Did he ask you anything about your father, or what he was working on?"

"No," said Arlo. "And I wouldn't know anything anyway." Arlo barely understood what his father did, beyond that it involved codes and computers. "Besides, we barely talked."

Arlo's mom looked at him strangely.

"You were talking for a couple of minutes, Arlo. I could see you from the kitchen."

That seemed impossible. How could Arlo have forgotten an entire conversation?

Don't say a word, Arlo Finch.

It was the man's voice, but it was in his head. Was it a memory, or his imagination?

I'm the only one who can help you.

Arlo tried to seem casual, to shrug it off. He didn't want his mom to worry.

"We didn't talk about anything important." While he couldn't remember the content of the conversation, he was certain this was a lie.

Then he added: "It was mostly about Rangers."

That part? That was true.

8
A WARNING

ARLO CONSIDERED CALLING INDRA and Wu to fill them in on what had happened at the diner. But each time he thought about telling them, the idea quickly evaporated. He could watch it melt away in his mind, like a snowflake on the back of his hand. Was it magic that was making it fade, or some kind of hypnosis? All he knew was that he couldn't keep the thought in his mind long enough to act on it.

Besides, Arlo reasoned, he'd be seeing them tomorrow on the bus to summer camp. No sense getting into it now. And he needed to get ready for the trip.

The packing list for Camp Redfeather was more extensive than for a normal campout. Arlo needed bug spray and sunscreen, soap and shampoo, notebooks and pencils. The sheet also called for a small battery-powered lantern. Arlo had asked Wu about it, puzzled. "Snaplights aren't really practical for the latrine," Wu had explained. "Believe me, you don't want to be in there in the dark."

Arlo had chosen a lamp with a strip of bright white LEDs. It hurt his eyes to look directly at it, but he figured it would protect him from toilet-related disasters.

Since the camp was two weeks long, it required more changes of clothes than a normal campout. So that evening, while his mom was making spelt dough for the pizza, Arlo started a load of laundry. He had just switched on the washer when he heard a gentle tapping behind him.

He turned to see a shadowed face at the window, and a finger rapping the glass. The girl pulled back her hood so he could see her clearly.

It was Rielle.

Rielle was Connor's cousin, kidnapped by the Eldritch when she was four. Now roughly Arlo's age, she lived on the far side of the Long Woods in a place she called the Realm.

Arlo hadn't seen her since the bonfire at the Alpine Derby, when he'd found himself beside her watching a fiery dragon. That visit, like all of his encounters with her, had seemed to happen in a dream space.

This was different. Rielle was really there, standing on the other side of the laundry room window.

She motioned for him to come outside, then walked around to the side of the house. He could hear her footsteps in the gravel.

Arlo's heart pounded, a sudden panic. He didn't know why she had come, but it couldn't be good news.

His hand hesitated on the doorknob.

So much of what had happened this past year had started exactly this way: someone or something suddenly appearing, beckoning him to follow.

But that didn't mean he had to. He could simply stay inside, where his mom was making pizza and another one of Uncle Wade's old tapes awaited. He could fold his laundry and pack for summer camp.

Not every call had to be answered.

It's my choice, he realized.

His heart slowed. His dread subsided. In the end, he opened the door because he wanted to, not because he had to.

"No one knows I'm here," she said. "I only have a few minutes."

They were standing behind the woodpile. Rielle was dressed in a tunic, cape and trousers, all of them covered with elaborate embroidery. She kept glancing over at the forest, as if expecting something to come charging out of it. For the first time, Arlo got a good look at her eyes. They were the same mismatched colors as his.

"What's going on?" he asked.

Rielle leveled her gaze. "What were you doing in the Long Woods?"

It felt like an accusation. Arlo deflected: "When?"

"A few days ago. You were in the Woods with your friends, the boy and the girl." Sensing his next question, she explained,

"The Council has spies all over the Woods: animals, spirits, even trees. You have to assume they see everything."

Arlo thought back to his feeling of being watched while at the Broken Bridge. He wasn't paranoid. Someone really was out there.

"They saw you take something," she said. "What was it?"

"I don't know. I mean, it was a flashlight, but there was something inside it."

"Whatever it was, the Council wants it. I've never seen them so panicked. I tried to listen at the door, but I couldn't hear much."

Arlo wanted to know what "the Council" was, but it seemed more important to understand why they were freaking out. "What *could* you hear? What were they saying?"

Rielle lowered her voice. "They said it could destroy the Realm."

Arlo wondered how something so dangerous could fit inside a rusted flashlight. Was it a virus? A spell? Some sort of magical nuclear weapon?

"I heard a name, too: Hadryn." She pronounced it *HAD*-rin. "I don't know who he is, but it sounds like he's really dangerous. Whatever the thing is, they're worried he's going to get it."

Hadryn. Could he be the man at the diner?

I'm the only one who can help you.

If the Eldritch were scared of Hadryn, what did that mean for Arlo? Was Hadryn an ally, or another enemy? Either way, it didn't seem like a good idea to reveal that Arlo had met him that afternoon.

"What are they going to do?" asked Arlo. "Are they coming after me?"

"I don't know. I'm not sure they've even made a decision. But if I were you, I would just give it to them."

"I can't! I don't have it!"

"Who does?"

Arlo didn't know how to explain. Then he realized Rielle might have the answer. "This is going to sound crazy, but are there parallel universes? Not just the Realm and the Long Woods, but maybe multiple worlds? Like this one, but different?"

"Like in a comic book?" she asked. "How in one universe, Superman is evil and Lex Luthor is good?"

Arlo was surprised: "They have comic books in the Realm?"

"Not really. But I have a stash. Whenever I come here, I bring back a few."

For the first time, Rielle seemed almost normal. Take away the strange clothes and jewelry and Arlo could picture her sitting next to him in class. If she hadn't been taken by the Eldritch, she would be in his grade.

How often did Rielle sneak away from the Realm? Did she visit her family? Connor had said that she came back twice a year. He'd also warned that Arlo shouldn't necessarily trust her.

Rielle looked back at the trees. "I need to go. They'll be looking for me."

"Okay, but what should I do?"

"I don't know. I assumed you still had it."

Arlo tried to imagine the encounter at the Broken Bridge from the perspective of a spy hiding in the trees. "If they saw me take the flashlight, then they know who I gave it to. They would have seen me toss it to them."

"And you trust them, the people you gave it to?"

"Absolutely." He said it with confidence, but immediately had second thoughts. He certainly trusted Indra and Wu. But did he really trust Other Indra and Other Wu, much less Other Jonas and Other Julie? They looked like his friends, but that didn't mean they were necessarily on his side. In a universe where Wu was patrol leader, everything was different.

Rielle seemed to recognize his mental backpedaling. "If there's one thing I've learned in the Realm, it's that you can't trust anyone."

"Even you?" Arlo asked with a smile.

"For all I know, they wanted me to tell you. I didn't know whether I should come."

"So why did you?"

She shrugged. "I just have this feeling we're in this together."

Right then, Arlo heard his mom shouting his name. She sounded upset.

"Be careful," Rielle warned. She turned and started running for the trees.

Arlo called after her: "How do I find you?"

She didn't answer. She didn't slow down. They might be in this together, but at the moment, he was on his own.

Arlo returned to the laundry room to find his mother switching off the washing machine. The tub had overflowed, an inch of water flooding the floor. He had forgotten his uncle's warning to check that the cycle started properly.

"I'm sorry!" he said.

"It's okay," his mom said. "Grab a bucket and start bailing."

Working together, it took almost an hour to get the water out of the laundry room. The carpet was still squishy. The dryer had shorted out, so Arlo had to hang his clothes on the line outside.

The smoke detector suddenly blared, reminding them they'd forgotten the pizza in the oven. It was unsalvageable, so they ate cereal instead. Arlo thought the milk tasted funny, but didn't want to complain. It was nine o'clock before they sat down to watch one of Uncle Wade's tapes. The movie was called *Smokey and the Bandit.* Ten minutes in, Arlo thought it was one of the funniest movies he'd ever seen. His mom agreed.

Arlo asked her what she was planning to do while he was at camp.

"I'll try to work some extra shifts," she said. "And there are a few books I've been wanting to read. It's weird—I grew up in this house, but I don't think I've ever spent a night alone here."

Arlo realized then that he was going to miss his mom. Not just as a parent, but as a person. "I had a good week," he said. "It was fun."

His mom agreed. "Definitely. It was cool hanging out with you, Arlo Finch."

9
THE PACK

SOMETHING IN RUSSELL'S BACKPACK was moving.

A bulge rippled under the nylon as some unseen creature shifted to a new location. Russell seemed completely unaware, chewing sunflower seeds and spitting out the shells.

Arlo was standing behind him in line, puzzled and intrigued. What could be hiding in the pack?

A squirrel? A snake? A white-footed groovel?

Had the pack belonged to any other member of the Pine Mountain Company, Arlo would have immediately given warning that a wild creature was nestled among the Ranger's socks and underwear.

But Russell Stokes was a jerk and a bully. He delighted in teasing "Arlo Flinch," sometimes drafting his Red Patrol buddies into the harassment. During a snowball fight that winter, Russell had pegged Arlo twice while he was lying helpless on the ground.

And though no one could prove it, Blue Patrol was pretty sure Russell had peed on their tent at the last campout.

So Arlo said nothing as the mysterious creature inside Russell's pack moved again.

It was Saturday morning, and the entire company was assembled in the church parking lot, where a rented school bus was waiting to drive them four hours to Camp Redfeather. But first, their backpacks needed to be inspected for contraband, which was why they were lined up.

"Remember, no electronics other than flashlights and lanterns!" shouted Diana from the back of the truck that would haul their gear. "And laser pointers are not flashlights! That was on the sheet."

Diana Velasquez was the new marshal. She'd been elected two months earlier to replace Christian Cunningham, who was off on his Vigil training for Bear rank. Diana was in tenth grade, with shiny black hair and perfect posture. Arlo had voted for her, but had never really spoken to her. She made him nervous. She felt more like an adult than a teenager.

Arlo suddenly realized that Indra's newly straight hair looked almost exactly like Diana's. She even had identical hair ties. Was Indra trying to copy her?

"And guys, I'm serious," Diana said. "Absolutely no peanut butter. That's why we're going through every pack one by one."

Arlo turned to Indra and Wu, who were waiting behind him in line. "What's the deal with peanut butter? Is it because of allergies?" Back in Chicago, there had been a girl in his class who was deathly allergic to peanut butter. Even a speck could send her into shock.

"Peanut butter attracts howlers," explained Indra. "They can smell even tiny traces."

"It's like sharks and blood," said Wu. He turned to Connor, their patrol leader. "Didn't something happen one year?"

Connor seemed sluggish this morning, like he couldn't quite wake up. "Yeah, back when my brother was a Squirrel. This kid in Green Patrol, he had a wrapper left over from a candy bar. At two in the morning, this pack of howlers shows up and rips the camp apart looking for it."

"Was anyone hurt?" asked Jonas, suddenly curious. He and Julie were at the end of the inspection line.

"No," said Connor. "But the howlers destroyed the tents. Sleeping bags were ripped apart. It was bad."

"I don't like peanut butter anyway," said Julie, as if that settled the issue.

Arlo had only seen howlers in *Culman's Bestiary*. In the illustration, they looked like a cross between monkeys and crows. They couldn't fly, but apparently they could leap from tree to tree so fast you couldn't outrun them. By the time you heard their terrifying howls, it was too late.

"Next!" called Diana.

The whole line moved up one step. Russell dropped his pack on the folding table so two of the Senior Patrol members could inspect it. Arlo leaned around to watch, eager to see Russell's shock as he discovered the creature hidden inside the pack.

Except Russell wasn't the one opening it. Leo McCubbin was. Arlo felt a sudden twinge of guilt and panic. What if a vicious beast was inside the bag, ready to strike? Leo McCubbin was already missing a fingertip from a hachet incident. What if the creature bit off another?

"Stop!" Arlo shouted, louder than he had intended. All eyes went to him. He pointed at the bag. "There's something in there. It's moving. I saw it."

Russell scoffed. "You're crazy."

Arlo ignored Russell, looking at McCubbin and the other inspectors. "Seriously. You have to believe me."

By this point, half the company was watching. Diana climbed down from the truck to intervene. "What's going on?"

"Flinch is just being a weirdo," said Russell.

Arlo looked Diana in the eye. "I was standing behind him. I saw something moving in his pack. Like a snake or a rat or something."

Diana seemed to believe him. "Is there anything in the bag, Russell?"

"No!"

"Okay," she said. "Why don't you open it for us, just to be safe."

Rolling his eyes, Russell began undoing snaps and loosening drawstrings. Arlo unconsciously took a step back, ready to get out of the way in case the creature sprang out. Meanwhile, everyone else circled around to watch.

Russell flipped open the top of the pack. He reached in with both hands, pulling out his sleeping bag. Then his poncho. His socks. His flashlight. His mess kit. He laid them side by side on the table.

With each new item Russell pulled out, it became increasingly obvious that there was no creature in the pack. Arlo felt a sinking sensation. Had he imagined the whole thing?

Once everything was out of the pack, Russell turned it upside down and shook it. "See! Nothing."

Leo McCubbin looked inside and confirmed that it was empty.

Russell smirked, the smug grin of vindication.

All eyes went back to Arlo. "Sorry," he said quietly.

"What's that, Flinch?"

"Sorry," he said louder.

He could hear chatter around him, but didn't look. He wanted to hide under the table until the bus left, then flee to the woods and start a new life, perhaps emerging ten years later with a full beard and a new name.

McCubbin waved Arlo up for inspection. While Arlo unpacked, Russell was putting everything back in his bag. He cinched the top shut and slung it on his back.

Suddenly, the pack's drawstring whipped into the hole, as if an invisible hand had reached out and snatched it.

Arlo was the only one who had seen it, but Russell evidently had felt it happpen. He glanced over at Arlo and shook his head slowly. *Don't say a word.*

Then he carried his pack over to the truck, handing it to the loaders. Arlo watched as they piled it with the other packs, no idea there was something very troubling hidden inside.

On the bus, Arlo sat next to Wu, leaning across the aisle to talk with Indra and Connor. He decided against saying anything more about Russell's mysterious backpack. He wasn't sure what he'd seen or how to prove it. Besides, there were plenty of other topics to discuss on the long drive to Camp Redfeather.

Indra got Connor caught up on the hidden flashlight and troll at the Broken Bridge, while Arlo filled in the three of them about Rielle's subsequent warning.

"So the Eldritch know who we are," said Wu, keeping his voice low. It was halfway between a question and a brag. He was clearly excited to merit the attention of shadowy forces.

"I'm not sure they know your names," said Arlo. "But they definitely saw you two at the bridge."

"On both sides of the bridge," Indra pointed out. "Wu and I were the only people on both sides of the canyon. So whatever's going on, we're a big part of it."

"So are Jonas and Julie," said Connor. All four of them peered over the seat backs to look at the twins sitting a few rows ahead. Jonas was reading a car magazine while Julie sketched in her notebook, both completely unaware they were being discussed. "I mean, I wasn't there and you told me. Shouldn't you tell them?"

Connor had a point.

Last winter, before the Alpine Derby, Jonas and Julie had been left out of the loop, which made them understandably upset during the battle with the hag in the Valley of Fire. After all, they argued, they were equal members of the patrol. Their lives had been just as imperiled as anyone's, yet they'd gotten no advance warning that they were at risk of death by supernatural creatures. Arlo might have been the target of Eldritch interest, but they were caught in the crossfire.

"What would we tell them, exactly?" asked Indra. "That they're somehow involved with a mysterious flashlight in the Long Woods?"

"For starters, yeah," said Connor. "Arlo, didn't Rielle say she thought the thing in the flashlight was a weapon, or at least something really dangerous?"

Arlo nodded. He hadn't said anything about his encounter with Hadryn at the diner. Each time he thought to bring it up, the words slipped away from him. He wasn't intentionally keeping it a secret, but he just couldn't say it somehow. The words were locked away.

"Go back to the Ranger's Vow," said Connor. "Loyal, brave, kind and true. Telling Jonas and Julie what happened is all four of those things."

Arlo immediately knew Connor was right. Indra and Wu nodded as well, a little ashamed. They decided they would tell the twins everything that night, once they had time and privacy.

For the next two hours, Arlo read through the chapter on firecraeft in the Field Book until his eyes got heavy. He listened to the chatter on the bus, not really able to pick out specific voices.

He felt the road beneath the tires and the sunbeam on the side of his face.

The brakes squealed as the bus slowed, then turned. Arlo opened his eyes to find Julie kneeling on her seat, calling back to him, "Wake up! We're here!"

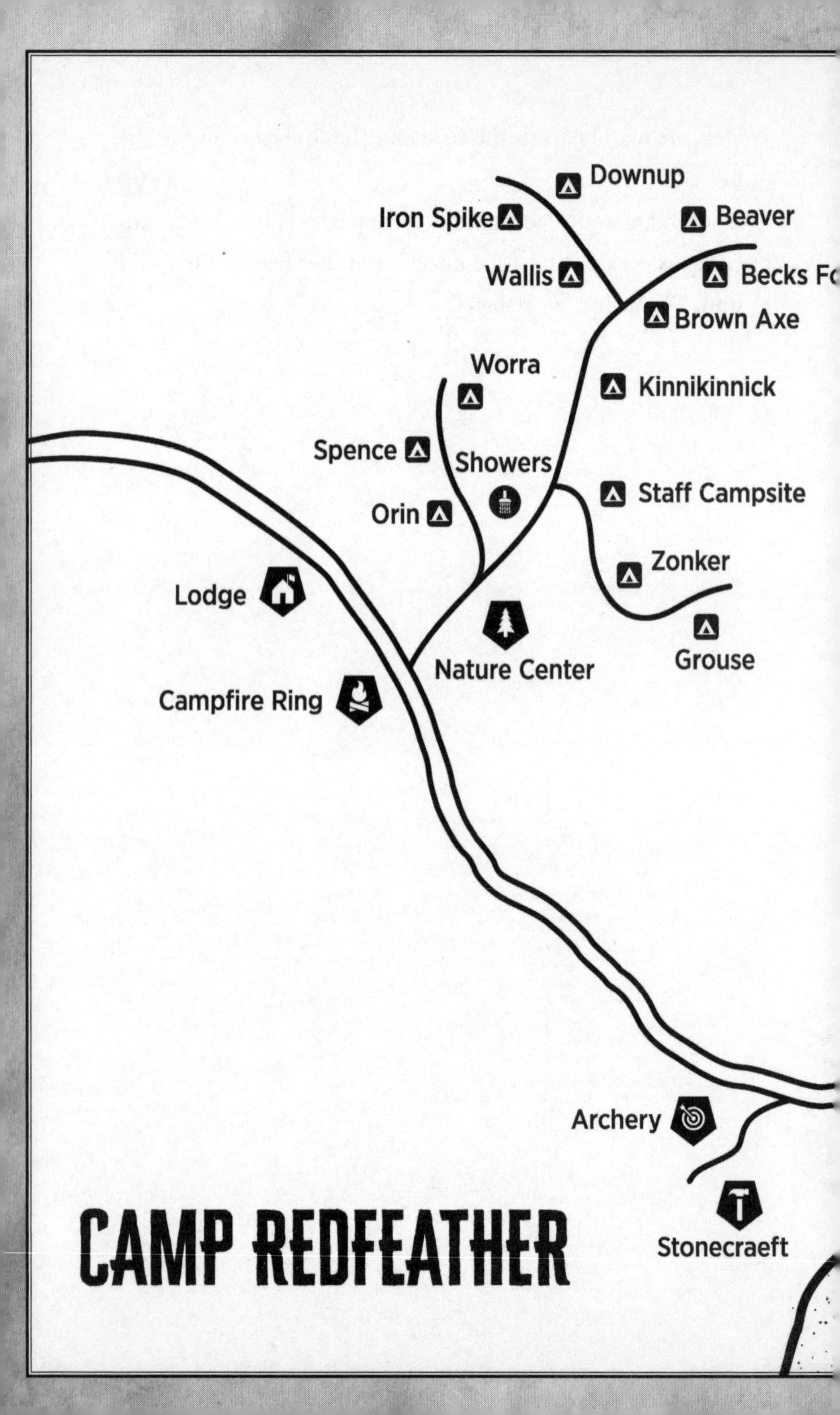
Downup
Iron Spike
Beaver
Wallis
Becks Fo
Brown Axe
Worra
Kinnikinnick
Spence
Showers
Staff Campsite
Orin
Zonker
Lodge
Grouse
Nature Center
Campfire Ring
Archery
Stonecraeft
CAMP REDFEATHER

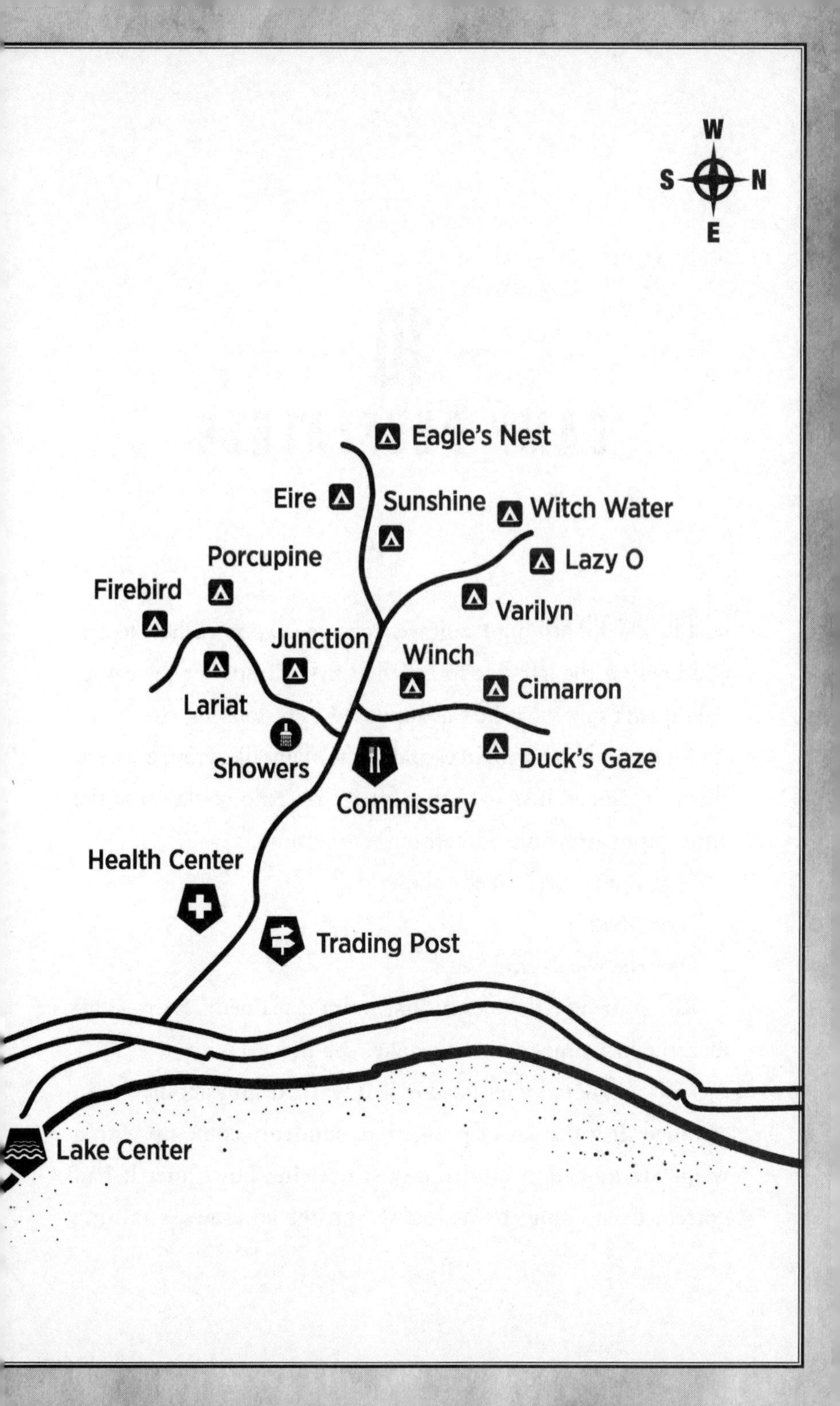

W
S
N
E
Eagle's Nest
Eire
Sunshine
Witch Water
Porcupine
Lazy O
Firebird
Varilyn
Junction
Winch
Cimarron
Lariat
Showers
Duck's Gaze
Commissary
Health Center
Trading Post
Lake Center

10
CAMP REDFEATHER

AS THE BUS TURNED onto a gravel road, everyone rushed to the windows on the left side to get their first glimpse of the camp. Arlo wasn't sure what he was supposed to be looking at.

All he could see were trees and the sunlight flickering between them. It seemed like any other forest. Yet Arlo could sense the anticipation growing. Something was coming.

"Are you ready?" asked Julie.

"For what?"

"For the wish!" said Wu.

Recognizing Arlo's confusion, Indra explained: "Every summer, the first time you see the lake, you make a wish."

Arlo wondered why no one had warned him about this in advance. It was a lot of pressure to suddenly come up with a wish. He looked around the bus, noticing how quiet it had gotten. Every Ranger was focused on the windows, straining to see something just beyond the trees. He didn't have much time.

His mind raced, trying to pick something worthy of a wish. *Happiness* felt too vague. *Oreos* felt too specific. He tried to remember previous birthday-candle wishes, but came up blank. *Is that why they didn't come true? Because I can't even remember what they were?*

Maybe he didn't need to wish for himself. He could wish for his father to come back from China. He could wish for his mom to get a job that didn't mean working so many hours. He could wish for his sister to be less grumpy all the time. (To be fair, that would benefit Arlo as much as anyone.)

Then, just as the bus was rounding a final curve, it came to him: *I wish I knew what was hidden in that flashlight.*

This was the thought in Arlo Finch's mind when he first saw Redfeather Lake. Then he gasped.

The lake was much, much bigger than he had anticipated. Like a forgotten sea, it filled the basin of the shallow valley, sunlight glinting off the water. Three massive rock islands dotted the surface, the largest resembling a clenched fist.

Stretching their arms out the windows, some Red Patrol boys threw snaplights, trying to reach the lake. Russell Stokes spooked a mule deer that was grazing near the water's edge. Luckily, it ran away from the bus rather than towards it.

"Guys! Knock it off!" shouted Diana.

Wu, who had been about to snap a light of his own, quickly pulled his hand back inside the bus.

Out the windows on the right side of the bus, Arlo got his first look at the camp itself. Tucked into the tree-lined hills at the eastern side of the lake were several buildings, mostly log cabins. Beyond them, trails led up to the campsites.

The bus passed by a patrol of Rangers from another company headed for the water. They were in swimsuits, carrying their towels.

"That's Cheyenne Company," said Wu. "The patrol that won the Alpine Derby."

Indeed, Arlo recognized one of the boys. He was blind, and waved in the direction of the bus. Arlo waved back. It felt rude not to.

This was the first time Arlo realized they would be sharing the camp with others. "How many companies are up here?"

"Six or seven," said Connor. "I think they're at capacity this session. Last I heard, they were scrambling to find room for everyone." Arlo did the math in his head: if each company had about 20 Rangers, that meant more than 120 kids were up on the mountain with them.

"But we still get Firebird, right?" asked Jonas.

"What's Firebird?" asked Arlo.

"It's the best campsite," said Wu. "We had it last year. It's a little bit away from the others, so it's more private."

"It's also farther away from the sinks and the latrine," added Indra. "So you have to walk more. But it's worth it."

"They won't announce sites until we get there," said Connor.

"But we're the smallest patrol, so they can put us anywhere. We'll just have to hope."

As they unloaded their packs from the truck, Arlo's patrol explained the basic layout of the camp to him.

At the edge of the parking lot stood two small cabins: the Trading Post and the Health Center. The former sold snacks and gear, while the latter was for first aid—everything from skinned knees to snakebites. "The Warden who runs it is pretty intense," said Wu.

Jonas agreed. "Last year, I cut my finger peeling potatoes. All I needed was a Band-Aid, but she started chanting and burning sage like I was possessed or something."

Further up the hill was the Nature Center, the meeting spot for several Ranger classes. Arlo had signed up for Elementary Spirits, which would be taught there.

At the top of the road was the Lodge. It was the largest building by far, a pine-clad box with a steeply pitched green roof. Twice each session, the whole camp ate together in its main hall—at tonight's opening dinner and again midway through.

Connor was at the far side of the parking lot, meeting with the other patrol leaders to learn who was assigned to which site. As he started walking back, he gave Blue Patrol a big smile and a thumbs-up.

"We got it! We got Firebird!" squealed Indra. "I knew we would."

"Was it your wish?" asked Wu. Indra nodded. "Mine too," he said.

Jonas was the first to notice that another Ranger was walking with Connor. "Who is that?"

It was a boy, small and wiry, with sandy blond hair. Arlo guessed he was twelve years old. He was definitely not from Pine Mountain; he wore a yellow neckerchief, which he was in the middle of undoing.

As they got closer, Connor introduced him. "So, guys, we have a new patrol member. He's from Texas. He'll be with us all camp."

For three long seconds, no one said a word. The whole thing had taken them by surprise.

Finally, the boy spoke. He had an accent. "Right nice to meet you all. I'm Thomas."

11
THE OUTSIDER

THOMAS HAD RUINED EVERYTHING.

Over the previous weeks, Blue Patrol had carefully planned every detail of camp life, from tent assignments to duty rosters to costumes for skit night. There had been meetings and debates, re-votes and compromises. The final plan had been unanimously accepted. The chore chart had been laminated.

But the sudden addition of a seventh patrol member threw everything into question.

While Thomas headed off to get his pack, the rest of the patrol circled around Connor.

"They can't do this, can they?" asked Jonas. "Just assign someone to our patrol?"

Connor was ready for their questions: "Rangers can choose to go to camps outside their region. It happens all the time." He stopped Jonas before he could interrupt. "And we're the smallest patrol. So they put him with us."

"Where will he sleep?" asked Wu. "Is he going to be in a tent by himself?"

"No one's allowed to bunk solo. It's camp rules," said Connor. "We'll squeeze a third cot in somewhere."

"With who?" asked Arlo. The plan had been for Arlo to bunk with Wu, Connor with Jonas, Indra with Julie. They certainly wouldn't put Thomas in with the girls, which meant—

"You're going to stick him with us, aren't you?" asked Wu, indignant.

Jonas jumped in: "Connor and I have a lot of patrol gear in our tent. There wouldn't be room."

"The gear could go in another tent!"

"Not ours!" said Julia. "We don't want you digging around in our tent all the time."

Arlo could feel a patrol-wide squall brewing, the likes of which they hadn't seen since the Alpine Derby. The twins would stick together. Indra would argue both sides. Connor would play the peacemaker—except he currently looked too exhausted to intervene.

If anyone was going to stop the drama, it would have to be Arlo. "It's fine," he said. "He can stay with me and Wu. We'll make it work."

Wu stared at Arlo, surprised and betrayed.

Arlo had done a quick calculation and decided it was better

to have one angry Ranger than five. Besides, Wu would forgive him. They were best friends.

As Thomas headed back their way, Julie suddenly thought of a new problem: "Guys, the duty roster is made for six people. What is Thomas going to do? There's not even a spot for him."

Connor sighed. "What Arlo said: we'll make it work."

Like Wu, whose full name was Henry Wu, Thomas went by his last name.

"My first name's kind of embarrassing," he said, hoisting his pack. "It was my daddy's, and his daddy's, but they didn't use it either. So who knows why they gave it to me."

"What is it?" asked Julie, intrigued.

"You're gonna have to guess," he said with a smile.

On the trail to Firebird, the patrol took turns speculating what his first name might be. *Marion? Clyde? Seymour? Snarklebutt?* The suggestions got sillier as they went. With each wrong guess, Thomas just shook his head.

Then Indra proposed *Alvin*. The way Thomas looked at her suggested she was close. They started shotgunning variants at him: *Albert, Allan, Alten, Elvin, Albin, Alien, Alice, Alva*—

He held up his hand to stop them. "Wow! You got it."

"Alva?" asked Wu in disbelief. "Really? That's a name?"

"I had an Aunt Alva," said Connor. "She was ninety-six."

"Very few people on Earth know my true name," said Thomas

with exaggerated seriousness. "Not at school, not in Rangers. Not even my dog back home, and he's seen me naked. So I'm trusting the six of you to take my secret to the grave. I can trust you all, right?"

Each of them swore to keep his name secret.

Thomas was from a small town in Texas near Laredo. His company only had two patrols—Yellow and Purple—with few good options for camping. "Basically, you got meadows with a river, or meadows without. Don't get me wrong; it's pretty. But it's all pretty in the same way, any direction you look." He had saved money from his paper route to come to Camp Redfeather, a place he'd only seen on the website.

It was his first time out of state. "Heck, it's nearly my first time out of Webb County. Closest I've come to climbing a mountain is walking up stairs."

Arlo decided he liked Thomas.

Part of it was situational. With Thomas joining the group, Arlo wasn't the newcomer anymore. Plus Thomas had a different energy from anyone else in Blue Patrol—looser, more easy-going. He wasn't interested in stirring things up.

Maybe Thomas was the Ranger they'd needed all along.

At first glance, the Firebird campsite was an unremarkable patch of dirt and pine needles. Four army-style canvas tents had been set up on wooden platforms, each holding two steel cots with ragged mattresses.

Nearby, a heavy wooden picnic table stood beside a half-barrel stove set in concrete.

In terms of basic features, it was no different than any of the other sites they'd passed on their way up the hill.

What made Firebird special was its location: it was completely hidden. You could walk right by it and not know it was there.

There were two trails in, but a dense tangle of trees made it so you couldn't see the tents themselves. An aspen grove formed the southern edge, white bark standing out against the bright green undergrowth. Indra pointed out a bonus trail through the grove that provided a shortcut to the Nature Center.

Arlo could hear birds all around and a creek burbling somewhere close by. He was certain that Firebird was the best campsite on the mountain, and maybe in all of Colorado.

As a patrol, they agreed to let Arlo, Wu and Thomas have the first pick of tents. They chose the one with the fewest gaps in the floorboards. ("That way, squirrels are less likely to come through," said Wu.) Carrying a cot over from the unused fourth tent, they placed it perpendicular to the others, forming a U. It was a tight fit, but it would work.

Thomas offered to take the back bed. "After all, I'm the interloper."

After months of camping in small nylon tents, these canvas tents felt spacious. Arlo could stand up in the center, or sit on his cot to take off his socks. On normal campouts, tents were for sleeping. These tents were for living. With the flaps tied open, they were like little rooms.

There wasn't time to fully unpack, because the whole company was headed to the lake for the swimming test. Arlo quickly changed into his suit and grabbed his towel.

"The water comes from a glacier, so it's really cold," explained Indra on the way back down the hill.

"There's also a plesiosaur named Ekafos," said Wu.

"It's not a plesiosaur," said Indra.

"How do you know?"

"Because I looked it up. Plesiosaurs are saltwater. Redfeather Lake is fresh water."

"So it evolved. He adapted."

Thomas interrupted. "Wait, are you all saying there's a dinosaur swimming in the lake? Like the Loch Ness monster?"

Arlo was happy that there was another patrol member to ask these basic questions. It was usually his job.

Wu said yes. Indra said no, but provided more context: "The story is that there's a dinosaur named Ekafos who's been stranded in the lake for millions of years. He only comes out at night when there's no one around to see him, which seems convenient."

"How do we know it's a boy dinosaur?" asked Julie. "All they've ever found are footprints, and you can't tell from that."

"The footprints are probably fake anyway," said Jonas. "It's all a silly camp legend."

"My brother saw it," said Connor. "A couple years ago, he and some friends were down at the lake after dark. The moon was really low in the sky and this fog started drifting across the water. Then out of the mist, they saw it: this long neck sticking out. The light was behind it, so they couldn't make it out that clearly. Christian sent a snaplight towards it and it just disappeared."

"We've got weird stuff in Texas, too," said Thomas. "My company, there's a lake we camp at—more like a marsh, if I'm being honest—and they've got some critters there that are definitely not from our side of things. These ones, they'll spray this purple gunk on you—"

"Faerie beetles," said Wu with a groan.

"Sounds like you have experience." Wu nodded. On Arlo's first day at school in Pine Mountain, Wu had arrived covered in purple goo from a run-in with one of these strange insects. It had taken hours of scrubbing to get the sticky, jingling substance off.

"The funny thing is, the grown-ups, they never seem to notice this stuff," said Thomas. "All these crazy things are right under their noses and they can't see 'em."

"We call it the Wonder," said Arlo.

Thomas nodded. "That's a good word for it. And from what I hear, these mountains have a lot of Wonder. That's half of why I wanted to come here, to see what I've been missing."

They were nearly at the lake. Arlo could see other patrols hanging their towels on the pegs by the dock.

Suddenly, Julie blurted out: "We were in the Long Woods last winter. A hag was trying to kill us, but then Arlo killed her."

Arlo winced. After their experience in the Valley of Fire, they had agreed not to tell anyone outside the patrol what had happened. Yes, Thomas was technically part of the patrol, but it felt too soon to include him on the secret.

Thomas looked over at Arlo, impressed. "Wouldn't have picked you for a killer."

12
ON THREE

THE WATER WAS SO COLD it burned.

With each step Arlo took into the lake, he felt a sharp sting as a new section of skin became submerged. Even his dry arms had goose bumps.

As the ripples rose over his kneecaps, he looked down into the murky green water. He couldn't see his feet, but he could feel the mud squeezing between his toes. The water began wicking up his swim trunks.

Indra waded past him. "You just have to go for it!" She crouched down and pushed off, joining a dozen other Rangers headed for the buoy fifty yards away.

Arlo knew how to swim. In a proper pool with lanes and chlorine and a temperature suitable for humans, he was actually pretty good. But this was altogether different.

Thomas came up beside him, hugging himself for warmth.

They exchanged a look of mutual sympathy and disbelief. Everyone else in the patrol had already passed them.

Arlo nodded in the direction of the buoy. "On three, we just go for it?"

Thomas nodded. Arlo steeled himself, then gave a slow three-count. He reached his arms forward, but the rest of his body refused to cooperate. He couldn't will himself to actually move.

Thomas laughed. He hadn't budged either. "I was waiting on you!"

"Okay, this time, let's promise each other we'll really do it." It was easy to break a promise to yourself. It was harder to break one to someone else.

"I'm in," said Thomas. "Cross my heart and hope to die. Or, not die, but . . ."

"Exactly." Arlo shook his arms loose. Took a few deep breaths. With a nod, he and Thomas counted in unison: "One. Two. Three!"

Arlo leaned into the water, letting it come up to his shoulders. His chest contracted. His ears rang. But the cold didn't kill him. He pushed his feet against the slimy lake bottom and started kicking.

Other than the temperature and the weird taste of the water, lake swimming honestly wasn't that different from swimming in the YMCA pool. He quickly found his rhythm. By the time he reached the buoy, he had made up a lot of distance, eventually passing Connor and Wu.

Toweling off on the shore afterwards, his skin felt electric. He sought out a sunbeam to warm up.

Everyone in Blue Patrol had passed the swimming test, which meant they were allowed to use the rafts, canoes and rope swing. In fact, the big board by the lifeguard tower had tokens for every member of Pine Mountain Company except one: Russell Stokes. He was sitting alone on a rock nearby. He hadn't even changed into a swimsuit.

Arlo asked Wu if he knew why.

"He says he's got a punctured eardrum. He's not supposed to get in the water."

Russell noticed Arlo watching him. He glared and gave him the finger.

Arlo wondered if there might be a different reason Russell wasn't getting in the water.

Dinner that night was in the Lodge, with more than two hundred Rangers and camp staff seated at long tables. Arlo was surprised to find companies from as far away as Ohio and Massachusetts, some of whom had had to drive for days to get to Redfeather.

Everyone was in uniform, but neckerchiefs proved to be a handy way of telling groups apart. Patrols ended up all over the color wheel. Tulsa's Blue Patrol was sky blue, while Pine Mountain's was closer to navy.

In order to get kids from different companies talking to each other, tables were assigned by drawing from a bowl. Arlo ended up next to the blind Ranger from Cheyenne. His name was Farhad, and he'd already gotten his Owl. Like Arlo, he was going for his Canoeing patch, so the odds were good they'd be in the same class.

Arlo hadn't met anyone who was blind before, and wasn't sure how much help to offer him. Ultimately, Arlo just described the bowls of food as they were passed around. Farhad was more than able to manage for himself.

A counselor named Jellybeans was assigned to their table. Apparently, all the staff went by nicknames; Jellybeans had chosen hers because they were her favorite food. "Honestly, it would be doughnuts, but there was already a Doughnut when I started last year."

Jellybeans was from Orem, Utah, and taught Pathfinding. She was in college now, but had gotten to Ram when she was in Rangers. "Most of the counselors have at least their Ram. There are a couple of Bears, though. And the Wardens know super advanced stuff, obviously."

Warden was a nebulous term that had confused Arlo at first. In general, it referred to any adult who was involved with Rangers. For Pine Mountain Company, four of the parents were listed as Wardens, but they didn't have any real responsibilities beyond driving and signing checks. On campouts, they set up their tents nearby but left the running of things to the marshal (originally Christian, now Diana) and the patrol leaders. Most Wardens didn't seem to know any special Ranger skills. Arlo doubted they could even cast a snaplight.

But there were some Wardens who were clearly different.

At the Alpine Derby, Arlo had seen three Wardens perform remarkable acts of firecraeft, bending the flames into impossible shapes. Connor had told stories of Wardens who protected ancient sites around the world using abilities that went far beyond anything in the Field Book—and perhaps any book. Apparently, a lot of their knowledge was only handed down from person to person, never written down lest it fall into the wrong hands.

Jellybeans motioned to the front of the room, where a Warden had stepped up onto the hearth of the fireplace. She was tall, with dark tanned skin and silver-gray hair that hung in a braid down her back. "That's the camp director," said Jellybeans.

The Warden was evidently preparing to speak, but the room was still noisy with a hundred conversations and clattering plates.

She put two fingers to her lips, then raised them up.

A moment later, a wave of silence swept across the room. It was unnerving. In just a few seconds, the volume dropped to almost zero, as noiseless as the moonlight on a snowy night. Arlo could hear himself breathing.

"What is this?" he tried to ask, but his voice was muted.

He would later learn this skill was simply called *hush.* It was mostly for stealthy tracking in the forest, but also worked on noisy kids.

"Good evening, Rangers!" she said with a broad smile. "I am Warden Mpasu. It is my pleasure to welcome you to Camp Redfeather."

She spoke with an accent Arlo couldn't place. Every word was crisp and deliberate. Even as the hush began to fade, she had everyone's rapt attention. It wasn't magic. It was the force of her personality.

"Over the next two weeks, I wish for each of you to have a remarkable experience, one that challenges you. Inspires you. You will learn much from your counselors and from your fellow Rangers. You will learn skills. You will learn leadership. You will learn how little you know. But this is not a school. This is a place of wonder and discovery and real danger. That is why we have rules."

She held up a phone. "There are no electronic devices allowed here. No phones. No games. No digital books. You are here to be in nature, not technology. So if these things are found, they will be taken, and both your company and your patrol will receive demerits. If you have them, you must give them to your marshal immediately after dinner."

Arlo noticed a few glances between Rangers—evidently some of them had brought things they shouldn't have.

Warden Mpasu continued. "There is also no peanut butter permitted at Camp Redfeather." She traded the phone for a shredded nylon backpack. "A Ranger was wearing this pack when the howlers attacked him. He lost an eye and an ear. The howlers were after a small bag of Reese's Pieces he had hidden in his pack. If you brought peanut butter to this camp, you have put yourself in grave danger," she said. "If it is in your tent, your tent is likely now destroyed."

She handed the backpack to a table of Rangers so they could inspect the damage. One kid put his hand through a hole.

"The final rule concerns where Rangers may and may not go. The boundaries of the camp are clear. But there are places within the camp you are not to go either. Such as the staff campsite. Such as my house on the road. Ask yourself, 'Is it appropriate for me to be here?' If the answer is no, then the answer is no."

She smiled. "If you follow these rules, you will likely never speak to me. And that is as it should be. I am not your mother. I am not your teacher. In the end, the confidence to solve your own problems is the most important skill a Ranger must learn. That is what this place can teach you, if you let it. May your path be safe."

The Rangers answered back: "May your aim be true."

With a small nod, the Warden stepped down from the hearth. The din of the crowd slowly grew as eating and conversation resumed.

Arlo had never heard an adult speak quite like that before. He found himself eager to impress Warden Mpasu while at the same time suspecting that that was impossible.

He wanted to ask Indra or Wu what they thought, but the rest of his patrol was spread throughout the room. The only member of his company anywhere nearby was Russell Stokes. He was sitting at the next table, with his back to Arlo.

As he was passing down a bowl of macaroni and cheese, Russell's neckerchief shifted. That's when Arlo saw it: a bloodstain soaking through his shirt, just below his collar. It was the size of a quarter, and fresh.

Russell adjusted his neckerchief, hiding the bloody spot.

As Pine Mountain Company hiked back from the Lodge, Arlo kept an eye on Russell. He didn't seem to be hurt. He was joshing with his Red Patrol buddies like always. But Arlo was certain that Russell knew he was bleeding. Twice, his hand slipped behind the neckerchief, as if scratching an itch.

Indra came up beside Arlo, keeping her voice low. "I think we should wait on telling them."

"Wait on telling who what?"

"Jonas and Julie, about the Long Woods and the Broken Bridge. It's already late, and now with Thomas in the patrol, it's going to be weird to pull them aside."

So much had happened that Arlo had forgotten about the twins and the decision on the bus. "That's fine."

"But we should tell them," said Indra. "I still think that's the right decision, don't you?"

Arlo nodded. "Definitely." He watched as Russell tweaked his neckerchief. Arlo was certain he was trying to make sure the stain was covered.

Once they reached Firebird, Arlo kept looking for a moment when he could talk to Connor alone, hoping to get his advice on Russell. But Connor headed straight to bed, barely saying goodnight.

Whatever was going on with Russell Stokes would need to wait until morning.

13
LAKE

ARLO WAS STANDING in Redfeather Lake, a few feet from the shore. Surprisingly, the water was crystal clear. He could see his toes flexing in the mud.

Golden sunlight glinted off the surface, so bright that Arlo had to squint.

He was alone.

"Do you know who I am?"

It was a man's voice. Hadryn. Arlo was suddenly back at the diner. The golden coin was spinning on the table. That was the light he was seeing.

This was a memory.

"Do you know who I am?" asked the voice again.

No.

"Do you know why I'm here?"

No. Arlo was whispering.

"I'm here to help you, Arlo Finch. I'm the only one who can help you. Say it."

You're the only one who can help me. As he spoke, Arlo felt himself holding the words in his hands, feeling their weight as if they were physical objects. He wanted to set them down, but there was no place to put them.

"The Eldritch, they want both of us. So you can't tell anyone I was here. Say it."

I can't tell anyone.

He was holding these words, too. They were even heavier.

Arlo was back in the lake. He was sinking into the mud. Or was he being pulled? It was up to his ankles. His knees.

He tried to pull his feet out, but every movement just sucked him in deeper. The mud was up to his waist. The water had nearly reached his chin.

"You wouldn't lie to me, would you, Arlo Finch?"

Arlo shook his head.

"Because I know where you live. I know your friends. I know your family."

Arlo struggled to keep his mouth above the surface. He gasped for air.

"Do you know what happened at the lake?"

Arlo held his breath as water suddenly rushed over his face. He could see a blurry shape of a man backlit by the sun.

Hadryn's voice echoed in his head:

"You made me."

14
WHAT WE BRING WITH US

ARLO WOKE SUDDENLY, gasping for breath. His heart was racing. It took a few moments before he realized he wasn't drowning.

It was dark in the tent, just a little moonlight spilling around the edges of the flaps. The heavy canvas walls were completely still. Arlo could hear Wu and Thomas breathing, and beyond that, the dull rush of the nearby creek.

He knew it was a dream. He hadn't really been drowning in the lake.

But the part in the diner, he was pretty sure that was real. Arlo had recalled a portion of the conversation with Hadryn. It was like finding a photo you didn't remember taking.

Arlo turned on his side—the bedsprings creaked—and fished under the cot for his water bottle. He found it. Empty.

Now he was thirsty.

Firebird looked different in the dark. Colder. Emptier. In moonlit monochrome, the white trunks of the aspen trees glowed. The dirt showed distinct footprints.

Arlo debated grabbing his lantern, but decided there was enough light to navigate his way to the sinks.

Everyone called it "the sinks," but in truth it was simply a pipe with six spigots suspended over a slab of concrete. It was the lone water source for Pine Mountain Company's four patrols, so it became a nexus of activity, from brushing teeth to filling canteens. When there was camp gossip, this was where it spread.

As he rounded the bend in the path, Arlo saw a single figure in the distance. Someone was standing at the sinks, scrubbing. Arlo froze.

It was Russell.

He had his uniform shirt under the running water, rubbing the fabric together. He was trying to get the bloodstain out.

Arlo considered backtracking into the trees, leaving Russell alone. In the morning, he could ask Connor's advice. Together, they would figure out the right thing to do and say.

But that would mean waiting. That would mean spending the rest of the night wondering where the blood had come from. Russell was here in front of him, alone. If Arlo wanted answers, there was no better time.

Unscrewing the top of his water bottle, Arlo walked to the sinks.

Russell looked up, startled. Once he recognized Arlo, he shook his head in annoyance, but didn't stop scrubbing his shirt.

Arlo filled his bottle from one of the spigots. He pointed at the shirt: "What's happening there?"

"Nothing you need to worry about, Flinch."

Fine. We'll play it that way. "There was something in your pack this morning. Then at the lake, you didn't go in the water. I don't think you really have a punctured eardrum. I think it's because you didn't want to take your shirt off."

Russell kept scrubbing.

Arlo continued: "Then at dinner, there was blood soaking through your uniform. Now you're scrubbing it out. So something's going on."

"I'm fine. Just leave it alone."

"Tell me what it is or I'll tell someone else. I'll tell Diana or a Warden if I have to, because if someone's hurting you . . ."

"No one's hurting me! It's just a thing."

"What kind of thing?"

Russell twisted off the spigot. The silence was jarring. Russell stared daggers at Arlo. Arlo held his gaze. He didn't flinch. Finally, Russell gave up.

"It's called a grisp," he said. "It's like a tick."

Arlo knew about ticks from the Field Book. They were tiny bugs that dug into your skin and could cause diseases like Rocky Mountain spotted fever. On campouts, Arlo was careful to check himself every morning. He and Wu looked through each other's hair.

Arlo knew this was no mere tick. Ticks were tiny, the size of a grain of rice. Whatever had been moving inside Russell's pack was much, much larger. But Arlo decided not to challenge Russell quite yet.

"The grisp. Where is it now?" Arlo asked.

Russell was silent for a long moment, then sighed. "It's on my shoulder." He stretched the collar of his T-shirt to show him. Arlo leaned in to look. But it was just skin, no bug.

"It's invisible," Russell explained. There was nothing in his tone of voice to suggest he was joking. "I can feel it, though. When it moves, and when it bites."

Arlo was skeptical, but his time in Pine Mountain had taught him that a lot of unlikely things were real. "Where did it come from?" he asked.

"Last month on the campout, I was out in the woods and I saw this squirrel staring at me. It was big, and just kind of weird looking. So I threw a rock at it." He said it like, *Of course I threw a rock at it, that's what you do when something looks weird.* "I hit it. Then I found the body, and I was leaning over it when suddenly I felt this little prick."

"On your neck?"

"On my leg first, right through my sock. But it's bit me all over now." Russell pulled up his T-shirt to show a bruise just below his ribs, and another on his back. Even in the moonlight, Arlo could make out distinct puncture marks. They had to hurt.

"You have to tell somebody," Arlo said.

Russell shook his head. "I looked it up in *Culman's*. A grisp only lives six weeks. It's already been four. I'll just tough it out."

"But what if *Culman's* is wrong? I mean, it doesn't know everything." *I've seen wisps and trolls in real life. They're scarier than in the book.*

"I'll be fine." Russell was clearly ready for the conversation to be over. He started squeezing the water out of his uniform shirt.

"Does anyone else know?"

"No. So if anyone says anything—if I even hear the word *grisp*—I'll know it was you." Russell didn't bother to make a specific threat. The beating was implied.

Then Arlo had an idea. He slipped off his left boot—it hadn't been tied—and started unlacing it.

"What are you doing?" Russell asked.

"You said it's invisible. Sometimes that's because things aren't actually in our world." He knew that sounded confusing. "Just trust me."

Arlo looped the shoelace in his hand and began twisting it, trying to feel that spot where the fibers started moving through themselves.

For the past few months, Arlo had been practicing his slipknaughts—the weird multidimensional knots he'd first encountered during the Alpine Derby. Tying them had become fairly straightforward; opening them was still nearly impossible. They invariably collapsed. He suspected that the large slipknaught he'd opened in the Valley of Fire had had something to do with the strange forces of the Long Woods.

But that didn't matter at the moment. For what he was doing, he only needed a small opening. With his fingernails, he carefully tugged the knaught into a circle no larger than a quarter. A thin film shimmered inside it, like a soap bubble.

"How are you doing that?" asked Russell.

"It's just something I can do." Arlo held the loop up to his right eye like a monocle, squinting. Through the slipknaught lens he perceived a shadowy reality. The focus wasn't sharp, but he could clearly see Russell—and the grisp.

Russell had told the truth: a bizarre creature really was on his shoulder. "I see it," Arlo said, trying not to react too strongly.

"What does it look like?" asked Russell. "*Culman's* doesn't have a picture."

Arlo took his time to find the right words to describe it. "It's white. Milky white. You know in science books, when they have magnified photos of bugs, like aphids or mosquitos, and they sort of look alien?"

"Yeah."

"It's like that."

What Arlo had said was true, but misleading. He'd left out the single most important detail: *the grisp was the size of a house cat.*

It wasn't just sitting on Russell's shoulder. It was hunched there, predatory. Its six bulging eyes stared in different directions, eyelids blinking independently.

Like an insect, the grisp's body was covered in a scaly exoskeleton. It had at least ten legs, each covered with barbs. Every part of it was white or translucent, except for two fangs—*mandibles?*—that were filled with blood.

Arlo carefully reached one hand forward to touch it. His fingers passed right through the grisp; it was insubstantial, just like Cooper the ghost dog.

A tiny thread of silver light connected the creature's thorax to Russell's shoulder. Arlo suspected it was tethered to him by that single point. *That's why Russell thinks it's small. He only feels that tiny part.*

The knaught suddenly collapsed, the film inside popping. Arlo couldn't see the grisp anymore.

Arlo debated how much he should tell Russell. He didn't want to panic him. "You should go to the Health Center," he said. "The Warden who runs it, maybe she would know how to get rid of it."

Russell shrugged. "Yeah. Maybe."

"You'll go?"

"I said maybe." He pointed a finger at Arlo. "But I'm not telling anyone else, and neither are you."

He waited until Arlo said: "Okay."

Russell left, headed back to the Red campsite with his uniform shirt.

Arlo stood alone at the sinks, listening to the spigot drip. The sky was beginning to purple. In a few hours, they'd hear the bugle sounding reveille. After breakfast, Arlo could pull Connor aside to ask his advice in a way that didn't break his promise to Russell.

Or he could figure it out himself.

Maybe it was time to stop running to others for guidance. After all, he already knew what Connor would say: *Loyal, brave, kind and true. What does the Ranger's Vow tell you to do?*

Loyal and *true* argued for keeping his word and saying nothing. That felt certain. But which was the *brave* choice—respecting Russell's wishes, or ignoring them? Was Arlo more afraid of Russell's anger at being betrayed, or of Russell being hurt by a creature he didn't fully understand? It was hard to say.

That left *kind*. On this point, the Field Book urged Rangers to consider the Golden Rule: treat others how you'd wish to be treated. If Arlo were being nibbled on by an invisible monster, would he want Russell telling others about it? Absolutely not.

While Arlo didn't have a bloodsucking grisp on his shoulder, he had things of his own he wasn't ready to share, including his encounter with Hadryn. Secrets—even painful secrets—belong to their owner. To reveal them without permission was a kind of theft.

Besides, Arlo suspected his own life was in much more danger than Russell's. Shadowy forces beyond the Long Woods were regularly conspiring to kill him. As creepy as the grisp was, it was just a bug. Russell deserved the time and privacy to deal with it himself.

The swirling thoughts in Arlo's mind quieted. He washed his hands. They weren't really dirty, but it felt right.

Then he walked back to his tent and slept until the bugle woke him up.

15
ALWAYS BLUE

THE MORNING DIDN'T GO as planned. For starters, their underwear was missing.

Digging through his pack, Arlo was able to locate his socks, his shorts and his camp T-shirts. But he couldn't find a single pair of briefs. Neither could Wu or Thomas.

"Guys!" shouted Indra from outside.

They opened the tent flap to find Indra and Julie pointing at the trees. Underwear was hanging from every branch. It was as if a cyclone had struck, sucking up all the undergarments and depositing them high in the surrounding trees.

Briefs dangled amid the pinecones. Bras swayed in the morning breeze. *Indra and Julie wear bras,* Arlo suddenly realized. That had never really occurred to him.

Something else was different: Indra's hair. Yesterday, it had been straight and shiny, just like Diana's. This morning, it was bigger and curlier than it had ever been. It was like a hood of hair.

"What happened?" he whispered, pointing to her head.

Indra sighed. "I think it's because of the swim test yesterday. I guess it couldn't get wet."

Retrieving his underpants from a branch, Wu was furious. "This had to be Red Patrol. We need to retaliate."

"We could tie their tents shut," said Julie. "And then fill them with bees."

Wu sparked to that idea. "There's a hive in the field east of the lake. They use it for Insectology. We just need a smoker and some kind of bag to hold the bees."

"What if someone's allergic to bees?" asked Arlo. "It could kill them."

Julie was icy. "Then Red Patrol will learn not to mess with our underwear."

"It wasn't Red," said Connor, stepping out of his tent. "It was pixies."

Connor had set up the standard wards around the site, but those wouldn't stop pixies. These invisible sprites were native to the forest, so you couldn't simply wall them off. "You have to bribe them," he explained as he used a stick to retrieve a pair of boxers from a branch. "They like shiny pennies and sunflower seeds. We should have set some out last night."

"Then why didn't we?" asked Jonas.

"I forgot," said Connor. He had a weariness that made him seem older than his fourteen years. "Sorry, I'm just really run-down. I think I'm getting a cold or something." He sat at the picnic table and laced up his boots.

It took teamwork to retrieve all their underwear, with some Rangers climbing trees while others lashed poles together. At Arlo's suggestion, they treated it like an Alpine Derby challenge, scoring one point for each pair of briefs, two for each bra. (The straps made the bras harder to snag, plus there were fewer of them.) Having it be a game also made it less awkward to be touching other people's underclothes. At the end of half an hour, they had ninety-seven points and a table full of garments to sort through.

Arlo was used to picking through laundry, but it felt weird to see all of his friends' underwear, especially the girls' stuff. Luckily, every piece had the Ranger's name written on the tag per camp instructions. Except—

"Who's Hicks?" asked Jonas, reading a pair of briefs.

"And who's Ramos?" asked Indra, looking at a different pair.

"They're both mine," said Thomas, taking them.

There was a long silence while the remaining six members wordlessly debated who was going to ask the natural follow-up question.

Wu took it. "Why do you have other people's underwear?"

Thomas didn't look up from his folding. Arlo guessed he was trying to think of the right way to answer.

Finally, Thomas set his pile aside. "So, a couple months ago there was a fire. No one was hurt, but my family's house burned down. And it's not like we had a lot of money before that, but it sort of wiped us out. The Rangers in my company, they threw a pancake breakfast and raised enough money to pay for me to come to camp here. They knew I had always wanted to come. But my pack, and all my stuff, it burned. So everything I have is theirs. I know it's weird to have other people's underwear, but it's what I got. And I feel so lucky to have it, because I know where it came from. I'm here because of Hicks and Ramos and . . ." He picked up a new pair, reading the tag. "Delgado?"

"That's actually mine," said Jonas. The underwear all did kind of look the same.

Thomas smiled. "I just know I'm lucky to have my friends back home, and you all here. The fire was awful, but it reminded me what's important."

Connor spoke for the patrol. "If you need anything, just ask, okay? You're one of us, and we stick together." He reached out his hand. Everyone stacked theirs on top of his.

"Always true!" said Connor.

"Always Blue!" the rest answered back.

16
THE TURN

IT WAS COMPLETELY OBVIOUS how to paddle a canoe until you actually tried doing it.

Just minutes earlier, on land, Arlo had felt confident that he and Indra had mastered the fundamentals. He knew how to grip the paddle and why it was important to keep it vertical when pulling back. They had practiced staying in rhythm and calling out turns.

But once they got on the water, all bets were off.

Simply getting into the canoe was surprisingly difficult. Standing ankle-deep in the icy lake, Arlo braced the stern while Indra slowly crept her way to the bow, where she kneeled on the aluminum shell. They weren't allowed to use the seats; staying on your knees gave more power, and made the canoe less likely to tip over.

Then it was Arlo's turn to climb in. Without anyone to steady the back, the canoe rocked wildly.

"Careful!" cried Indra unhelpfully.

The life jacket made the whole process extra clumsy, riding up against Arlo's ears as he hunched over. The fabric was scratchy and smelled like algae and sunscreen. He transfered his weight as evenly as he could, but a little water still rushed over the edges of the canoe.

Reaching his designated spot, Arlo sat back on his wet sneakers and used his paddle to push off from shore. They were finally floating free.

They were the sixth out of ten canoes in the water. Thomas and Wu were already far ahead. They barely seemed to be paddling, yet their boat cut a fast, silent line through the water.

Meanwhile, Arlo and Indra were struggling. Each stroke sent them veering left or right, then overcorrecting, until they ultimately found themselves facing in the wrong direction, staring back at the docks.

"Finch! Jones!" called their instructor, Trix. She had pigtails and a megaphone. "Use your J-strokes!"

Arlo remembered those: the paddle needed to flare out at the end of the stroke, creating a J shape. He thought he had been doing that the whole time, but now he redoubled his effort, scooping deep into the water.

But they weren't turning. If anything, they were lurching the wrong way faster.

Then he realized the problem: Indra was doing the same stroke at the front of the canoe.

"She means me!" Arlo shouted. "J-strokes are for the back."

"Then what do I do?"

"Don't do anything. Let me fix this."

Indra rested her paddle across the frame, clearly annoyed. Arlo knew she wanted to be in control, but canoes were steered mostly from the stern. That was one of the first things Trix had taught them half an hour ago, back when they thought they'd mastered canoeing.

Arlo kept paddling, switching sides from left to right. The canoe barely budged. It was like they were floating on pancake syrup. Plus his knees hurt from the grit rubbing into his skin.

With each stroke, he questioned the basic premise of canoeing, an activity that had clearly been created to frustrate and humiliate. *Why does anyone need to canoe anyway? Aren't rowboats better? Their oars are locked into place. There probably isn't even a Ranger patch for rowing because there's no skill to it. You just . . .*

"Stop!" shouted Indra.

Arlo looked up to see they were headed towards a thicket of reeds at the edge of the lake. Flies and moths flitted between the cattails. Oily foam floated on the water.

They needed to stop, but how? Canoes didn't have brakes.

Indra looked back. "We need to do fan strokes to turn."

"We haven't learned those yet."

"They're in the Field Book. You go clockwise. I'll go counterclockwise."

She demonstrated, sweeping her paddle across the surface of the water in a wide arc. Arlo did the same. To his relief, the canoe began to twist in the water. Yet they were still headed for the reeds. Arlo wasn't sure if it was momentum or the wind pushing them.

"Why is this so hard?" he asked.

"I don't know," she said. "We're doing everything right."

That couldn't be true. None of the other teams were having nearly as much trouble. Even Farhad and his patrol mate from the Cheyenne Company had found their rhythm, the blind Ranger smiling broadly as he paddled at the front of their canoe.

No matter what they tried, Arlo and Indra kept drifting towards the marshy grass. As the canoe slid amid the reeds, startled grasshoppers jumped into the boat, pinging against the aluminum shell like popcorn kernels. Arlo tried to shoo them out, to no avail.

Then he looked up and saw Indra. He let out a single laugh.

"What?!" she demanded, turning back to face him.

Indra's hair was completely covered in fluffy white cattail fuzz. It made her look like a kindly grandmother, or Mrs. Claus.

"What's so funny?!"

Arlo made a pinching motion towards his hair. Indra reached up to her own hair and plucked off a single bit of fluff, letting the wind carry it off. She assumed that was it.

To Arlo, this just made it all the funnier. Which made Indra angrier: "This isn't funny! We're going to fail Canoeing."

"This isn't a test," he pointed out. "We're not being graded."

"Of course we are! They're just not telling us."

In that moment, Arlo felt he suddenly understood Indra better. She never seemed particularly worried about tests and homework in school. She got As and Bs and an occasional C. In P.E. class, she wasn't particularly aggressive. But when it came to Rangers, she was obsessed with placing first. She had memorized huge portions of the Field Book and practiced knots blindfolded. Wu had called her a "super Ranger," and that felt accurate.

Arlo wondered if Indra's selective competitive streak had something to do with her older sister, who not only made it to the national fencing championships three years in a row, but was also ranked as one of the top high school clarinetists in the country. Indra had quickly given up on fencing, and while she played piano, she wasn't particularly good.

Rangers was the one thing she excelled in. So to be bad at canoeing was unforgivable.

"I'm sorry," Arlo said. "Let's just try to get out of here."

Indra shushed him.

"Do you hear that?" She pointed up.

Arlo rested his paddle and listened. Over the buzzing insects and trilling birds, he heard it: a low rush, like a washing machine in the spin cycle. "What is it?"

"I'm not sure. Maybe a plane?"

Waving the bugs out of his face, Arlo craned his neck up to look over the reeds. He couldn't see anything, but the sound was definitely getting louder. It was coming from the south.

He looked out at the other canoes on the lake. One by one, the teams stopped paddling, all of their attention focused on the southern peaks. Wu was pointing to a spot in the sky.

Something was coming.

Closer.

Louder.

Suddenly, the noise was deafening. Arlo put his fingers in his ears.

A bright red helicopter zoomed directly overhead. Arlo felt his body shake.

The surface of the lake rippled and shimmered from the force of the blades. The chopper slowed as it approached the gravel parking lot, preparing to land.

That's when Arlo saw the white cross on the side of the helicopter. This was an air ambulance.

His heart sank into his stomach. He felt sick.

He knew why they were here.

"We have to go," he said. "Right now!"

Arlo ran as fast as he could, wet sneakers squishing with every step. He shed his life jacket, dropping it on the trail.

There hadn't been time to bank the canoe properly, or to explain to Trix why he was racing out of class. He'd heard snippets of conversation as he passed other counselors at the waterfront—

"—a kid from Pine Mountain—"

"—never seen anything like it—"

"—just hope they caught it in time—"

It had to be Russell. He must have gone to the Health Center that morning. Or maybe he'd collapsed somewhere else. The only thing Arlo knew was that he had to get to the parking lot before the helicopter took off. He had to tell them what he knew about the grisp.

No matter what he'd promised Russell, if it really was life or death, he needed to let the doctors know what they were dealing with.

It wasn't just Russell who was in danger. The parasite might latch onto someone new. Or maybe it was laying eggs inside Russell's body that would suddenly burst forth, infecting an entire hospital. He had to warn them.

But first he had to get there. The trail to the lake hadn't seemed so long this morning. Now, running, it seemed endless.

Arlo saw the medical techs loading a stretcher into the helicopter. They slid the door shut. Warden Mpasu waved back a dozen onlookers as the helicopter's blades began to spin up again.

"Wait!" shouted Arlo. "WAIT!"

He was too far away, and the engines were too loud. He kept running.

Diana Velasquez spotted him. She moved to intercept him, taking him by the shoulders.

"It's okay!" she shouted over the helicopter roar. "He'll be okay."

Arlo squinted in the rising dust. "Do they know what it is?"

"They think so. They'll do an X-ray at the hospital to make sure."

Arlo wondered if a grisp would really show up in an X-ray. He supposed it was possible; X-rays did show invisible things. But he had a hard time believing a normal hospital was really equipped to deal with a supernatural parasite from the Long Woods. Maybe they were taking him to a specialty clinic.

He covered his ears as the helicopter lifted off the ground. The wind was so strong it rattled his teeth. Diana shielded him from the worst of it. She was a foot taller than him.

The helicopter turned, then passed directly overhead, lights blinking along its belly. It flew south, back across the lake.

Quiet slowly returned. Arlo watched as dozens more campers streamed in from their classes to watch the departing chopper. Indra, Wu and Thomas were running down the path from the waterfront.

And then Arlo saw him, standing by the Trading Post: Russell Stokes.

He was standing with his Red Patrol buddies, watching the helicopter fly away. But if Russell was here, then—

Arlo grabbed Diana by the arm. "Wait—who was in the helicopter?"

"Connor," she said. "He's really sick. They may have to do surgery."

Arlo blinked hard, disbelieving. Then he looked back to the south, where the helicopter was just a black dot in the sky.

Indra, Wu and Thomas arrived, winded.

"What happened?" asked Wu.

"Connor's gone."

17
LOYALTIES

LUNCH THAT DAY WAS cheese sandwiches with apples and potato chips—but no one was eating much. Sipping his watery red punch, Arlo glanced around the picnic table, making occasional eye contact with the other five members of the patrol. He suspected everyone was thinking the same thing, but no one wanted to say it.

Finally, Julie broke the silence. "If Connor dies, it's our fault. Patrols are supposed to look out for each other, and we didn't."

"We're not doctors," said Jonas. "We couldn't have known."

"But we should have wondered. I mean, something was definitely wrong from the moment we got on the bus. He was tired and probably already sick, but none of us said anything, because we never worried about Connor. He just worried about us. And now he's in a hospital somewhere because we were too busy thinking about our own problems."

Julie had a knack for saying the wrong thing the wrong way at the wrong time, but in this case Arlo thought she was absolutely right. They had taken Connor for granted. They had failed him.

"Connor's not going to die," said Indra. "Diana said they think it's his appendix, or maybe his spleen. If that's it, they'll do surgery to take it out. He'll be okay."

"But he won't be back," said Jonas. "At least not for the rest of camp."

"No. He won't," she agreed.

"So who's in charge now?" asked Wu.

The Field Book was surprisingly unhelpful on this question. The chapter on patrol life suggested that if leaders knew they were going to be absent for a meeting or campout, they should designate a temporary patrol leader in advance. But Connor hadn't picked anyone before being whisked away. It was unclear what was supposed to happen.

"Jonas and I are the highest rank," said Indra. They were both Owls, while everyone else was a Squirrel. "So it should probably be one of us."

Jonas shook his head. "No thanks. I don't want to be patrol leader. I just want to have fun."

"Summer camp isn't about fun," said Indra. "I mean, fun is fine, but it's not just that."

Wu pointed to Thomas. "Thomas is an Owl, too."

"Thomas isn't really in the patrol, is he?" asked Julie, as if he wasn't sitting across from her. "He's just visiting."

"Technically, I think he is in the patrol," said Indra. "He's on our roster, and Connor gave him a neckerchief."

Thomas waved away the attention. "Look, I'm happy to be part of Blue Patrol. But there's no way I should be your patrol leader. It's gotta be one of you. And Indra, she seems to know a lot and have a strong sense about how things should be."

"So she's patrol leader?" asked Julie.

"No, we should definitely vote," said Indra. "To make it official."

"I agree," said Arlo. Voting felt orderly and disciplined, like coiling a rope rather than leaving it tangled on the ground. Once Indra was elected, they could start figuring out how to function without Connor.

Jonas seemed satisfied. "All in favor of Indra being patrol leader?"

Thomas held up a finger to stop them. "But before we vote, I'd just say maybe we're overlooking someone else who might be great at the job, and that's Henry Wu. I've seen he has a lot of good ideas, and sometimes people aren't really listening." He turned to Wu. "This morning, you were talking about the duty roster. What were you saying?"

Wu was surprised to be on the spot. He swallowed his bite of sandwich. "It just seems like we're all assigned jobs based on a formula, not what we want to do, or what we're good at. Like, I'm really good at fire, and Jonas is really good at cooking, so why aren't we just always doing that?"

"Because we have to rotate jobs," said Indra.

"But why? Fire and cooking are the hardest things, so if Jonas and I want to do them . . ."

Julie interjected: "And I don't mind KP. I like washing dishes. I'm always happy to do that."

"It's not about what you *want* to do," said Indra. "It's what you *need* to do."

"But why does anyone need to build a fire if I'm always willing to do it?" asked Wu. "Or cook? Or wash dishes?"

"Because then the other people are stuck carrying water or doing Commissary runs."

"You can help me wash dishes if you really want to," offered Julie.

Indra scoffed. "I don't want to help! I want it to be my job or not be my job. That's why we have a duty roster. I don't know how to make it any more basic so you can understand."

Arlo winced. Julie glowered. Wu and Jonas exchanged a look. Indra seemed completely unaware of how her words were coming across.

"For what it's worth, back in Texas, my patrol never had duty rosters," said Thomas. "Stuff still got done. Everyone pitched in. We got along just great."

Jonas gestured to Wu. "If you were patrol leader, what would you do?"

"First thing, I'd tear up the duty roster. Everyone does what they want to do."

Indra was exasperated. "That's crazy! If you don't assign jobs, they don't get done. Besides, we all agreed on the duty roster together. It's not like this was forced on any of us."

Thomas gestured to Arlo. "What do you think?"

Arlo hated being called on. "I can see both sides," he said. He hoped that would be enough, but everyone seemed to expect him to say more. "I mean, it's good to know who is doing what, but some people are better than others at some things. And we're going to have to redo the duty roster anyway because Connor's gone. Maybe people could trade shifts or something, so they can do some jobs more often."

"Or we could just throw the duty roster in the fire and forget about it," said Wu. Arlo noticed that Wu had progressed from tearing up the roster to incinerating it.

"What you're proposing is anarchy," said Indra. "It would never work."

Wu snapped. "How do you know!? Why are you so sure I'm wrong?"

She shrugged. "Because you usually are."

Arlo shut his eyes and wished he were in the Long Woods. He would rather be chased by a troll than be in the middle of this argument.

"I think we should vote," said Jonas. "All in favor of Indra being patrol leader?"

Arlo felt his chest tighten. He was literally being forced to choose between his best friends. No matter which one he chose, the other would feel betrayed. *What would Connor do? He'd say to think about the Vow. Loyal*, *brave* and *kind* could go both ways, but if he focused on *true*, that tipped the scale. Indra was truly better prepared for the job.

He slowly raised his hand. He was the only one to do so.

He had expected Julie to vote for her tentmate, but she kept her arms crossed.

Wu stared directly at Arlo, a look of sadness and betrayal. He shook his head.

"All in favor of Wu?" asked Jonas.

Now Jonas, Julie and Thomas raised their hands. That was enough. He'd won.

"Congratulations," said Indra in a falsely happy tone. "I'll let Diana know." She then got up from the picnic table and walked away.

Wu untacked the duty roster from the tree and placed it on the fire. The patrol gathered around him, watching as the lamination bubbled and melted. In less than ten seconds, it was reduced to flakes of ash.

"We need to get you your stripes," said Thomas, pointing to the spot on Wu's sleeve where a patrol leader patch would go.

Arlo thought back to the encounter on the Broken Bridge, when he wondered why Other Wu was patrol leader rather than Other Indra. It had seemed impossible at the time.

Maybe it had happened like this.

18
TWO TRAILS

ARLO CAUGHT UP with Indra as they were headed down the hill to their afternoon classes. It was the first moment they'd had alone since Wu was picked as patrol leader.

"Are you okay?" he asked, walking alongside her.

"I'm fine," she said. "You shouldn't have voted for me."

"I wanted to. You'd do a better job."

"It doesn't matter. They were clearly going to vote for Wu. You should have let it be unanimous."

"Why?"

Indra stopped walking. "Because now I'm a loser. If everyone had voted for Wu, then it would have been consensus. Like I never ran. But now I clearly lost, three to one. And that's because of you."

Arlo couldn't believe she was blaming him. "I voted for you! I'm on your side!"

"It's the wrong side. Four against two. And now Wu's mad at you."

"No he's not."

"Of course he is! You picked me over him, which is exactly what he said you'd do at the bridge."

"That wasn't about me. That was about you being bossy." Arlo immediately regretted saying it.

Indra shook her head. "I hate that word. No one ever calls Connor bossy."

Arlo had to admit Indra was right. "Connor's older, though. He's also really good at listening."

"That's great feedback. Thanks." She started walking again.

Arlo followed her, not sure what to say. This whole argument seemed to be about Indra's fear of failure, but pointing it out didn't seem like a good idea. "Look, it'll be okay. Everyone's going to forget about it by tomorrow."

"They don't have to. I'll be fine, seriously. I already talked to Diana. After camp's over, I'm going to transfer to Green Patrol."

Arlo stopped short, stunned. "What do you mean?"

"I'm leaving. Green Patrol's a better fit for me anyway."

"But there won't be enough people left in Blue."

"New kids always join in the fall. There'll be someone to replace me."

They'd reached a fork in the path. Indra was headed left to the Lodge, while Arlo was headed right to the Nature Center.

"You won't be happy in Green Patrol," warned Arlo. "They're too perfect. Too smiley. They'll drive you crazy."

"I'll be fine. Don't worry about me."

Indra took the left fork, heading up the road to the Lodge. As he watched her walk away, Arlo admitted that he wasn't especially worried about Indra. She was right. She'd be fine in Green Patrol.

He was worried for himself. He didn't know how to do Rangers without her.

19
BIG BREEZY

ELEMENTARY SPIRITS was a required patch for Owl, so pretty much every Squirrel at camp was taking the class, including Julie and Wu. They joined a bunch of other Rangers from various companies, all sitting on the dry grass behind the Nature Center, squinting in the afternoon sun.

The class was taught by Darnell Jackson. He was seventeen and African American, and hailed from a company in Denver.

"And to answer your first question, yeah, we've got Rangers in Denver. People think because there's tall buildings there's no Wonder. It's there. You just gotta look harder for it. Up here in the mountains, you're tripping over Wonder. Down there, you seek it out."

Darnell said he had been coming to Camp Redfeather since he was twelve. This was his second year as a counselor.

Wu raised his hand. "Why don't you have a goofy name like all the other counselors?"

Darnell shrugged. "Why would I want to be Booger or Flapjack when I can be Darnell Jackson the Third? My name is who I am. I'm not going to run from that."

Arlo immediately liked Darnell. He was relaxed and confident in a way Arlo had never seen in a non-adult. Arlo decided right then that if he ever became a camp counselor, he would stick to using his own name.

"Who can tell me what a spirit is?" asked Darnell.

A redheaded boy named Stevens called out: "A ghost. Or a phantom."

Darnell shook his head. "You're just calling it different names, not telling me what it is."

"It's a thing that's not really there, but sort of is," said Julie.

Darnell feigned confusion. "Well, which is it? Are spirits there, or not there?"

"They're there, but they're not *really* there," she answered.

"That's like saying ice is *really* icy. You're not defining your terms."

"They're invisible," offered Wu.

"Okay, *invisible*. That's something. So no one ever sees spirits?"

"I've seen them," said Arlo. He felt all eyes turning to him. "I've seen wisps. They're a kind of spirit. And there's a dog who's dead but still hangs around our house. I see him sometimes. I even heard him once."

"What's your name?" asked Darnell.

"Arlo Finch."

"So, Arlo Finch. If you've seen spirits, maybe you can tell us what they are."

Arlo struggled to find the right words, ones that Darnell wouldn't pick apart for being too vague. "Spirits are . . ." *Creatures? Things?* ". . . *beings* that exist in our world and also sort of sideways to our world. That's why you don't usually see them. Because they're not fully here."

"That's what I said," complained Julie.

"Yeah, but he said it better." Darnell picked a long stalk of grass, splitting it in his fingers as he paced. "Finch here called spirits *beings.* That's probably a good word for them. Lots of people get hung up on whether spirits are quote-unquote alive, and I'll tell you what: They're alive enough. They're alive like a tree is alive, like a forest is alive."

Stevens raised an objection. "But he said one of the spirits was a dead dog. If it's dead, it's not alive."

"You need to get over that kind of black-and-white thinking," said Darnell. "Just because something doesn't fit into your tidy little boxes doesn't make it any less real. Fact is, some spirits *are* the leftovers of things that used to be conventionally alive. They're the echoes. Shadows." He pointed at Arlo. "This dog you see. What does he do?"

"He walks around. Barks at something that isn't there."

"Same pattern, same routine? Like he's stuck in a loop?"

"Exactly." Arlo felt his pulse quickening, excited to hear someone confirming his theory.

"I can promise you, that dog isn't barking at nothing," said Darnell. "Something happened in the past. Something big. Most likely something bad. And that dog is repeating the same moment, over and over."

"That's sad," said Julie. "It's like he's trapped."

Arlo wouldn't have put it in such grim terms, but it was true that Cooper did seem stuck. "Is there any way to set him free?" he asked. "Like a ritual or something?"

Darnell tossed aside the remains of the grass stalk. "Look, this is Elementary Spirits," he said. "Let's not get ahead of ourselves."

Over the next thirty minutes, Darnell explained that while some spirits were the remains of living creatures, most spirits were part of nature itself. They arose spontaneously, and didn't have any distinct form. You could only see them by their effects.

"People focus too much on what spirits look like," said Darnell. "But what matters is what spirits *do*. They're more like verbs than nouns, if that makes sense."

Spirits were also highly local. With rare exceptions, spirits didn't travel more than a mile from their origins. And their ranges overlapped; a single mountain spring might have several different spirits, each with a different personality. "For example, there's a creek a little bit west of here. If you try to cross it, nine times out of ten, you're going to get your boots wet because this one particular spirit thinks it's hilarious to suddenly surge the water when you don't expect it. But just around the bend, another spirit's in charge. That one will leave you be as long as you don't try to fish. She hates fishing."

"How do you know it's a *she* if you can't see it?" asked a freckled girl named Sophia.

"You don't. Truth is, spirits don't really have a gender. We give them names and talk about them like they do, but that's just convenience. So don't be thinking that spirits are like people or even animals, because they're not. They're their own thing."

Darnell said Camp Redfeather had more than one hundred distinct spirits, ranging from a singing stone to a shaft of sunlight that appeared only after a rainstorm. But the most important spirit at Redfeather was a wind known as Big Breezy.

"You can find her everywhere in the valley," he said. "And believe me, if you get on Breezy's bad side, she can make your life difficult. Just try building a fire. Try setting up a tent. If you're not treating Breezy right, she's gonna let you know. So first thing we have to do is make sure she feels respected."

"How do we do that?" asked Wu.

Darnell smiled. "You give her a present."

He directed them over to several crates full of supplies. They crowded around, pulling out pie tins, nails, streamers and bells. There was a natural instinct to hoard these items even before they knew what they were supposed to do with them.

"Each of you is gonna make an offering to Big Breezy, something she'll enjoy. So be thinking about what you'd like if you were the wind. Then make that for her."

By the time Arlo got to the crates, a lot of the best stuff had already been taken. But he felt good about what he chose: a rusted bike wheel, a stack of black feathers, a bag of bottle caps and a ball of coarse twine. He took a seat against a fallen log and started planning his work. He figured the wind might like twirling things, so he would let the feathers dangle freely from the twine. The whole thing could even spin if he could find a way to balance the wheel.

Wu had just finished rummaging through the crates and was looking for a place to sit. Arlo gestured to the empty space beside him. Wu paused, then turned and sat with a group from another company.

Arlo wasn't entirely surprised to be rebuffed. He'd recognized the hurt look in Wu's eyes after the patrol leader vote. Still, it was crushing to be snubbed by your best friend. Arlo wasn't sure how they were going to get past this. The Field Book offered detailed instructions for splinting broken bones, but nothing on how to mend broken friendships.

Darnell gave the class fifteen minutes to work on their offerings. Then he led them up the trail to Coral Rock, a jagged promontory that looked out over the lower valley. Several kids dared each other to approach the edge, but Arlo was happy to stay safely back. He could too easily envision falling, his body smashed on the rocks below.

Three wooden posts, each about six feet tall, had been positioned in a line. Based on the rusty nails and bits of string, Arlo guessed they had been used for offerings for decades.

Darnell explained the process. In groups of three, Rangers were to attach their creations to a pole, then let Big Breezy check out their work. "If she likes what you've done, you'll see it," he said.

Arlo was assigned to the final group. He sat down and waited his turn.

Idly picking at the dirt around him, he came upon a piece of chalk-white stone no bigger than a fingernail. One side was ridged, but the other was smooth and shiny. It seemed oddly out of place. He showed it to Darnell.

"What do you think this is? A tooth?" he asked.

Darnell studied it. "It's a seashell," he said. "Piece of one, at least."

"Why would someone bring a seashell to the mountains?"

"These weren't always mountains. All of this used to be underwater, probably for millions of years. Some of these spirits, they were around back then. Nothing is old to them. They remember things from before there were words."

The first group—Stevens, Sophia and a girl with bright blue elastics on her braces whose name Arlo hadn't yet learned—had finished attaching their works to the poles. "What do we do now?" asked Stevens.

"Nothing," said Darnell. "Breezy knows we're here. She'll come."

The three Rangers stepped back, joining the rest of the class.

The air was completely still. Arlo wouldn't have noticed, except now he was anticipating the wind. It was like listening for a sound in the middle of the night. Instead of straining his ears, he was straining his skin to feel any disturbance, any ripple.

But there was nothing. *Dead calm,* he thought. He suddenly understood what the term meant. The stillness felt like the opposite of life. A vacuum. A void.

He wiped away the sweat beading on his forehead.

"Give her a sec," said Darnell. "Could be the helicopter threw her off. Bet she didn't like it coming through her valley, chopping up the air like that." Arlo tried to imagine what a helicopter felt like to the wind. Was it like a knife? A whisk? A blender?

Darnell held up a finger. "Hold on. Here she comes."

Sure enough, the streamers dangling on the first pole began to sway. They lifted and twisted, as if an invisible cat was batting at them with a paw.

A murmur went through the Rangers. It wasn't disbelief, exactly; they'd all encountered snaplights and thunderclaps and other remarkable things. This tiny wind was simpler, more primal. And a little unsettling. It felt like watching a ghost.

Then the wind shifted to the next pole, where it jingled several strings of bells hung by Sophia. It spent longer with this offering, trying different combinations. *She likes this one better,* Arlo thought, though it felt weird to be calling the wind "she."

He remembered his conversation with Merilee on the last day of school. She had described the wind behind her house, and how it liked to blow through her hair. Was Merilee not crazy? Had she actually been talking to a spirit?

Finally, the breeze reached the third pole. This was Stevens's offering, a collection of aluminum pie tins nailed in a triangle. The thin metal crinkled back and forth slightly, but otherwise there was no sign of Breezy's presence.

"She doesn't know what to do with it," said Darnell. "There's nothing for her to move. Remember, you're not making things that seem cool to you. You want something that's cool to her."

With a screech, Stevens's triangle suddenly ripped free from the pole and swirled up in the air. It hung there, revolving in place faster and faster until it became a blur. Everyone gasped.

Wu was the first to call it: "It's like a fidget spinner."

Then the offering dropped to the ground, tossed aside. The wind had moved on.

"Those get boring fast," said Darnell.

Three by three, the class tacked up their offerings on the poles. The wind investigated each design, swirling and spinning and smashing as appropriate.

Wu had fashioned a series of dangling sticks, which Big Breezy banged against the post in a staccato rhythm. Julie's offering was simply a coffee-can lid piled high with flower petals. The breeze gently lifted the petals into a funnel that snaked high into the sky before floating down upon the class.

Finally, it was Arlo's turn. He chose the middle spot, where a leftover nail in the top of the post could serve as the axle. After seeing how the others had fared, he had decided to set his bicycle wheel horizontally—like a merry-go-round rather than a ferris wheel. He gave it a careful spin, watching the feathers swirl and listening to the bottle caps clink.

Arlo's offering had sight *and* sound. Big Breezy was sure to love it.

He stepped back with the other two Rangers and watched as the wind toyed with the humdrum streamers dangling on the first pole. As the ribbons settled, Arlo's pulse quickened. He was next in line. He watched and waited for Breezy to visit his wheel of wonder.

But nothing happened.

The feathers weren't swirling. The wheel wasn't spinning.

Arlo looked over to Darnell, who shrugged. The class seemed just as confused. Breezy had clearly enjoyed some offerings more than others, but she had at least tried them all.

"Why isn't she doing anything?" asked Julie.

"No idea," said Darnell. "It's weird."

Arlo caught eyes with Wu, who offered a mix of puzzlement and sympathy. That was heartening. A little of his iciness seemed to be thawing.

"Look!" said Stevens, pointing.

The yarn and popsicle sticks on the third pole had begun twisting. The design was nothing special, but Breezy was checking it out, pulling and poking at it. Yet the whole time, not a stray gust touched Arlo's offering. His wheel sat unturned, his mobile immobile.

Maybe she's saving mine for last, thought Arlo. *Like dessert.*

But as the third offering's popsicle sticks came to rest, Arlo could sense the moment had passed. The wind was gone. The air was completely still.

"Did you do something, Finch?" asked Darnell. "Are you on Breezy's bad side for some reason?"

"No!" said Arlo, more defensive than he had intended. "I mean, I don't think so. This is my first year. I didn't know she existed until an hour ago."

Darnell shook his head, confused. "I've never seen her skip someone. Not once. Far as I know, that just doesn't happen."

"Maybe she didn't like his offering," said Stevens.

"She never tried it," pointed out Julie.

Arlo gave the wheel a gentle spin, just to make sure it actually worked. It squeaked a bit, but definitely turned. "Do I still get credit?" he asked Darnell.

"For the patch? Sure. The requirement is just to *make* an offering to a local spirit. Doesn't say anything about having it accepted."

Darnell dismissed the class. As the Rangers headed back down the trail with their offerings, Arlo deliberately lagged behind. At each twist in the path, he let the gap grow a little longer, until the rest of the class was finally out of sight. Then he doubled back to the cliff. He was determined to figure out why Big Breezy had shunned him.

With salvaged nails and a rock, Arlo tacked his wheel up on the first pole. He gave it a powerful spin, watching the black feathers twist. He listened to the tinkling bottle caps.

There was no question in his mind that his offering was fun. The wind didn't know what she was missing.

"Try it," he said. "You'll like it."

It felt strange to be talking to the air. *Like a crazy person,* he thought. He suddenly missed his mom and his room and Uncle Wade and his normal life—even his sister to some degree, though he'd never admit it. He hadn't felt homesick since arriving at camp, but the combination of Connor's departure, Russell's spectral parasite and the patrol leader drama had taken a toll.

And now the wind hated him.

It was all too much. He felt like he was failing. Flailing. Drowning. He wanted to go back to the way things had been.

But how far back? he wondered. If he could rewind his life, where would he stop?

A few days would put him in that happy week between the end of school and the start of camp. But he could also go back further, perhaps to the day he'd found the Broken Bridge. If he hadn't been tromping around in the Long Woods, he wouldn't have dragged Wu and Indra into this new Eldritch drama. Maybe his friends would still be speaking to each other.

If he really wanted a fresh start, he could go back to his first days in Pine Mountain. Or even earlier, before his dad left for China. Everything was easier then. Arlo didn't have any worries or responsibilities. No one was plotting against him. (Or if they were, he was happily unaware.)

Once you began what-if-ing the past, there seemed to be no stopping. There would always be a time when things were simpler, when choices mattered less, until eventually you ended up as a newborn baby staring helplessly at the ceiling. You got what you wanted by erasing your life.

The bicycle wheel slowed, then stopped. One of the black feathers came undone, slowly spiraling down to the ground.

Arlo reached over to pick it up. That's when he noticed something strange.

The feather was floating.

A tiny eddy of air was keeping it aloft, gently twisting a few inches off the ground. Arlo could feel the faintest ripple on his fingertips.

This had to be Big Breezy.

"Hello?" Arlo asked. "Are you here?"

As if in answer, the feather gently rose until it was right in front of his face, slowly drifting back and forth. *She's handing it to me,* he thought. He reached up and took it.

The feathers on the wheel were starting to swirl now, the wind toying with them. The bottle caps clinked together. The metal wheel turned, gradually picking up speed.

Big Breezy had finally taken Arlo's offering, but there was no one around to see it.

"Why didn't you do this before?" he asked the air.

The wind grew stronger. Arlo could feel it on his face. It rushed through his hair like a comb made of whispers and sunlight. He smiled.

The wheel kept spinning faster. Pine needles and little bits of dirt flew up as the wind widened its range. Even a straggly tree in the distance started to bow.

Arlo had envisioned the spirit as human-sized, but it was clearly much larger. Or was that even the right way to think about it? *They're more like verbs than nouns,* Darnell had said. Verbs didn't have size. They had force. Energy. Power. *How powerful is Breezy?* Arlo wondered.

The wind grew stronger. The wheel spun faster, until the feathers ripped free of their knots. Arlo watched as they sailed out over the valley.

He instinctively crouched a bit, bracing himself. He didn't want to get knocked over the edge of the cliff.

The wheel was now spinning so fast that sparks crackled along the axle. A low hum kept climbing in pitch, like a teakettle just about to whistle.

Feeling his feet sliding in the gravel, Arlo grabbed hold of the post. He squinted as tiny rocks pelted him. His ears ached.

One by one the strings of bottle caps broke off, whipping away at enormous velocities. Arlo wrapped a second hand around the post, keeping an eye on the wheel spinning above him. It was moving so fast, it looked like a solid disk, the spokes blurring together. He wasn't sure how long the rusty nail was going to last.

It was hard to breathe. The air was getting sucked out of his lungs. As the whirring whine climbed higher and higher, he used what little breath he had left to shout: "STOP!"

The wind obeyed. The air was abruptly, eerily still.

The wheel kept spinning overhead from residual momentum.

Straightening up, Arlo tried to catch his breath. His ears were buzzing. His eyes were stinging.

Suddenly, a massive blast of wind hit him square in the chest.

Arlo found himself flying backwards. He grabbed for the pole, but couldn't quite reach it.

Midscream, he looked down over his shoes to see the edge of the cliff. The wind was carrying him up into the sky. Higher. And higher.

He frantically tried to swim against it. He flailed his arms. He twisted. He fought. But there was nothing to push against. It was just air. Just wind. He couldn't break free of its grasp.

He flipped over, looking down. He was flying hundreds of feet above the valley. He saw treetops and streams and the roof of the Lodge. If he'd had any control—a parachute or a hang glider—the view would have been thrilling. But he was helpless, no different from Julie's flower petals, caught in the swirl.

Breezy is trying to kill me, Arlo realized. *She's going to drop me, or smash me against the rocks.*

Arlo saw figures on a trail. Rangers. It was Darnell and the class, almost back at the Nature Center. Arlo tried to yell to them as he passed overhead, but all that came out was a croaking gasp:

h e l p

No one heard him. No one looked up.

Arlo knew he needed to get someone's attention. He willed his trembling fingers together and waited. He sailed over the empty parking lot. The marshes. The dock. He spotted a lifeguard and a few canoes out on the lake.

This was his chance.

He cocked his arm and threw a snaplight in their direction. It arced over their heads, unnoticed against the bright sky.

The wind was dropping him lower. They were now only a few feet above the water. *She wants to drown me,* he thought. *Hold me underwater.*

Up ahead, a rocky spire poked out of the lake. Back on the bus, he'd heard the other Rangers call it Giant's Fist. He was headed right for it. He'd be smashed against its knuckles.

Then suddenly, the wind let go.

Arlo skidded across the lake like a fallen water-skier.

The impact stunned him. He swallowed lake water as he struggled to swim, not sure which way was up. His clothes and his shoes were weighing him down. The shock of the cold made his lungs seize.

But he was alive. He was treading water. Giant's Fist loomed over him, silhouetted in the afternoon light.

Arlo swam towards it.

20
GIANT'S FIST

ARLO CLAWED AGAINST the rocks, trying to find a handhold, some way to pull himself out of the water. His fingertips were already white and wrinkly. His shoes slipped against the slimy moss. There was no way up.

Circling to his right, he discovered a narrow fissure. He wedged a foot in, using it to push higher. His hand found a grip, and then another. Inch by desperate inch, he hoisted himself out of the lake, fighting the weight of his wet clothes. Muscles straining, he finally made it all the way onto a rocky slab.

He collapsed onto his back, staring up at the white sky, trying to catch his breath.

Giant's Fist was aptly named. Its massive stacked stones really did look like the clenched fingers of a hand holding a missing torch. Arlo was lying on a sloping section of the giant's palm, the only "beach." Unfortunately, it faced away from the rest of the camp. If anyone had spotted him flying overhead—if anyone was coming to get him—he would have no way of knowing.

He was on his own.

Sitting up, Arlo debated trying to swim for the shore. He estimated it was easily ten times farther than his swimming test, but he could probably do it if he rested first.

But waiting might be even more dangerous.

He was already shivering. It was summer, but it got cold at night in the mountains. He considered taking off his wet shirt. What had he read in the Field Book about hypothermia? *Cold kills more people than bears. Hypothermia makes people confused. They think they have to take off their clothes to get warm. They find people frozen to death in their underwear.*

He decided to keep his shirt on. There were still hours before dark. His clothes would eventually dry. If he was going to die, he wouldn't die in his briefs.

Arlo emptied his pockets to see if he was carrying anything useful. He found a pen, two dimes and his Ranger's compass. Tucked into the very bottom of a pocket he discovered the seashell fragment he'd shown to Darnell.

No matches, no flint. Nothing to help him build a fire. But as he looked around, he realized there was nothing to burn, anyway. Except for occasional patches of lichen, nothing was growing here. It was just a pile of rocks.

So why was he here? Big Breezy had whisked him off the mountaintop and carried him to Giant's Fist. But for what purpose? Was she trying to strand him, like a survivor on a deserted island? Was she hazing him? Punishing him?

Or was there something here she wanted him to see?

This last question was like a spark landing in the tinder of his imagination. *That's why she didn't take your offering during class. So you'd keep trying. She wanted you here alone.*

Arlo quickly forgot about hypothermia. He forgot to shiver. His curiosity was keeping him warm.

Giant's Fist was taller than his house in Pine Mountain. The three bottom "fingers" connected to the palm, but thirty feet up there was an open space between the thumb and the index finger. It seemed just large enough for a person to squeeze through.

This was an easier climb. He took his time, feeling for handholds. His sneakers squished but held their grip. Eventually, he reached a perch atop the third finger. He pulled himself up. And smiled.

He had reached the entrance to a hidden cave.

It was small, no wider than a camp tent and perhaps twice as deep. Covered by a rocky overhang, the space was sheltered on all sides. The only way to spot it was to climb.

But Arlo Finch hadn't been the first to find it.

In the dim light he saw the remnants of a campfire, along with tabbed aluminum rings from old-fashioned soda cans. He only recognized what they were because Uncle Wade had a bucket of them out in his workshop: "You can link them together to make chain mail. One of these days, I'm going to do that."

It was only as Arlo's eyes adjusted to the dark that he saw it:

a single letter had been scrawled on the back wall of the cave: an uppercase *A*.

He crawled over to it, careful not to bump his head.

The lines were very faint. At first, he thought it had been done with chalk, but it seemed thinner and scratchier. On a hunch, he pulled the seashell fragment from his pocket and scraped it against the rock. It left the same kind of mark, a bumpy white scratch.

Someone had scratched an *A* on the wall of this cave, and also on one of the fallen stones at the Broken Bridge. But why? Who was behind it?

"Arlo!?"

A boy's voice was yelling from outside. Arlo straightened up, whacking his head.

Moving more carefully, Arlo backed out of the cave. He looked down at the water below to find an aluminum canoe. The figure standing in it was backlit by the water's glare. Arlo couldn't see his face.

"Are you okay?" the boy yelled. "I saw you flying overhead." Arlo recognized the voice. It was Wu.

"I'm fine," said Arlo. "I found something."

After securing the canoe, Wu climbed up to investigate the cave with Arlo. There was no mention of class, or Wu's silent treatment. The excitement of a new mystery seemed to have set that aside for now.

Wu pushed against the stone wall with the *A* on it as if looking for a hidden compartment or a secret door to unlatch.

"I'm pretty sure it's just rocks," said Arlo.

"Maybe it's some kind of portal," said Wu. "Try your compass."

Arlo took out his Ranger's compass. The needle was pointing due north, just as expected. "I don't think it's a Long Woods thing. I can usually feel that."

"Maybe you're not trying hard enough."

The tone in Wu's voice took Arlo by surprise. It had an edge of accusation. But Arlo was wary of starting an argument with a friend who had just come to rescue him. "We should probably get back to camp. We need to get started on dinner."

Wu shook his head. "There has to be something here. Why else would she bring you out here?"

"I don't know."

"Well, what's your sense? Do you feel anything?"

"Cold," said Arlo. "And tired. I need to go back."

Wu sighed, clearly frustrated. "Fine. But we need to keep this secret."

"Why?"

"Because we don't want anyone else coming here until we figure out what's going on."

"We need to tell Indra."

"No. Definitely not."

"Look, I know you and her aren't getting along, but she's good with this kind of stuff."

Wu was about to say something, then stopped himself. He tried a different tack. "Arlo, I know you like her, but the more you tell her, the more you're putting her in danger, too."

That felt like a strange thing for Wu to say. "The three of us are always in danger," said Arlo. "That's sort of our thing."

21
PINEREADING

ARLO AND WU had just finished hoisting the canoe back onto the rack when they heard a familiar voice yelling in the distance:

"Arlo!"

It was Indra. She had evidently just spotted him and was now running down the path to the lake.

Arlo glanced back at Wu, anticipating a groan or some disparaging comment. But Wu had already circled behind the lifeguard shack. He was going to avoid her completely. Maybe that was for the best. Arlo hung up the paddles.

Indra slowed as she approached, catching her breath. She pointed to her notebook as if to indicate that this was what she wanted to talk about first.

"I found something. Something incredible."

"So did I."

She tapped her notebook. "Mine's better."

Arlo knew with one hundred percent certainty that his news was more important. An invisible wind spirit had just thrown him off a mountain. He could have died. Whatever Indra had written in her notebook couldn't compare. Still, he decided it was better to let her go first. "Fine. We should head back to camp, though."

They walked side by side. The sun was low in the sky, catching the pollen in the air.

Indra jumped into her story. "So this afternoon I had Pine-reading, which meets in the Lodge, which seems like a weird place for the class—why not have it outside where the trees are?—but that's where they keep all the reference logs. So I'm there, and the counselor is explaining the very basic stuff like tree rings, which everyone already knows."

"I don't," said Arlo. Over the past year, he'd gotten better at admitting when he didn't understand what Indra was talking about. It saved time in the long run.

"Oh," said Indra, surprised. "Well, every year, trees grow a new layer. So if you cut a tree down, you can count the rings to see how old the tree was. For example, the tallest trees at Red-feather are three hundred to four hundred years old."

"How long can trees live?" asked Arlo.

"Up to a thousand years. But what usually happens is there's a fire that burns all the trees and new ones take their place. It's a cycle. First the aspen grow, then the pines. There was a big fire in this valley exactly one hundred and seventeen years ago. We know that because we can look at the trees that survived and see that there's a ring that's a little bit burned. It's the same number of layers back in every tree, so we know that's when it happened."

"That's really cool."

"That's nothing, though. The next part is where it gets crazy."

Indra suddenly wandered off the trail, searching the forest floor. She picked up a fallen branch about as long as her arm. Carefully peeling back the bark, she showed Arlo the gray wood underneath.

"You see these marks? The ones that look like squiggly lines?"

Arlo took the branch, examining it closely. There were tiny grooves carved into the wood, a random scribble that crossed itself in places. He'd noticed marks like these before, but never paid attention to them. "What are they?"

"It's called *coneiform*. It's writing. All the scratches and grooves, the places where they cross, they all mean something. It's a record of everything that's happened in the valley."

She paused, letting that sink in.

"You mean, like a history book?" asked Arlo.

"Exactly."

"But who's writing it?"

"Bark beetles, technically. They're chewing the wood. But they're just the tools, sort of the pencils. It's the forest itself that writes everything down. Every tree has a piece of the story, and it's copied again and again. That way, if one tree falls or burns, there's always a backup."

Arlo studied the swirling marks in the wood. While he couldn't make sense of them, the whole idea was really no crazier than cursive, which he had struggled to learn in third grade. "What does this say?"

Indra turned the stick over in her hands, trying to figure out where to begin. After a few false starts, she confessed, "I can't really read it yet. We're only on our first class. And anyway, there are druids who spend their whole lives studying it. It's really complicated."

"Still. It's cool." The idea that the trees around them were recording everything that happened was mind-blowing. He wanted to ask a hundred more questions about pinereading, but—

"That's not what I wanted to tell you. This was all just setup for what I found out." She stopped, looking around to make sure they were alone. Whatever she was going to say next clearly was for Arlo's ears only.

"So in the Lodge, they have samples that are already translated so you can start to learn some of the glyphs." Anticipating Arlo's question: "*Glyphs* are what they call the individual characters. It's not like our alphabet. It's more like Chinese, I guess, where it's a bunch of marks all put together. Anyway, we had to pick three logs to study. First you do a charcoal rubbing and then you use this key to help you translate. I'm on my second sample and here's what I find."

She opened her notebook, showing Arlo what looked like a

blurry map—smudged pencil around bright white lines. Indra had circled six sections. Beneath them she'd written a chain of words:

brown green eye boy lake moon

Arlo shrugged. "What does that mean?"

"It's you! Arlo, you're the 'brown green eye boy.' You have one brown eye and one green eye."

Arlo wasn't so sure. "Or it could mean a boy with brownish-green eyes. You know, hazel. Lots of people have those."

"There's more, though." Indra flipped the page, where the same charcoal rubbing continued, with three additional words marked:

fox wind knife

Indra studied his reaction. "Didn't you say that the man who came to see you last winter was named Fox?"

Arlo took the notebook. *Fox* definitely made sense. And *wind* could be referring to Big Breezy.

"What was Fox, exactly?" asked Indra. "You said he vanished. Was he just in your head, the way Rielle used to be?"

"No, I touched his jacket. He was really there. He wasn't Eldritch, but he wasn't human, either." *I'm not people. I just dress up sometimes.* "He might literally be a fox. I remember he had really sharp teeth."

Indra took her notebook back. "What I can't figure out is how the forest knew you were coming."

"What do you mean?"

"This sample is thirty years old. So anything written there has to be at least that old. It's like you've always been destined to come. It's fate."

Arlo didn't like the word *fate*. It sounded too much like *fatal*. Plus it implied that whatever he did next was predetermined. That his choices had already been made for him.

"Maybe you mistranslated," he offered. "You said yourself that druids spend their whole lives studying pinereading."

"I'm sure there's more to it. I just thought you should know, since things are always trying to kill you."

Arlo took that as an opening to tell her everything that had happened that afternoon. Indra didn't interrupt as he described making his first failed offering to Big Breezy, circling back for a second attempt, and being whisked off the top of Coral Rock. His heart was racing just from retelling it.

When he got to the part where Wu rescued him on Giant's Fist, he left out Wu's insistence that they not tell Indra about the events. He didn't want to get in the middle of their drama again. By the time he'd finished, they had nearly reached Firebird.

"One thing doesn't make sense," said Indra.

Arlo was surprised it was only one thing.

"How did Wu find you?" she asked.

"He said he saw me flying overhead."

"But he would have been with the rest of the class, right? You said they were still headed back to the Nature Center."

"I guess."

"Then why was it just Wu? Wouldn't Julie have come? Or the counselor? I mean, if they saw a kid flying overhead, you'd think they'd all investigate."

Arlo didn't have a good answer.

"And another thing," she said. "How did Wu get out to Giant's Fist?"

"In a canoe."

"By himself?"

"Yeah."

"Okay, but we've all had exactly one day of canoe lessons. Do you think you could canoe by yourself?"

Arlo admitted he probably couldn't. "What are you saying? You think Wu is lying?"

"No," said Indra. "I don't think that was Wu at all."

22
SUSPICIONS

"SO WHAT DID EVERYONE do this afternoon?"

Indra asked the question just as the patrol was sitting down for dinner. Arlo was careful not to look immediately at Wu for his reaction.

"I had Archery," said Jonas. "You know how you sometimes see archers with those straps on their arms? This is why." He held out his left forearm, where a purple bruise ran from the inside of his elbow to his wrist. Everyone grimaced.

"Is that from the bowstring?" asked Wu.

"Yup. Thwack! Right along the skin."

"I've done that," said Thomas. "Hurts like the devil."

Thomas then told a story about learning archery with his company in Texas, and how one of the older girls was able to hit three bull's-eyes in a row. Arlo tuned out most of it. He was focused on trying to figure out if the Wu sitting across from him was his friend or an evil shape-shifter who'd taken his form: a doppelgänger.

Arlo had first heard that word before the Alpine Derby, back when Indra and Connor were speculating on ways the Eldritch might try to kill him. According to them, a doppelgänger was a creature that could make itself look and sound like anyone. (*For all you know, one of us could be a doppelgänger, just waiting for you to fall asleep so we can smother you.*) Now Arlo was facing the possibility that the Wu he'd seen on Giant's Fist was actually one of them. Indra said she didn't know much beyond the basics, but had suggested they track down a *Culman's Bestiary* to learn more. It stood to reason that Camp Redfeather must have a copy in order to teach Beast Lore.

As Thomas finished his archery anecdote, Indra passed the potatoes to Julie. "What about you? What did you do this afternoon?"

"I had Elementary Spirits with Arlo and Wu. We had to make an offering to Big Breezy, this wind spirit."

"Julie's was the best," Wu said. "Super simple, but it looked the coolest."

Julie smiled, surprised to be singled out.

"What did you guys do after class?" asked Indra.

"I just came back to camp," said Julie.

Wu didn't answer. He was chewing a piece of kabob meat. But that could have just been to avoid the question.

"Has anyone heard about Connor?" asked Thomas.

Wu nodded, holding up his finger as he swallowed. "Diana

said that Connor had surgery to take out his spleen, but he's okay."

"When did she say that?" asked Arlo. He blurted it out a little too quickly. He worried it sounded accusatory.

"At the patrol leaders' meeting."

"When was that?" asked Indra.

"Right after class. We're planning a Capture the Flag game."

Arlo and Indra exchanged a glance. If Wu was at a meeting, he couldn't have also been at Giant's Fist.

"Can you live without a spleen?" asked Jonas.

"I guess," said Wu. "I mean, they took it out, so I hope so."

"The spleen helps you fight infection," said Indra. "But yeah, you can live without it. You just have to be more careful."

Julie explained to Thomas: "Indra's dad is a doctor."

"No kidding," said Thomas. "My dad was an army medic."

Thomas explained that his father had been injured in combat and now drove long-haul trucks for a living. He was often gone for weeks at time. It reminded Arlo of his dad living in China, still part of the family but remote.

For almost a minute, the patrol ate without talking. Arlo was hungry. The combination of altitude and adrenaline had made him ravenous.

As he went back for a second helping of corn, he noticed Indra signaling with her eyes towards Wu. She wanted Arlo to keep asking questions. But it would seem suspicious to keep drilling him on his timeline.

"Wu, um . . ."

He aborted the question he'd considered asking. Now Wu was looking at him, puzzled. Then—

"I forget what your dad does. What does he do?" He relaxed a little. It was a reasonable thing to ask, and on topic.

Wu seemed unfazed by the question. "He writes for magazines. But mostly he keeps my grandfather from burning down the kitchen. He says he's trying to re-create this barbecue pork his family used to make, but I think he's sort of a pyro."

Wu's story felt very specific and plausible. But just to be sure—

"Remember when we were building the sled?" asked Arlo. "What your grandfather said about it?"

Wu smiled. *"Hen hao."*

Thomas seemed confused about why the five of them were smiling. "That's how our sled got its name," explained Jonas.

"I thought that was supposed to be a secret," complained Julie.

"Thomas is in the patrol now," said Wu. "So he gets to know all our secrets." Thomas smiled at that.

Conversation then shifted back to camp. Julie and Indra speculated out loud about which counselors were secretly dating; they seemed to notice things that were completely invisible to the boys. "Like, Darnell asked Waffles if she wanted a soda from the Trading Post, but he had just come up the hill from there, so it's not like it was on his way," said Julie. "That's classic."

Indra agreed. "All the girls have a crush on Darnell. When he walks by, you can see them tracking him with their eyes, but their heads don't move."

Jonas seemed genuinely perplexed. "Why do they like this guy? Is he good-looking or something?"

"It's mostly because he's confident," said Julie.

"And he doesn't have a goofy camp name," added Indra.

This inspired them to spend the next twenty minutes assigning each other camp names. Indra was dubbed Ringlet for her hair. Wu was Pyro in honor of his firemaking prowess and his grandfather. Jonas wanted to be Football, but was outvoted and settled for Velcro. Julie was happy to be crowned ChapStick for her ever-present lip balm. Thomas accepted Alamo in honor of Texas.

That left Arlo.

"What about Tooble?" proposed Julie. It was the name the hag had called him in the Valley of Fire, evidently referring to his mismatched eyes.

"That's kind of morbid," said Indra. "I mean, she was trying to kill him."

"She was trying to kill all of us," pointed out Jonas.

"How about Compass?" proposed Wu. "That's what he's especially good at. He can find his way out of anything." Everyone agreed it was the right choice.

With dinner finished, they dug into the cherry crumble they'd made for dessert. As Arlo looked around the table, he realized that in trying to unmask an intruder, he and Indra had inadvertently brought the patrol back together.

Arlo was brushing his teeth at the sinks when Indra came up beside him. She wet her toothbrush. They were alone.

"So what are you thinking?" he asked, keeping his voice low.

"You first," she said.

He spit and rinsed. "I think Wu is really Wu. I mean, the guy at dinner tonight knew stuff only the real Wu would know."

"Agreed."

"But the thing is, the fake Wu from this afternoon, he looked so much like the real one. I don't know how I would tell them apart. I almost want to take a black marker and scribble something on Wu's arm. But then I think, if this doppelgänger can look like Wu, it can look like any of us."

"We ought to have a sign," Indra said. "A code word to let us know we're really us."

"Like what?"

"You pick," she said. "It should be something random that no one would expect. But not so weird that it's suspicious."

While Indra brushed her teeth, Arlo racked his brain. Why was it so hard to pick a single word out of thousands? Finally, it came to him: "Rocky Road." It was his favorite flavor of ice cream.

Still brushing her teeth, Indra smiled and nodded.

Arlo spotted flashlights headed their way. They didn't have much more time to talk in private.

"I'm guessing there's a *Culman's Bestiary* at the Nature Center," he said. "Tomorrow before class, I'm going to see if I can find out anything about doppelgängers. Maybe they have a weakness we can use. Like they're allergic to silver or something."

"Smart."

Arlo had one last question, one not related to supernatural beings. "Are you still thinking about Green Patrol?" Indra seemed confused. "You said you talked to Diana about transferring."

Indra waved it off. "Oh, I was just upset. I'm fine now. All good."

Arlo was relieved that she had given up on that idea. Maybe all they had needed was a new mystery to solve. He grabbed his stuff to head back to his tent. "G'night."

"Hey, Arlo Finch," she said.

He turned back.

"Rocky Road." She smiled.

23
PAGE 57

THE NEXT AFTERNOON, Arlo found Darnell Jackson in the tiny, cluttered office of the Nature Center. The counselor was sitting perfectly still on a wooden stool, his back to the door.

A large black fly was buzzing around the room, occasionally alighting on an antler or a rolled-up map. Darnell didn't seem to pay it any mind.

Not sure whether to knock, Arlo scuffed his shoes on the concrete floor, hoping to make himself heard. Darnell didn't react.

Arlo was about to fake a cough when the giant fly suddenly zoomed towards the door. Arlo stepped aside to let it out, but the insect began circling him. It buzzed past his ears, so close he could feel it on his skin. He batted at it with his hand, but nothing would deter it.

"It's Finch, right?" said Darnell. Arlo looked into the office. Darnell was still facing away from the door.

"Yeah," he answered. "Arlo." The black fly changed course, disappearing through an open window.

"What time is it, Arlo Finch?"

Arlo checked his watch. "Twelve thirty." Darnell still hadn't turned around. It was unsettling to be talking to his back.

"Class isn't for another half hour."

"Sorry. I wanted to ask you something."

Darnell's posture softened. The lanky counselor slowly turned around, still sitting on the stool. His eyes seemed hazy and unfocused, like he'd just woken up from a nap.

Arlo had come to ask about *Culman's Bestiary*, but suddenly that wasn't his top question. "How did you know it was me behind you?"

"That's the question you wanted to ask?"

"Well, now it is." Although it sounded crazy, Arlo decided it was better to forge ahead with his half-considered theory: "Were you . . . seeing . . . through that fly's eyes?"

Darnell gave a small nod. "It's called shifting."

"How do you do it?"

"Like anything. Practice."

"Can you teach me?"

Darnell smiled. "That's right. You're the impatient one. The one who wants to dispel spirits when you can't even get them to come in the first place."

"I did, though. I went back, and she finally . . ." He hadn't meant to get into the situation with Big Breezy. He didn't really understand it himself. "I'm not here about that. I wanted to see if you have a *Culman's Bestiary*."

"Yeah, we got one." Darnell never broke eye contact. It made Arlo nervous.

"Okay, great. Can I see it? I need to look something up."

"What did you find?"

Arlo didn't want to say *doppelgänger*. He could imagine that word opening a line of questions and answers that would make him sound absolutely crazy. *I think a shape-shifting creature was impersonating my friend after a wind spirit threw me off a mountain and into the lake.* So instead Arlo said:

"Is it okay if I tell you after I look it up?"

Darnell considered, then shrugged. He stood up, taking his keys from his pocket. He went to unlock one of the file cabinets, and seemed surprised that it wasn't necessary—the drawer was already slightly open. From it, he pulled out a battered copy of *Culman's Bestiary* and handed it to Arlo.

It looked to be the same edition as the one in the Pine Mountain Elementary library, but with years more weather and rough handling. The book was organized alphabetically, so Arlo opened it to a page about one-fifth of the way through. He ended up on the entry for *Faerie Beetle*. He worked his way backwards, flipping past *Dvergr* and *Duende* to *Cyclops* and *Chupacabra*.

But no *Doppelgänger*.

Arlo gave a little *huh*.

"What is it?" asked Darnell.

"I just thought it would be in here." Arlo flipped forward to the index, running a finger along the list:

Chimera

Chupacabra

Cyclops

Doppelgänger

Dryad

Duende

Dvergr

The index listed a page for *Doppelgänger*: 57. The only problem was . . .

"This page isn't in the book," Arlo said. He flipped back to make sure no pages were stuck together. They weren't. This copy of *Culman's Bestiary* skipped directly from page 56 to page 59, *Cyclops* to *Duende.*

The sheet holding pages 57 and 58—*Doppelgänger* and *Dryad*—was missing.

Darnell motioned that he wanted to see. Arlo handed the book over. Darnell laid it flat on the desk, leaning in to take a closer look.

"You're right. Someone's pulled a page out of the book. You can see right here, there's a little ripped edge of the paper." It was less than a millimeter wide, a fuzzy remnant of the missing sheet.

Darnell shook his head. "I know exactly why they did it, too."

"You do?" asked Arlo.

"You know what dryads are?"

Arlo didn't.

"They're tree spirits," explained Darnell. "They look like women. Like, really hot women not wearing any clothes. I mean, they're sort of covered in bark, but, you know. If you're a fifteen-year-old guy and you're flipping through this book, you see this illustration and you're thinking, that's a pretty good-looking girl, never mind the leaves and the roots."

"You think they wanted the picture?" asked Arlo.

"That's why we keep it locked up."

"But it wasn't locked. It was already open."

Darnell shrugged. "Some counselors forget to relock the cabinet." He closed the *Bestiary* and put it back in the drawer. "So, what, you thought you saw a dryad? Or did you just hear about the picture?"

"No!" said Arlo, a bit embarrassed. "It's not like that at all."

Darnell locked the cabinet. "Look, it's fine. No one's judging."

Arlo decided not to say anything more about it. Any attempt to defend himself would just dig him in deeper.

Darnell sat back down on the stool. "What you saw before, what I was doing with the fly, looking through its eyes. That was pretty cool, right?"

"Yeah."

"It's also easy to imagine a lot of ways that could be used. A lot of inappropriate ways. Particularly by a guy who wanted to see some things he shouldn't be seeing. So part of the reason we don't teach young Rangers how to shift is that it takes some maturity to understand how to use it responsibly. Why you don't want to be flying in to eavesdrop on a conversation, or spy on someone showering."

"I wouldn't!"

"That's good! And that's easy to say when you can't. But someday, you'll be able to do that and lots of other things. And before that time comes, it's important you learn that just because you have the power to do something doesn't mean it's the right thing to do." Darnell lowered his voice a bit. "You're gonna find there are some Rangers—former Rangers—who learned the skills, but not the lessons. They do what we do, but not for the same reasons. They're only out to protect their own interests."

Arlo suddenly thought of Hadryn. Back in the diner, before he started spinning the coin, he'd said he was in Rangers. "Do you know any of them?"

"Hell no," said Darnell. "And it's not like they're organized, some sort of gang of evil ex-Rangers. They're all free agents. They've got no loyalty to anything. And the truth is, they didn't wake up one day deciding to be bad. They got there bit by bit, choice by choice. That's why you have to choose well."

Arlo nodded.

For a moment, Arlo Finch considered telling Darnell everything. He would tell him about Big Breezy and Hadryn and Fox and the doppelgänger and the flashlight he'd found at the Broken Bridge. Darnell was smart. He'd have great advice. He reminded Arlo of Connor in that way.

But could he really trust Darnell?

The doppelgänger—or whatever it was—had been able to

flawlessly impersonate Wu, one of his best friends. If it could do that, it could disguise itself as anyone. For all Arlo knew, he was talking to the creature right now. *Darnell could have ripped that page out of the* Bestiary.

In that moment, Arlo wondered if he could trust anyone but himself.

"Thanks for your help," he said.

"No worries. I've got my eye on you, Arlo Finch."

24
THE EVIDENCE

THAT NIGHT, Arlo was halfway to the latrine when he realized he'd forgotten his lantern. The nearly full moon provided enough illumination for him to find his way there, but he definitely didn't want to be in there without a proper light. He turned around and headed back to his tent.

Thomas had moved in with Jonas, taking Connor's spot. "I figure you and Wu have been friends all this time. Makes sense for you to stay put." Thomas didn't mention Wu's snoring, but that was likely also a factor.

Arlo opened the tent flap to find Wu sitting on his cot, his face lit by the glowing screen of his cell phone.

For a long moment, neither boy said anything. Then Wu motioned for Arlo to step inside. Once Arlo had taken a seat, Wu tied the tent flaps shut.

"Why do you have that?" asked Arlo, keeping his voice low.

"It's a huge infraction if they find it. They could send you home!"

"I know!"

"Then why do you have it?"

"It's for *Galactic Havoc 2.* I have to manage my league. They're counting on me."

"How much are you using your phone?"

"Only three times a day. Twenty minutes, max."

"How are you even charging it?"

"At the Trading Post. I plug it in behind the Coke machine."

Arlo couldn't believe the gamble Wu was taking. "If you get an infraction, that counts against the patrol and the company. We could lose the spirit award."

"I know! So you can't tell anybody."

Arlo wasn't about to let Wu throw this back at him. It was Wu's mistake. Arlo shouldn't be the one covering it up.

"Look, I'm sorry," said Wu, almost pleading.

"Don't apologize. Just stop using your phone."

"I can't! I can't abandon my league."

"They're strangers. We're your friends."

"I know. I'm sorry."

They sat in silence for nearly a minute. Finally, Wu picked up his phone and started typing.

"What are you doing?" asked Arlo.

"I'm resetting my passcode." Wu handed him the phone. "Pick a new number. Something I won't be able to guess. That way I can't use my phone."

Arlo was suspicious, but it did look like the same kind of lock screen as his sister's phone. He chose four digits—his mom's birthday—making sure Wu wasn't watching. He then handed it back.

"I really am sorry," said Wu.

"I know."

Suddenly, there was a voice outside the tent: "Guys! Guys!" It was Jonas.

Panicking, Wu hid the phone under his leg. Arlo then untied the tent flaps. Jonas was winded. He'd clearly just been running.

"What is it?" Arlo asked.

"Down at the lake. They found something."

As they reached the base of the trail, Arlo and Wu saw a growing crowd at the edge of the lake. There were Rangers from every company, many of them in pajamas, with flashlight beams sweeping in every direction.

According to Jonas, a kid from Illinois had been skipping rocks in the moonlight when he discovered a massive footprint in the mud. It was more than six feet long, with four distinct claw marks.

Thomas joined up with them. "It's gotta be a hoax, right? I mean, why would there be just one footprint?"

"It could have snatched something off the shore, like a deer," suggested Jonas.

"If it's a plesiosaur, it wouldn't leave footprints at all," said Wu. "They have flippers."

Arlo spotted Indra conversing with a group of Green Patrollers. Despite what she'd said at the sinks about staying with Blue Patrol, she had been spending a lot of time at the Green campsite, coming back only for meals and bed. Arlo wondered if she was reconsidering her decision.

Along with Wu, Arlo pushed his way through the crowd to see the print itself. It was fairly unimpressive, just a cluster of indentations quickly filling with water.

"Totally fake," declared Russell to one of his Red Patrol buddies. For once, Arlo agreed with Russell.

Eventually, Warden Mpasu came over to break up the crowd and send everyone back to their campsites. When asked if the footprint was real, she answered only, "I have never seen a one-footed dinosaur, and I suspect I never will."

Back at Firebird, Arlo was tying the tent flaps shut when Wu said, "Someone's been in our tent."

"What do you mean?"

Wu held up his phone. "I put my phone under my sleeping bag. But just now, it was on top. You didn't move it, did you?"

"No," said Arlo.

"Well, someone did. Someone knows I have it."

25
TENT LOGIC

THIS TIME, Arlo Finch knew he was dreaming. He remembered falling asleep, but not waking up. Plus in real life he couldn't fly.

He was floating through the forest, gradually descending to make a perfect superhero landing amid the towering trees. It was a hot day, and pine sap hung in the air like honeyed smoke. The bird songs began to fade as Arlo became aware of a gritty, scratching sound. It was coming from the trees.

Arlo pressed his hand against a massive lodgepole pine. He could feel movement under the rough bark. With his fingernails, he began ripping the bark away until he revealed pale wood and thousands of tiny larvae, each smaller than a grain of rice. They were chewing paths in the wood, creating the intricate patterns Indra had shown him from her Pinereading class. *They're pinewriting,* he thought with a smile.

"There's more to it," said a man's voice. Arlo looked over to see a small fox sitting in a sunbeam. "Dig deeper," said the fox.

Arlo went back to peeling off bark, exposing more and more of the design. The branching squiggles formed an image. Two towers and a fractured arch between them. The Broken Bridge.

A heavy object suddenly fell at Arlo's feet. It was the rusted flashlight. Arlo picked it up. He tried to open it, but it wouldn't budge.

Arlo peered up into the trees, trying to figure out where the flashlight could have come from. Sunlight danced through the branches in bright dapples. Arlo watched them, transfixed.

The gold coin was spinning on the table in a shaft of sunlight.

Arlo was back in the diner. Hadryn was sitting in the booth, but Arlo couldn't look over at him. His focus was locked on the coin.

This was a memory. Hadryn was asking about the flashlight: "It was hidden in the Long Woods, right? That's why the Eldritch couldn't find it."

I don't understand, Arlo said.

"The Eldritch can't go into the Long Woods. That's why they need spies and henchmen to work for them."

Do you work for them?

"No. No, I definitely do not." Just the thought of it seemed to amuse him. "Do you know why they're so interested in you, Arlo Finch?"

Because I'm special.

"You're not that special. You're good at finding things. That makes you useful. Valuable, even. Like a hunting dog or a race-horse. But don't think that makes you special. You're disposable."

Why were they trying to kill me?

"So I couldn't find you."

Who are you?

With all his might, Arlo tried to turn his head to face Hadryn. As he moved, he heard a rumble, as if the world were growling.

He saw Hadryn's hands. His arms, with tattoos peeking out beneath the rolled-up sleeves. A crystal hanging from a cord around his neck.

But Hadryn's face was missing. In its place was a smooth oval with small indendations for the eyes and mouth.

"I'm the only one who can help you."

Arlo woke up just then. As he'd expected, he was in his tent.

Around the edges of the canvas door flap, he could see the first light of day. He figured it was around five A.M. Wu was still asleep on the next cot. That was the growling he'd heard.

Arlo had become an expert in Wu's snoring. The noises could be divided into two basic categories: wet and dry. The wet snores came mostly on the inhale, alternating between the snuffling gobble of a ravenous pig and the desperate gasps of a drowning badger. The dry snores ranged from wheeze, to growl, to ghostly moan.

Tonight was a pig-moan cycle. Arlo didn't really mind. After the strange dream, Wu's snoring was comfortingly familiar. This really was Wu. No shape-shifting creature could replicate these sounds.

Arlo stared at the ceiling of the tent. It wasn't Wu's snoring that was keeping him from falling back asleep, or any one specific thing. Rather, it was all the little unanswered questions swirling in his head. The moment he tried to focus on one issue—Hadryn, Big Breezy, the Eldritch—another worry pushed its way into the foreground. He didn't even know where to begin.

You've gotta start at the edges, said Arlo's dad.

Arlo heard his father's voice in a memory. He could see the pile of jigsaw puzzle pieces dumped on the coffee table in the little house in Philadelphia. Arlo was six, and seven, and eight. It wasn't a single event he was recalling, but a collection of Sunday afternoons spent assembling puzzles with his dad while his mom and sister were off at basketball practice.

Arlo's dad loved all sorts of puzzles, from crosswords to number games to Rubik's Cubes. But he had a special affinity for jigsaw puzzles.

None of their puzzles were in their original boxes. Whenever he'd buy a new one, Arlo's dad would immediately dump the pieces into a plastic bag and discard the box. "The point of a puzzle is to discover the answer," he'd say. "It's the mystery, the process, the surprise. If you're just trying to re-create the image on the box, then what's the point?"

They'd always started with the edges, picking through all the pieces to find the ones with flat sides. Then they each took a corner and tried to link together as many edge pieces as they could. Arlo's favorite moment was when he'd discover that the next piece he needed was already at the end of one of his dad's lines. They'd carefully slide their chains until they could be snapped together. In just a few minutes, they'd see the perimeter of the puzzle—generally a square or a rectangle, but occasionally a circle. From chaos, they would have created order.

Arlo and his dad had always stopped at this stage to speculate what the final image might be. Which way was up? Did the blue along one edge represent water or sky? Could those little brown marks be claws?

Arlo's dad said that the work he did with computers was about teaching them how to sort through trillions of pieces of data to find things that would otherwise be imperceptible. "It's like if you had a blizzard, and you needed to find a single specific snowflake while it was blowing around. You couldn't just stop everything and look at each one. They'd fall. They'd clump together. You'd want to find a way to embrace the wind."

Embrace the wind.

His dad had meant it as a metaphor, but after the events of the previous afternoon, it seemed all too possible. The wind was a real entity. It had carried him off the mountain for a reason. He just needed to figure out why.

Arlo's mind drifted back to the present, and the questions swirling around him. He wondered if he could answer them the same way he and his dad had solved jigsaw puzzles. He'd start with the corners and try to figure out the edges of the problem.

One corner had to be Camp Redfeather. Both Big Breezy and Giant's Fist were specific to this valley. Plus, if Indra was right about what she'd discovered in Pinereading, this forest knew who Arlo was. Whatever was happening, Redfeather was a crucial part of it.

Another corner might be the Past. A lot of old things were suddenly cropping up, including the rusted flashlight and the ancient seashell. If bark beetles really had etched Arlo's name into the wood, maybe that was how the chain linked back to Redfeather.

A third corner could be the Broken Bridge. That's where Arlo had found the flashlight and seen the other versions of Indra, Wu, Jonas and Julie. Of all the mysteries, this was still the most perplexing. Who were they? Were they his friends, or impostors? And why didn't they have an Arlo with them?

The final corner was Hadryn. What was he, exactly? Was he a shape-shifting doppelgänger like Indra had suggested? Was he Eldritch? Or could he be human, a former Ranger gone bad, like Darnell had described? Whatever he was, he clearly had skills that went way beyond snaplights and thunderclaps. If Darnell could shift his sight into a fly's eyes, what else was possible?

He wanted to ask Diana, or a camp counselor, or even Warden Mpasu. But he knew he couldn't trust them. Hadryn had successfully impersonated Wu. That meant he could be anyone. Arlo could never be sure of who he was talking to.

Wu suddenly snorted and grunted as he rolled over, then

quickly settled. His new snoring pattern was the classic badger-wheeze.

Arlo rolled over as well. He wished he had the cardboard box with the puzzle's picture on it so he could know exactly what he was facing. Still, he felt better for the progress he'd made in sorting it out.

There were more pieces of the puzzle to find. At least now he knew where they might fit.

26
STORM WARNING

THE THUNDER CAME FIRST: a deep, low rumble, like a mountain waking up.

Arlo was a mile into the forest when he heard it. He had spent the last hour searching for a spirit-haunted spring on the list Darnell had provided to the class. This water spirit was the fifth and final type of nature spirit he needed to identify. (He'd already found fire, wind, stone and tree.)

A flash of light. This time, the thunder was sharper. Closer. Like the sky was cracking open. If he hurried, maybe he could get back to camp before the rain. But Arlo was determined to find this water spirit first.

He had followed the illustrated instructions in the Field Book to fashion a dowsing rod—a Y-shaped section of bendy branch that, when used properly, would point to nearby water spirits and their associated bodies of water. According to the Field

Book, dowsing rods were crucial tools for survival in deserts and dry canyons.

Making the dowsing rod had been easy enough. Actually using it seemed to require a finesse Arlo couldn't quite master. The end of the rod never dipped or quivered, at least not in any way that seemed helpful.

Arlo tossed the useless rod aside and reconsidered his options. He had started retracing his steps when his left boot suddenly plunged ankle-deep into icy water.

He'd found the spring. He had walked right past it at least four times.

Arlo followed the tiny stream to its source: a mossy opening in the hillside just a few inches wide. According to the list, this spirit was called Frostbourn. He wasn't sure if the spirit was *in* the spring or *near* the spring or *was* the spring. Regardless, the name made sense. There was a noticeable chill in the area. Tiny crystals of ice clung to the stones. The water that spilled forth was perfectly clear and numbingly cold.

In the *Notes* section on his spirit checklist, Arlo wrote *clear* and *cold*.

Next to the spring, a clay bowl held a few dozen coins. Arlo scrounged in his pocket to find a quarter. He rubbed it on his shirt to shine it, then added it to the collection. "Spirits can't use money, obviously," Darnell had explained. "But they like coins all the same. It's a tribute. They know coins are valuable to us, so offering them is a sign of respect."

Rangers were allowed to offer spirits tributes like coins and food and songs. Sacrifices were strictly forbidden. "No blood. Not yours, not any living creature's. You do that, you're headed into dark territory." Darnell hadn't elaborated—maybe the full explanation was part of Advanced Spirits—but Arlo got the impression there were people who were willing to do sinister things to win favors from spirits.

Arlo heard the rain before he felt it. Giant drops *plop-plop-plopped* on the forest floor. So much for beating the downpour.

The Lodge was the largest building at Redfeather, and also the most stereotypically camp-like. It looked to be constructed from a giant set of Lincoln Logs. Arlo didn't stop running until he'd made it under its eaves.

It was only once he was out of the rain that he realized how completely soaked he was. His socks slumped around his ankles. His T-shirt clung to him like a film. Arlo pulled the spirit checklist from where he'd tucked it into his waistband, hoping it had stayed somewhat dry. The ink was blurry and the paper had started to tear at the creases, but he suspected it was salvageable.

On the road to his left, Arlo spotted a patrol of Rangers walking past wearing ponchos. They looked like green Halloween ghosts, with just their boots visible under hooded plastic robes. Arlo envied them, and cursed his decision to leave his poncho in his tent. It had been sunny just an hour before.

He decided to wait it out under the eaves until the worst of the rain had passed.

Then the wind came.

The rain began blowing sideways in thick sheets of water like at a carwash. Arlo was no longer safe under the eaves of the Lodge. If anything, he was trapped. There was nothing to duck under or behind. He braced himself as the rain needled his back.

Trying to protect the spirit checklist, he made his way along the wall until he rounded the corner of the building. Here he was mostly protected; the wind was blowing at a ninety-degree angle. Until it shifted. Suddenly, the rain was coming right at him again.

"Come on!" he shouted in frustration.

It seemed that Big Breezy wanted him wet or drowned for some reason. The only solution was to get out of her reach.

The door banged shut behind Arlo, echoing in the empty hall.

Arlo hadn't been inside the Lodge since the first night. That dinner had been crowded and noisy, a constant din of knives and forks and conversation across long tables. Now the room was eerily quiet, with just the gentle hush of rain and occasional thunder.

"You can't be in here!" called a man's voice. "We're setting up for dinner."

Arlo followed the sound to a swinging door on the far wall,

where the silhouette of a burly man was backlit by the harsh fluorescent lights of a kitchen. Arlo assumed he was the cook.

"Sorry, I . . ." Arlo didn't know how to finish the sentence. It didn't seem like a good idea to tell a stranger that the wind was bullying him.

Just then, Arlo noticed a single Ranger was sitting at one of the tables near the massive fireplace, his back to them. Arlo pointed at the boy as if to ask, *Why does he get to be here?*

"You in Pinereading?" asked the cook. "All right, but fifteen minutes. Then you're out."

"Okay," Arlo answered.

The cook stepped back into the kitchen. The door swung shut behind him.

Surprised by this reprieve, Arlo slowly made his way over to the Ranger sitting at the table. The boy had a collection of sticks and logs arranged in front of him, and he appeared to be taking notes. The kid turned around.

It was Russell Stokes. His lip curled like he smelled something foul.

"You're not in Pinereading, Flinch."

"I know."

"So why did you lie?"

Arlo held his ground. "I didn't lie."

"You let him think you were in the class. That's basically a lie. What would Connor say? What would Diana say?"

"They wouldn't say anything," answered Arlo, "because you're not going to tell them."

The kitchen door swung open again. Both Arlo and Russell looked over as the cook wheeled out carts with pitchers and plates and began setting up the far tables. But he wasn't alone. Warden Mpasu was with him, evidently supervising the preparations.

Tonight was the Feast of Fives, an annual all-camp dinner. Indra had explained that the name referred to the five sides of Rangers' pentagonal patches. Jonas said it was to make sure every Ranger was eating at least five vegetables over the course of camp.

Russell glared at Arlo. He seemed to be considering yelling over to Warden Mpasu.

Arlo dropped his voice to a whisper. "If you say anything, I'll tell people about you and the grisp." He was surprised and excited to hear himself making a threat. It didn't feel like him. But he liked it.

Russell held his stare, then shrugged. He went back to his work.

Arlo took a seat across the table from him. He picked up one of the sticks, examining the intricate patterns twisting across the wood. He wasn't sure where to begin reading it, or even which direction was up or down.

"That's right," whispered Russell. "You can't even read English, can you?"

"I can read fine." That was mostly true. Arlo read more slowly than most kids, but he understood what he read, and did okay in school.

Arlo watched as the Warden and the cook headed back into

the kitchen. As the kitchen door swung shut, Arlo felt a stirring in the air. It was subtle. He wondered if it was just his imagination.

Then he heard it: a soft, deep drone. It was spooky and hollow, like air blowing across the mouth of a bottle. The sound seemed to be coming from the giant unlit fireplace.

Russell followed Arlo's gaze. "It's just the wind, Flinch."

"I know." He knew the wind well. He knew it had an agenda, and that it was best not to ignore it.

Arlo carefully approached the dark fireplace. The drone was steady. A few drops of rain dripped into the ashes.

Then, a rattle. Metal banging, like a lid on a boiling pot.

That got Russell's attention. He didn't stand, but he slid down the bench closer.

"It's probably the damper," he said. "The thing that closes off the chimney. It's like a door."

It was too dark in the room to see what might be inside the fireplace. Cocking his wrist back, Arlo threw a snaplight. The glowing spark hit the blackened bricks at the back of the firebox before gradually fading out. Whatever was making the noise was higher up.

"There's a handle," said Russell. "You have to reach in and pull it open."

The rattling grew louder, as if the wind had been listening to Russell.

"You scared, Flinch?"

"No," he lied. In truth, Arlo could imagine himself being

sucked up the chimney, or pelted by stones. Big Breezy seemed angry at him for hiding inside the Lodge, out of her reach.

"Then do it," said Russell. "Open it up."

Steeling himself, Arlo stepped up onto the hearth. The fireplace was large enough that he could stand up inside it, but he thought it was safer to just lean in.

With his left hand firmly gripping the mantel, Arlo reached his right hand up into the darkness. He blindly fumbled until he felt a knob. A handle. A latch. It was vibrating. Banging.

This had to be it. This was the damper. The door. Arlo took a deep breath to steady himself. Then he pulled.

The damper clanged open.

Arlo squeezed his eyes shut as a blast of wet wind hit him square in the face. It smelled like smoke and rot. The whistling drone was closer now, and higher-pitched.

Something whipped past Arlo's ear, dragging across his cheek. Wiping off his eyes, he turned to look.

Russell was standing, staring up in wonder. Arlo followed his gaze.

A single black feather was swirling above their table, held aloft by invisible currents of air. It looked to be from a raven or a crow. Russell reached for it, but it floated higher, always just out of his grasp.

As Arlo stepped down off the hearth, he heard the kitchen door open. The cook was back with another cart of table settings. Arlo and Russell watched as he worked, wondering if he would notice the feather floating impossibly over their table.

Arlo slid back into his seat at the table, pretending to look at one of the Pinereading logs.

"It's a wind spirit," whispered Russell.

"I know." Arlo glanced over at the cook, who was bobbing his head as he moved. Arlo assumed he was listening to music on headphones. The cook unloaded stacks of plates, then wheeled the cart back into the kitchen.

The moment the door swung shut, Arlo and Russell were both out of their seats. The feather was still floating overhead, as if in a holding pattern.

Arlo climbed up on the table. He reached for the feather, but it suddenly shot like an arrow aiming straight for the far wall. When it hit, it stuck in the wood.

Both boys hurried over to investigate.

The feather twitched and wriggled, its downy barbs twisting into a hole in the wall at waist level. Arlo carefully reached out and grabbed the feather's shaft like a pencil. The moment he touched it, the feather went still. It was just a normal feather again.

The hole in the wall had metal edges, along with a narrow slit. It was easy to overlook.

"It's a keyhole," said Russell.

That seemed unlikely. *Why would there be a keyhole without a door?* Arlo wondered. But then he looked down at the floor, where the molding seemed a bit off. Russell was already running his fingers along the vertical seams in the wooden paneling.

This could be a secret door.

"Hold on," said Russell. He quietly dashed across the room, nabbing a fork from one of the tables. On his way back, he started bending the tines.

"What are you doing?" whispered Arlo. The cook could be back at any moment. Or worse, Warden Mpasu.

Russell nodded towards the kitchen. "Watch the door." He then kneeled down in front of the keyhole and inserted the fork. As he probed, he occasionally reset the tines. He was picking the lock. He seemed to know what he was doing.

A scrape. A click. A door-sized section of wall swung back, squealing on its hinges. Beyond it, a steep staircase led up into darkness.

His heart pounding in his chest, Arlo looked back at the kitchen. "They could come out at any second."

"I know," whispered Russell. "We should close it behind us."

27
THE ATTIC

AT THE TOP of the narrow staircase, Arlo found a light switch covered in cobwebs. He could feel the metal scrape as he flipped it. One by one, a series of dusty lightbulbs came to life, their filaments glowing like the inside of a toaster.

This attic ran the length of the Lodge, the stairs intersecting it at the midpoint. With its peaked ceiling and graduated shelves, the room was shaped like a pentagonal hallway. Cardboard boxes were shoved in all available spaces, leaving only a narrow path down the center. Based on the thick layer of dust on the floor, Arlo suspected that no one had been up here in years.

Russell pushed past Arlo. "There's gonna be cool stuff, like contraband." Arlo had never used the word *contraband*, but he knew it meant things no one was supposed to have.

While Russell was lifting flaps of random boxes, rooting around inside them, Arlo was content to read the writing on the outsides of the boxes. *Parents' Weekend 1993. Gordian Knots. Totems (Broken).*

Suddenly, Russell shrieked. Two rats scurried over his feet, darting to a new hiding place.

Arlo looked down the stairs to the hidden door. They had shut it, but left it unlocked. The Warden or the cook could find them at any moment.

That is, if they had heard the scream. Had they? Could they?

Arlo and Russell exchanged a silent look, both straining to hear any movement from downstairs.

"Should we go?" whispered Arlo.

"No!" Russell whispered back. "They'd see us coming out. Better off staying here, at least for a while."

Arlo suspected he was right. They clearly weren't supposed to be up here. If anyone saw them sneaking out, there would be a meeting with Warden Mpasu at the least. Still, it felt weird to be in league with Russell.

Russell resumed rummaging, a little more carefully this time. Arlo headed left, his attention focused on a shelf of dated file boxes. The most recent was from five years earlier, but they stretched back decades. Arlo thought back to his tent logic session, in which he had decided he needed to keep "finding the edges." One of those edges was the past, and these boxes held a record of that. There might be answers inside them.

It took Arlo a considerable amount of time to do the following math:

Arlo was twelve, almost thirteen.

His Uncle Wade was forty-something. Maybe forty-two?

Wade had been a Ranger. So if Wade had attended Camp Redfeather when *he* was twelve, that would have been thirty years earlier. Arlo just needed to subtract thirty years from the current year to find the appropriate file box.

Luckily, the box he was looking for was already on the floor, so he didn't have to risk pulling it off a shelf. Inside, the file folders were divided by region. He quickly found Pine Mountain Company. The folder was an inch thick. Inside were pink camp waivers rubber-banded together by patrol: Green, Blue, Red, Senior . . .

. . . and Yellow.

Arlo's heart skipped. *There* was *a Yellow Patrol.* Uncle Wade had always avoided answering questions about the existence of a Yellow Patrol, even when asked about the yellow neckerchief. But here was proof in Arlo's hands.

Arlo looked over at Russell, who was now way at the other end of the attic. He wanted to show him, to get independent verification that the forms really did say Yellow Patrol. But Russell wouldn't know or care about any of it. He was too busy swinging a double-headed ceremonial ax he'd found.

The patrol's sheets were bound together with an old rubber band that crumbled when Arlo tugged on it.

Leafing through the pages, Arlo read the names on the forms: Jason Pulver. Doug Ramos. Deroy White. Chuck Cunningham. *He has to be related to Connor and Christian,* Arlo thought. *Is he their father? An uncle?* It was strange to realize that the kid who filled out this form was likely now a parent with a son the same age.

The next name was even more familiar: Mitchell Jansen. *Mitch the mechanic.*

At dinner one night, Mitch had claimed he was in Red Patrol, yet the proof was here, hand-printed with a ballpoint pen: Mitch had actually been in Yellow Patrol. *Why would he lie?* Arlo wondered. And what did it have to do with the strange look he had exchanged with Uncle Wade?

The final form was for Wade Theodore Bellman. Uncle Wade. Arlo recognized the handwriting; it hadn't changed much in thirty years. The address listed was Arlo's house on Green Pass Road. Even the phone number was the same.

At the bottom of the stack was a large manila envelope. Arlo bent open the brass clasp, then reached in to pull out a glossy photo. It showed the entire patrol gathered at their campsite. The colors were faded, but there was no question that their neckerchiefs were yellow.

Arlo immediately recognized Wade by his lanky build and red-blond hair. Mitch was similarly easy to spot. He looked like a smaller version of his adult form, a boyish Clark Kent. Arlo couldn't identify any of the others. One boy had been caught in midsneeze, his face a blur.

The Rangers were all in uniform, which made the photo seem strangely timeless—Arlo couldn't identify any fashion details to anchor it to a specific year. Except for the faded color, it could have been taken yesterday.

It was only then that Arlo noticed something odd in the photo. Not the boys, but the location. The campsite sign read SUMMERLAND.

Arlo was certain there was no Summerland campsite at Redfeather. So where was this photo taken? Where was Summerland?

Just then he heard a scrape. A squeal.

He froze. Someone had opened the door at the bottom of the stairs.

"Hello!" called a woman's voice. "Is someone up there?"

Arlo recognized the accent. It was the Warden.

Russell was just as panicked as Arlo. The older Ranger ducked behind some boxes, then waved for Arlo to do the same.

Arlo had a choice. He could reveal himself to the Warden and face whatever punishment he was due—possibly even being sent home—or he could hide and risk getting caught anyway. Then he'd be in even more trouble.

Maybe it was the adrenaline. Maybe it was the thrill of having found details about Yellow Patrol. But Arlo didn't feel like turning himself in.

He folded the photo, tucking it into his waistband. Then, as quietly as he could, he put back the file box and tucked himelf into a small nook. It was a pretty good spot. From the top of the stairs, he was completely concealed. But if the Warden decided to really investigate, he would certainly be found.

He held his breath, listening. Hoping.

The stairs creaked. The Warden was coming up. He could hear each footstep.

By pressing against a sloping roof beam, Arlo could see Russell at the far end of the attic, equally freaked out. Shifting, Arlo felt something on his hand. He thought it was a snake—he nearly gasped—but then realized it was braided leather. A whip.

Arlo looked at the coil. It was as supple as a rope, and smoother. He picked with his thumbnail at a flat strand. That's when he had a thought: *tie a slipknaught.* It wasn't quite a rope, but it was close enough that it might work. It might be a way to escape.

He carefully picked up the whip, feeling along its length to find the thinnest part.

More footsteps. The Warden was at the top of the stairs. Arlo couldn't see her, but he could envision where she must be standing.

Then she began to move in his direction. Arlo held his breath, watching as she walked right past him to the very end of the attic. The storm outside was rattling an air vent. She pulled it shut with a clang. With the Warden's back turned, Russell had a clear path to the stairs.

Showing impressive stealth, he snuck over to the stairway. Arlo caught a glimpse of him as he descended.

Now Arlo was alone in the attic with the Warden. Worse, she was almost certain to see him on her return trip. From this angle, there was no real way to hide.

Working on the whip, Arlo felt a familiar warmth in his fingers. A crackle. But the knaught wasn't forming on the surface like it usually did. Instead, his right thumb pierced the leather, disappearing into it. Arlo pressed his left thumb in as well.

The whip begin splitting open, a silvery shimmer between the leather threads. He'd formed a kind of slipknaught without the normal knot part.

The Warden was approaching. Step. Step. Step.

Arlo stretched the two sections wider apart, then lowered the gap over his head. Given the cramped space, it took a lot of contortion, like changing your socks in your sleeping bag. But he finally got the opening all the way down to his feet.

As his hands let go, the leather strands fused back together.

When the Warden reached his hiding place, all she would see was an uncoiled whip and footprints on the dusty floor.

28
HAUNTED

ARLO WONDERED if maybe he was dead.

He couldn't get warm, and food had lost its flavor. No matter how much salt and pepper he added, it all tasted like cardboard.

The dining room was crowded and noisy, with two hundred boisterous Rangers celebrating the Feast of Five. Yet everyone felt distant. It was like Arlo was watching it on TV rather than actually being there. A spectator in his own body.

It had been three hours since he had slipped away from Warden Mpasu, walking right past her as she searched the attic in confusion. He had been invisible and *incorporeal*—a word Indra had used to describe her experience after they'd used the slipknaught in the Valley of Fire.

Incorporeal meant "without a body." Basically, a ghost.

And that's what it had felt like. The effect had only lasted a few minutes, just long enough for him to get down to the main dining room. Then *pop*, *whoosh*, and the shimmer faded. He'd returned to the real world.

Mostly.

Arlo could touch things. He could lift his fork and be heard. By all outward appearances, Arlo Finch was completely normal. It was only on the inside that something was very wrong.

Everything felt flat. Hollow.

"It's interesting that you didn't fall through the floor," said Indra. She kept her voice low. The room was loud enough that no one could really eavesdrop, anyway. "Because if you think about it, why would the floor be solid when everything else isn't?" She speared another green bean. It bounced on her fork as she gestured. "But then again, the hag's hut was solid to us. And you said Big Breezy couldn't pass through the walls, either, so there must be something about how spirits interact with human structures. We should look it up, or ask. I bet they teach it in Advanced Spirits. Or, I don't know, this might even be beyond that. I suppose . . ."

Indra was sitting next to Arlo, close enough that her hair occasionally brushed against him. But she might as well have been in a different country. It felt like Arlo's weekly video chat with his dad in China: an approximation of being there, but not the real thing. Indra's voice seemed to be coming from a lifelike puppet of the girl he knew.

Arlo realized that Indra was still speaking. He had zoned out, and only caught the last sentence: ". . . or really, we should just do some experiments tomorrow and see what is and isn't solid."

"I can't do it again," he said.

Indra finally ate the green bean. "Oh, you don't need to use that whip you found. Just a normal rope, like before."

"I can't do it again," he repeated, more forcefully this time. "I mean, I *could*, but I don't think I *should*."

"Why not?"

"Because I don't think we're supposed to go to that place. It's not safe."

Safe. Safety had always been Arlo's top priority. It was why he planned escape routes from his bedroom. It was why he stayed back from the edges of cliffs. He'd lived his whole life in a state of constant vigilance, looking for threats.

But after his adventures over the past few months, and his many brushes with death, Arlo Finch had stopped playing it so safe. Each time he'd survived, he'd become more confident. Cocky.

Indra was talking again, something about precautions they could take.

Arlo thought about astronauts on space walks. They had suits to protect them from the radiation, along with heaters to keep them warm and oxygen tanks to let them breathe. Without that technology, they'd die in less than a minute, because humans aren't built to live in an icy vacuum.

Arlo hadn't traveled to space, but he'd walked through a realm of ghosts and spirits. Why hadn't he considered how dangerous it could be? Not just because of the creatures who lived there, but the place itself?

"Maybe the reason they don't teach slipknaughts in Rangers is because we shouldn't use them," he said. "They don't mention them, even to warn about them, because they know that if we knew, it was possible we'd be tempted to try it."

Indra considered that idea for a moment. Arlo could see it was hard for her to shift gears. She'd been so excited to explore the physics of slipknaughts that it was frustrating to be told that they shouldn't.

Thomas reached over to take the macaroni and cheese. He and the rest of the patrol had been busy discussing theories about Ekafos, and whether the legendary lake monster was a plesiosaur, a crocodile or simply a myth.

"What are you all talking about?" he asked. "You're always so serious."

Indra restated the issue as a question: "Do you think there are things that are useful, but so dangerous that people shouldn't use them?"

"Like steroids?" suggested Jonas, taking the bowl from Thomas. "Steroids can give you an advantage in sports, but they can also mess up your body. That's why they're not allowed."

"It's because they're unfair," countered Wu. Apparently, the whole patrol was joining the conversation. "If everyone had steroids, then that would be fine. Everyone would be equal."

"People aren't equal, though," said Jonas. "Some people are just faster than others. Or taller. Steroids aren't going to change that."

"Drugs are bad," said Julie, taking the final spoonful of macaroni.

"That's ridiculous," said Indra. "You can't say all drugs are bad. Lots of drugs save people's lives. That's why we have medicine."

Julie rolled her eyes. "You're just saying that because your dad's a doctor."

"Yes! And so's my mom." Then she added: "A psychiatrist is a kind of doctor. You can look it up."

"One of our uncles did drugs, and he died," said Julie. Jonas nodded. "He was really nice. He used to make homemade ice cream in all these great flavors, and he built us this tire swing that was crazy long. Like, scary. But then he hurt his back and the doctors gave him drugs for the pain, but he couldn't stop taking them. He started stealing things so he could afford to buy them—"

"He stole computers from the school," said Jonas.

"Wait, that was your uncle?" asked Wu. Jonas nodded.

Julie continued. "And then for a while he wasn't doing drugs. But my mom went to check on him one day and he was dead on his couch. He had overdosed." She looked heartbroken remembering him. So did Jonas.

"I'm sorry," said Indra. "It's awful that happened. But if your uncle had drowned, you wouldn't say 'All water is bad.'"

"He didn't drown," said Julie. "Were you even listening?"

Thomas intervened. "Guys! Something's wrong with Arlo."

Everyone's attention turned to the end of the table, where Arlo Finch had stood halfway up. He was swaying, dizzy. His skin was sweaty and pale. His mouth was moving as if he was trying to speak, but no words came out.

Arlo could see them, too. But they seemed to be receding

down a long tunnel. The edges of his vision became blurry. His body felt heavy.

Then everything went black.

A ceiling fan. Shelves. Wood paneling.

Black.

A woman's necklace. A single bear claw. A washcloth.

Black.

People were talking. Their voices were just a hum. "Don't try to sit up," said the woman. The woman with the necklace? Arlo wasn't sure.

Arlo looked at his hand. Light spilled between his fingers. The creases in his palm looked like river valleys. Chasms.

The Broken Bridge. Arlo reached his hand under the heavy stone. He smelled the wet earth. His fingers touched the flashlight.

Black.

The fourth time Arlo Finch woke up was different. He was still weak, but the confusion had passed. His thoughts seemed organized in natural patterns rather than dream logic.

He was lying on a cot in the small back room of a log cabin. It was night. The sky was dark outside the window.

Over his toes, through a half-open door, he saw a woman sitting at an old computer. She had her back to him, headphones on her ears. Arlo recognized her as Warden Jeannette, the camp's assistant director, who primarily ran the Health Center.

On the shelves around him, Arlo saw boxes of bandages and bottles of antiseptics, all the standard first-aid supplies. But there were also jars filled with more exotic ingredients, and candles in every shape and size. On the table by the bed, a stick of incense was burning, its long ash drooping into the shallow wooden tray.

He heard movement. A *pitter-patter* on the floor. Then the door slowly, silently swung shut.

"Now," said a man's voice. "It's important you don't shout, or she'll be right in here."

Confused, Arlo propped himself up on his elbows to see where the noise was coming from. A man rose from the floor, stretching his neck and cracking his knuckles. He was wearing dark jeans and an olive-green sweater and had an elaborate mustache that twisted up at the ends. Arlo hadn't seen him in six months, but immediately recognized him.

It was Fox.

29
A WARMER SEASON

FOX CHECKED that the door was really shut. He kept his voice low as he turned back to Arlo.

"You're in quite a spot here," he said. "But then again, you're not entirely here, and that's the root of the problem." He began looking through the jars and satchels on the shelves, searching for something specific.

"What happened?" asked Arlo. "Did I faint?"

"You're *faint*, all right. A pencil line when you should be ink. Have to make sure you don't get erased altogether." Fox sniffed the contents of a jar, then tasted one of the leaves inside.

"It's because of the slipknaught, isn't it?"

"It's not *not* the knaught, but the real issue is the string." Fox chewed on a piece of bark, assessing its flavor. He spit it out.

"What string?"

"The silver string. Your string. You're stretched too far. Your kite might fly away without you, and then where would you be?"

Arlo was genuinely confused. "I don't know."

"Exactly!" Fox examined a bag of herbs, then pulled the gold drawstring from it. He kneeled down beside Arlo, holding out two fingers. His fingernails were especially long and sharp. "Everyone you know has two parts: a body and a spirit. Most times, they're bound together nice and tight." Fox wrapped the gold string around his two fingers, pulling them together.

"But if a clever young man were to mess with knaughts, he might loosen that connection. Suddenly, his body and his spirit aren't quite as together as they should be." Fox opened a space between his fingers. "That's how you are right now. You've come undone."

"That's why I feel this way? Because my spirit's not in my body?"

Fox scoffed. "In. Out. You're not a box. It's just that your spirit's unbound, and that's bound to be trouble."

"Can you fix it?"

"Perhaps! Let's see if we can cinch you up a bit."

Arlo wasn't sure he liked the sound of that. "How?"

Fox went back to poking through the items on the shelf. "A ten-year process of study and meditation ought to do it. Ideally, one in complete seclusion and tranquility."

Arlo shook his head. "I can't—"

"—wait that long. Yes, I agree. We've been waiting much too

long as it is." Fox stood up, pulling a copper bowl from a shelf. "We'll have to do it the quick way, despite the dangers."

"What dangers?"

"Your string could break. It's already quite thin."

"What happens if it breaks?" asked Arlo. "Would I die?"

"No, no," said Fox. "It would be like you are now, but much worse, and forever. Well, not *forever.* Human lives are so short." Fox added a series of herbs and tinctures to the copper bowl. He didn't seem to be measuring particularly carefully.

"What are you, exactly?" asked Arlo. He'd been wondering that for months.

"I told you! I'm Fox. I'm all the foxes, and none of them."

"Are you a spirit?"

"I am! Quite a spirited spirit, I'm told."

"But you can talk. Big Breezy can't talk. Frostbourn can't talk."

Fox smiled. His teeth were as sharp as his fingernails. "So human to think that you can understand one little piece of something and thus understand all of it. My friend, there are as many kinds of spirits in the world as there are plants and people and animals. But no one asks why humans can talk and apple trees can't. Or why birds fly and fish swim. We simply are what we are."

Fox stirred the contents of the bowl with his finger. He seemed satisfied. "Now, let's get you reeled in. Can you stand up?"

"I think so." Arlo swung his feet off the cot and pushed himself to sitting. With a deep breath, he slowly stood up, wobbling a bit. He pointed to the copper bowl. "Do I have to eat that or something?"

"No! This is for me. I'm famished." Fox ate the herbs by messy fingerfuls, bits of green sticking to his lips and teeth. "It's hard to find this stuff out of season. But here it is, all neatly lined up on the shelf. So convenient." Fox licked the bottom of the bowl clean, then handed it to Arlo. "Now, which hand do you use for snaplights?"

"My right hand," said Arlo.

"Then hold the bowl in your left hand. With your right hand, I want you to almost cast a snaplight, but not quite."

"I don't understand."

"You do understand. You're just being stubborn."

Arlo realized Fox was right. He did know what he meant.

When throwing a snaplight, there was a moment just before the energy left your fingertips. It was like static electricity. A buzz. Arlo concentrated. He cocked his hand back, ready to snap. And then held it. He could feel the crackle and warmth. It was like a tiny spark held in the friction of his fingerprints.

"I have it."

"Now, move it in a clockwise circle around the rim of the bowl."

Arlo did as instructed. The moment his finger touched the metal, he could feel a vibration in the bowl. As he slowly traced a circle, the bowl began to softly ring. It reminded Arlo of how his dad had sometimes played melodies on the rims of wine-glasses at dinner.

"Faster," said Fox. "That's not quite it."

Arlo swirled his finger faster, as if he were mixing cake batter. The ringing grew louder. What started as a single pitch became two, then three. The tones climbed at different and discordant intervals.

"You're nearly there."

Arlo wasn't sure how much longer he could keep going. His fingertip had gone numb. His wrist was aching. Plus the heavy emptiness was growing. He worried he might faint again.

And then the notes reached a perfect chord. It was eerie and beautiful and haunting. Arlo was sure he'd never heard it before. In fact, he was certain no musical instrument could ever duplicate it. It seemed to be the universe itself humming.

Arlo stopped swirling, yet the tone continued. He looked into the bowl, where veins of energy crackled along the surface. Only then did he realize he wasn't holding it anymore. The bowl was floating in place. The hum was now coming from deep within Arlo's body.

"Brace yourself," said Fox.

The metal bowl suddenly crunched in on itself, contracting into a small copper ball. It hung in midair for a moment, then fell to the floor.

Arlo looked at Fox, confused.

Suddenly, Arlo found himself thrown back against the wall. It was like being hit by an invisible truck. He felt every bone in his skeleton ringing, every fiber in every muscle vibrating. It was like being tossed into the icy lake—but also *being* the lake.

Fox was back at the door, peeking out to see if Warden Jeannette had noticed the commotion. She was still at her computer, headphones on her ears.

Arlo slowly picked himself up. His body ached, but more importantly, he felt himself back inside it. The hollowness was gone.

"Told you to brace yourself," said Fox after carefully shutting the door. "It's a shock to bind one spirit, much less two."

Arlo was confused. "What do you mean *two*?"

"You're a tooble." Fox said it like it was obvious, such as *you're a Ranger* or *you're a boy.* "You have two spirits instead of one."

Tooble. Arlo had always thought the word sounded like a cross between *two* and *double.* Maybe he'd been right. "You're saying there are two spirits inside me right now?"

"Of course not! One spirit *is* you and one spirit is something else altogether. That's why your eyes don't match. It's uncommon, but not altogether rare."

He took Arlo's chin, tilting his head into the light so he could see Arlo's eyes better. "It's definitely a forest spirit, something quite old, I'd say."

"Is it like a parasite?" Arlo asked. The Field Book had a page on common parasites like giardia and tapeworms that Rangers might get from drinking untreated water.

"Spirits do sometimes hitch a ride with humans, but you were definitely born with this one. I suppose your parents are druids, Wardens, mystic types?"

"No! Not at all."

Fox seemed surprised. "Well, this spirit came from the Long Woods, so it got there somehow. Tell me: Do you hear voices? See strange words?"

Arlo's heart skipped. "Yes!" Even before he had moved to Pine Mountain, Arlo had occasionaly heard odd voices and had trouble reading.

"That's the other spirit trying to do its thing. Imagine what it must feel like for it, stuck inside your tiny body, unable to control anything. All that pent-up energy."

From the other room, a chair scraped across the floor. Warden Jeannette was getting up.

"I should go." Fox made his way to the window, unlocking it.

"Wait, no! I have questions."

"And she'll have questions if she finds me here."

"Just one!" He grabbed Fox's arm. The man's eyes narrowed, and he gave a low snarl. Arlo pulled his hand away. "Why did you come now?" Arlo asked. "You could have told me this anytime."

"This is when you told me to come. You said that you'd be ready."

Arlo was confused. "But I'm not ready. And when did I say that? I've only met you once before."

"Funny, that." Fox opened the window. "Still, next time we meet, it will be at the anchor."

"What anchor?"

"*The* anchor. Can't imagine there'd be two. Doesn't make sense for there to even be one."

Arlo heard the door opening behind him. He turned to see Warden Jeannette. She was wearing a bear-claw necklace and a lot of turquoise jewelry.

"You're up!" she said, surprised.

Arlo looked back at the window. Fox was gone.

"You gave us quite a scare." She put a hand on Arlo's forehead to check his temperature. "No fever," she said. "That's good. Been looking up your symptoms, checking all the Warden boards. At first I thought it might have been that a waxbee stung you, but there haven't been any in these parts for years."

"I feel better now," said Arlo. "I'll be fine."

"Let's give your mom a call. I've been talking to her, and she's understandably concerned."

30
THE CALL

THE PHONE IN THE HEALTH CENTER was avocado-green plastic. The receiver was surprisingly heavy. Arlo looked for the buttons to dial the number, but it was just a circle with holes in it.

"You know how to use one of these?" asked Warden Jeannette.

Arlo nodded. "I've seen it in movies." He set his finger into the number-three hole and then turned the dial clockwise until it stopped. Then he released it, watching as it slowly spun back to its starting place. He repeated the process for the rest of the digits in his home telephone number.

A series of clicks. Silence. He wondered if he'd messed it up, but then the call went through.

His mom answered on the second ring. "Hello?!" She sounded panicked, like she was expecting bad news.

"It's me," Arlo said. "I'm okay."

He heard her exhale. "Really? You're not just saying you're okay so I won't worry?"

"I'm really okay." He felt bad for making her worry.

Arlo tried to picture his mom. She was definitely in the kitchen—they only had one phone. Was she sitting at the table? Was she leaning against the wall? It was after eleven. Was she dressed for bed?

"So what happened?" she asked.

"I guess I fainted." He didn't want to lie, but he didn't want to tell her too much, either.

"Have you been drinking enough water?"

Arlo was relieved she'd given him a plausible excuse. "Probably not. I will, though."

"You really scared me, Arlo. I was about to drive up there. But the nurse-warden person said she'd call back, so . . ."

"Don't you have work tomorrow?" he asked.

"I have one son. That's more important than work." She said it with an *isn't that obvious?* tone.

"I'm fine, though."

"So you said. But I'm allowed to worry."

Arlo sat down in the Warden's chair. "Is everything okay there? Have you heard from Jaycee?"

"We video-chatted yesterday. She's having a great time with your dad in China. I'm sure she won't want to come back."

"How about Uncle Wade?"

"No, but you know." Arlo knew. His mom and his uncle didn't really talk much even when they were under the same roof.

"I'm sure he's fine. He'll suddenly show up and be angry about some ridiculous thing."

Arlo was conscious of Warden Jeannette listening to their conversation. He probably wasn't supposed to stay on the phone very long. "I have to go," he said.

"Promise me you'll take care of yourself. Don't push too hard. Drink plenty of water."

"I will," he promised.

"And have fun. That's what camp's for. Enjoy yourself."

Arlo half smiled. It was hard to remember a time when this had all been just fun. When he wasn't worried about spirits and doppelgängers and silver strings. He wanted to rewind the clock back to one week earlier, when it was just him and his mom hanging out.

"Love you," he said.

"Love you more."

31
NEGATIVE YEARS OLD

THE NEXT MORNING, Arlo woke up a few minutes before reveille. The air was wet and cold, but his sleeping bag was dry and cozy. He was in no hurry to get out.

Sunlight was streaming through tiny pinholes in the canvas tent. He listened to the bird songs.

"Are you awake?" whispered Wu.

Arlo looked over. Wu had just his face poking out of his sleeping bag. "Feeling better?" he asked.

"I'm fine. All good." Arlo had gotten back to Firebird just before midnight. He hadn't had the energy to explain about Fox and spirits and silver strings. "Should we get up?"

"Probably."

Neither boy made any effort to rise. They smiled conspiratorially.

"You dropped something last night," said Wu. "In the Lodge,

after you fainted." He snaked one arm out of his sleeping bag and reached under his cot to retrieve a folded photograph. He handed it to Arlo.

It was the photo Arlo had found in the attic, the one that showed young Wade and Mitch and Yellow Patrol at a campsite called Summerland. Arlo had nearly forgotten about it.

"Where's it from?" asked Wu.

"Somewhere here at camp, I think." He pointed to the tallest boy. "That's Uncle Wade."

"No way! It's weird to think of him ever being a kid."

Arlo pointed to another boy. "And that's Mitch, the guy who runs the garage in Pine Mountain."

"The one your mom's dating."

The words hung in the cold air. Arlo felt he could almost see them. Touch them. He had never heard anyone talk about Mitch and his mom that way.

"They're not dating," he said. "They're just friends. My mom does his bookkeeping."

"Sorry. I didn't . . ." Wu trailed off. He seemed uncertain how to finish the sentence.

Does everyone in town think they're dating? wondered Arlo.

A bugle blared. Reveille. It was time to face the morning.

Breakfast was eggs and bacon and corn cakes—pancake mix with leftover canned corn from the night before. Everything tasted amazing, even the little charred bits. Arlo was just happy that food had flavor again.

Indra was fixated on the photograph. "This proves there was a Yellow Patrol. So why was your uncle being so evasive about it?"

"He's sort of weird about everything, though," said Wu. "I mean, no offense, Arlo, but your uncle is really strange."

Julie looked over Indra's shoulder. "Why are there no girls in the patrol?"

"It's from before they allowed girls in Rangers," explained Indra.

Julie was aghast. "That's crazy. Girls are better at most things."

"No they're not!" said Jonas.

"We are," said Julie. "We just don't want you to feel bad."

"Everyone in this photo is in their forties now," said Indra. "Some of them probably have kids our age."

"Our mom was twenty when she had our sister," said Julie. "If I had a baby at the same age that she had a baby, then right now my baby would be negative seven years old."

"People can't be negative years old," said Wu.

"Sure they can. Right now, Jonas and I are thirteen. But fifteen years ago, we were negative two. That's how math works." Julie liked to point out facts about math. She and her brother were homeschooled, and already in their second year of algebra.

"You weren't anything fifteen years ago," said Wu. "You weren't even an idea."

"Yes I was! Our parents had already picked out names. Julie if it was a girl, Jonas if it was a boy. So they got both."

Wu wasn't going to let this go. "You could have just as easily not been born, or been born later. When you're in the past, everything else is the future, and the future is uncertain."

"No, I think she's right," said Thomas. "You say the future is uncertain, fine. But the past is locked down. You can't change it. Whatever happened, happened. So let's say it's fifteen years ago. Heck, let's say it's thirty years ago, when this photo was taken. You can say, 'The future is uncertain.' But *their* future—these kids in the photo—it's still the past to us. It happened. It's not gonna change."

Arlo paused chewing in order to better concentrate on Thomas's explanation.

"And whatever happened is what's brung us to right now. So it's not 'uncertain' that Julie was going to be born. Far from it. It was guaranteed. So when Julie says she was negative two years old, then she's correct, and the proof is that she's sitting right here with us."

Everyone sat silent for a moment, trying to find a hole in Thomas's logic. No one could.

"You're really smart," said Julie.

Thomas smiled. "Yeah, well, people underestimate me because of my accent."

Indra returned to the photograph. "Thirty years ago, there were six kids in Yellow Patrol. We know two are still around. But what happened to the rest of them?"

"I think the answer is here at camp somewhere," said Indra. "We just have to find Summerland."

Wu's campaign pledge to get rid of the duty roster had led to an informal and chaotic system for getting work done around camp.

As promised, Jonas was doing almost all of the cooking. Julie had offered herself up as the primary dishwasher, but the gap between "wouldn't mind doing" and "actually doing" had grown wider each day. At lunch and dinner, there would still be unwashed dishes from breakfast. Jonas would grumble that he needed a clean pot, and all food preparation would stop until somebody quickly scrubbed and rinsed it.

Arlo found himself doing a little bit of every job—and some days, more than a little. He'd gather firewood; he'd fetch water; he'd return the food crates to the Commissary when they'd stack up next to the picnic table. Wu, Indra or Thomas would sometimes offer to help him, but only after they witnessed him doing the chore by himself.

Rather than a duty roster, Blue Patrol was organized around guilt and inertia.

After Canoeing that day, Arlo and Indra returned to camp to discover that no one had gone to the Commissary to pick up the lunch crates. Wu and Thomas were playing checkers. Jonas was reading on his cot. Julie was drawing in her sketchbook.

Indra sighed. "It's fine. We can go back and get it."

She wasn't making a big fuss about chores, which puzzled Arlo. He could see she was frustrated, yet she never complained, never pointed out how Wu's anything-goes leadership style had made a mess of camp life. Instead, Indra just shrugged and smiled with her lips pressed tightly together. "Fake-happy" is what Julie had called it once when Indra was off at the sinks.

Arlo suspected that Indra knew it looked fake-happy, and that *she* knew that *they* knew she knew. Her toothless smile was both resigned and enraged. She was certain she was right, and certain it didn't matter. She wasn't ready for another fight she expected to lose.

Indra dropped off her daypack and headed back down the trail. Arlo followed her.

At the Commissary, Arlo and Indra received a lecture from the supply master, who pointed out that all of the other patrols had picked up their crates half an hour earlier. They knew there was no point explaining that the speech should be directed at the other four members of Blue Patrol.

While the man was talking, Arlo's attention drifted to a large map tacked on the wall. It showed the whole camp, with each campsite named and numbered based on how many tent platforms it held. He quickly spotted Firebird's four tents, and the other campsites used by the different patrols in Pine Mountain Company.

But something else caught his eye: a yellowed edge of older paper peeking out from the bottom.

His rant finished, the supply master went outside to answer a call on his walkie-talkie. If Arlo wanted to see what was hidden, this was his chance. He carefully pulled out a tack, lifting one corner of the map to reveal an older one beneath. It seemed to show Camp Redfeather as well, but the layout was completely different.

"What are you doing?" asked Indra in a whisper.

Arlo pulled out another tack, revealing more of the hidden map. He spotted some familiar names, including Firebird. But there were also a half dozen other sites with names he didn't recognize: Columbine, Toad's Hollow, Wit's End, Paladin, Claw-foot . . . and Summerland.

By now, Indra was looking over his shoulder. "Wait—where is that?"

The map showed the lake, but everything around it was off. The Lodge and the Nature Center were in the wrong places. Even the mountains had moved.

Arlo figured it out first: "It's rotated."

The regular camp map placed north on the right-hand side. This made sense because all the campsites were west of the lake and therefore "up" on the map, just as they were uphill from the lake.

This older map was oriented with north at the top. The road to the Lodge ran down to the lake, with trails branching off it to the left.

But another trail split off to the right, wrapping around the east side of the lake. That's where these six other campsites were located, including Summerland.

"That's impossible," said Indra. "There's no trail there. And definitely no campsites."

"Not now," said Arlo. "But maybe thirty years ago, there were." The map had no date on it, but it seemed like it could easily be that old.

Arlo and Indra shared a look. They could tell the rest of the patrol and investigate together, likely after a prolonged discussion and debate that would reignite old tensions. Or . . .

"We could go now," said Indra. "Just us."

Arlo agreed. They quickly delivered the food crates to the patrol, but didn't stay for lunch. They were on their way to find a lost campsite.

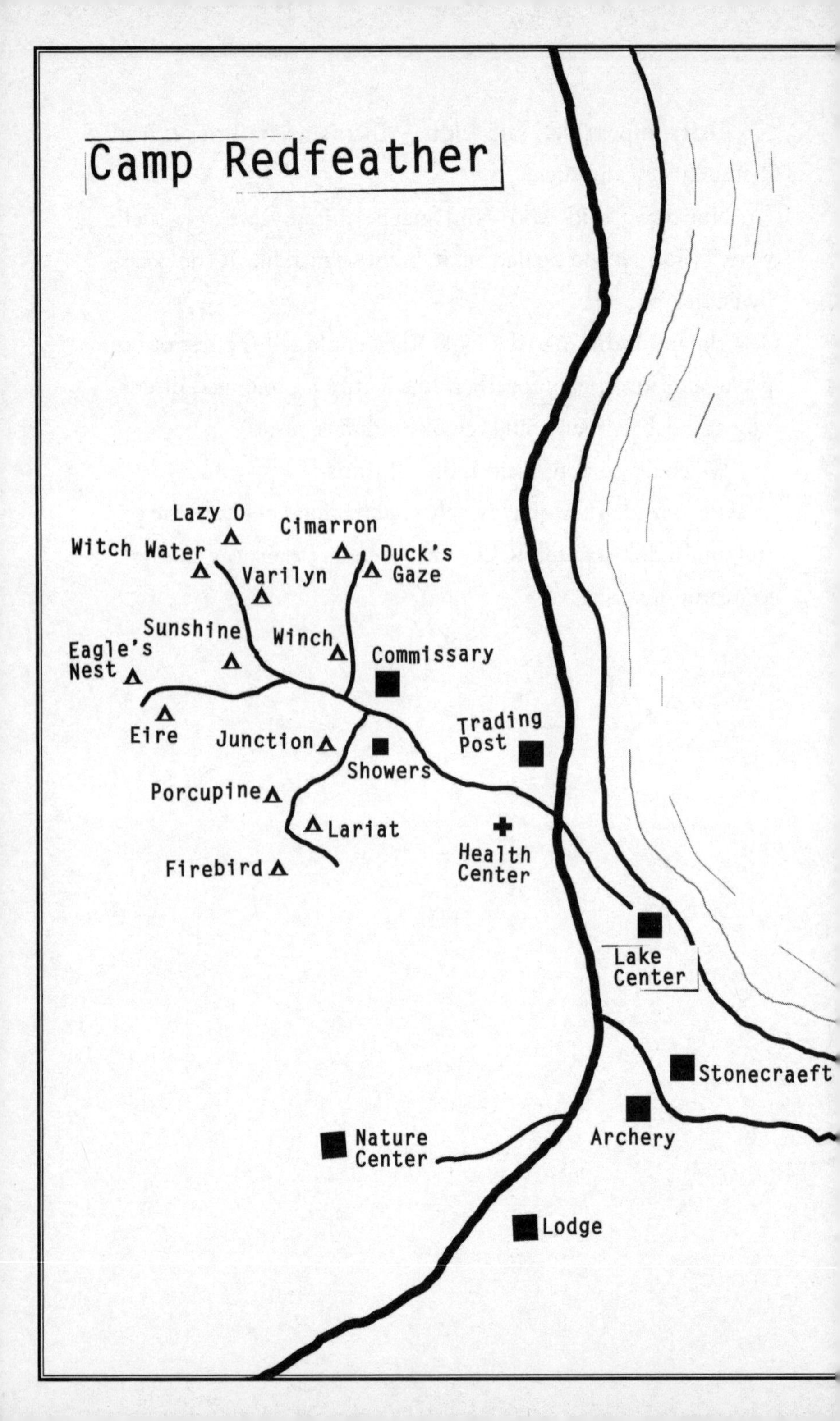
Camp Redfeather
Lazy O
Cimarron
Witch Water
Duck's Gaze
Varilyn
Sunshine
Winch
Eagle's Nest
Commissary
Eire
Junction
Trading Post
Showers
Porcupine
Lariat
Health Center
Firebird
Lake Center
Stonecraeft
Archery
Nature Center
Lodge

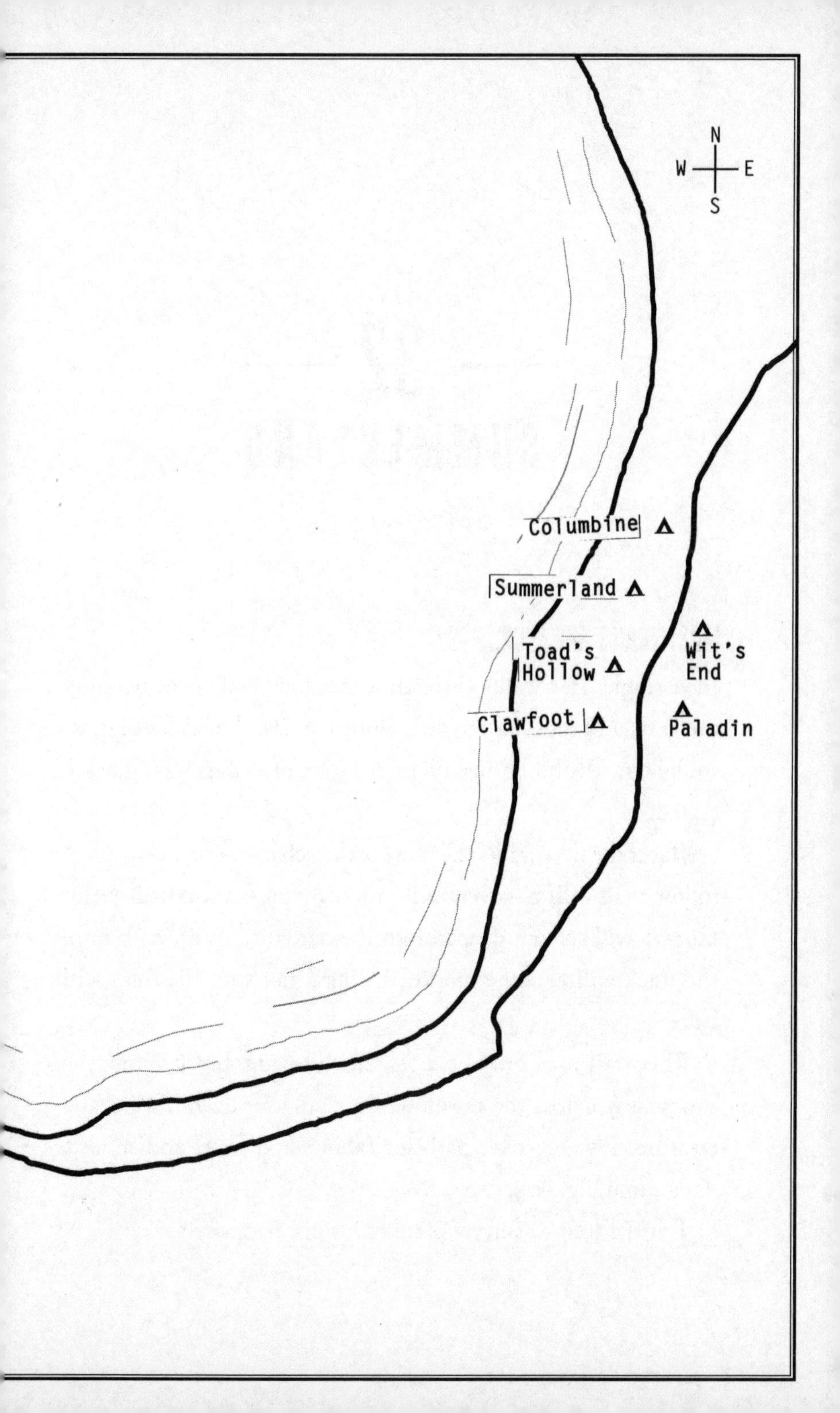
N
W
E
S
Columbine
Summerland
Toad's Hollow
Wit's End
Clawfoot
Paladin

32
SUMMERLAND

MOST TRAILS ARE ACCIDENTS.

A single deer walks through a meadow, its hooves bending the grass and scuffing the dirt. Within a day, the blades of grass straighten. The hoofprints fill in. All trace of its passing is quickly erased.

But if the deer walks the same path each day—or if other deer follow it in a line—eventually the tiny grass roots will yield. Hooves will scratch deeper, into the bare dirt. With each rain, the track will become muddy. Under a hot sun, the mud will bake.

This trail may only be a few inches wide, but it's now the easiest way across the meadow—not only for deer, but for any creature. It's a quicker path for rabbits and foxes and moose. An animal highway.

But the trail was never planned. It just happened.

In the Field Book, Arlo had read a lot about trails. In Tracking, Rangers were taught to recognize animal trails. In Venturing, they were warned to be careful when hiking as a patrol so as not to accidentally trample delicate areas. And in Pathing, they were taught how to build and maintain proper Ranger trails.

While most trails occurred by accident, the trails at Camp Redfeather showed clear signs of pathing. Stones marked the edges. Arrows and colored markers indicated forks. Logs had been embedded in slopes to prevent erosion.

These were the clues Arlo and Indra were looking for as they searched for a trail that would take them to Summerland.

At the moment, all they saw was marsh. The area east of the lake was flat and fetid, the tall grass and shrubs buzzing with insects. The ground was wet and sticky. Arlo's boots were caked with an inch of mud.

"There's no way they'd put a campsite here," said Indra.

Arlo agreed. "It must be further on. Like up there." He pointed to distant trees rising on a slope. "But how do we get there?"

"Let's think about the map. We know the Lodge was on it, so they must have had a way to get there. Maybe with a bridge or something."

They backtracked, circling south towards the Lodge. That's when Arlo spotted it: a splintered log, half-sunk in the muck. A second log lay parallel to it, three feet away. It had evidently been a wooden walkway, sort of like a dock, but all the boards had long ago rotted away. What was left was just a series of logs snaking into the marsh.

Arlo tried walking along it like a balance beam, but it was so rotted and slippery he kept plunking his boots into the muck.

Indra suggested they walk side by side, each on their own log, bracing each other for balance. That did the trick. It was like an obstacle course or Alpine Derby challenge. Once they'd figured out the technique, it wasn't that difficult.

The log path ended at a hillside covered with scrubby brush. Here they found two rows of stones set at an angle, spaced three feet apart. The edges of a proper Ranger trail.

They also found a huge metal sign mounted on a pole set in concrete. It was rusty, but the text was clear.

DANGER!
KEEP OUT

A year earlier, before moving to Pine Mountain, Arlo Finch would have obeyed such a sign without question. After all, it had clearly been placed here for a good reason, and at considerable effort and expense. The sign makers must know best. But after ten months in Rangers, living in a state of near-constant peril, Arlo's perspective had changed. He still took the sign seriously, but it was more cautionary than prohibitive: First, it reminded him to be alert for unexpected threats. Second, it told him they were getting close to something interesting.

He looked over at Indra. "We're going, right?"

"Of course."

Arlo led the way, ducking under the sign. Indra followed him.

A few moments later, a large black crow landed on the sign. It didn't caw or otherwise make itself known. It simply blinked its glossy black eyes and watched as Arlo and Indra headed up the path into the trees.

On the map in the Commissary, the Summerland campsite looked to be close to the lake, so Arlo and Indra searched for forks in the trail that would lead them towards the water. As they came over a small rise, they stopped short.

Massive pine trees lay strewn across the slope. They hadn't been felled with an ax or a saw. Roots had been ripped from the ground. Trunks were shattered, leaving jagged stumps. The dead trees leaned against each other at odd angles like a forgotten game of pick-up sticks, forming shadowy nooks.

Birds chirped. A woodpecker rattled in the distance. Yet Arlo felt a hush, the eerie quiet of a cemetery. Something terrible had happened here.

"What do you think did it?" he asked. "A bomb, maybe?" He remembered watching a video in science class of an atomic blast in a Russian forest. Suddenly, he wondered if the sign they'd ignored was warning of radiation.

"I guess? I mean, I don't know if even a tornado could do this," said Indra. Then she sparked with a new idea: "But we can figure out *when* it happened."

She led the way down to a broken-off stump. With her

pocketknife, she scraped away moss and dirt until she could see the rings of the tree.

"Remember I said there was a big fire a hundred and seventeen years ago? Well, there was a smaller one forty-nine years ago. All the trees at Redfeather have a mark from it." She poked at a narrow band that was just slighly darker than the others. "So all we have to do is count forward from that ring to see how long ago this tree fell down."

As Indra counted, Arlo noticed a single crow alight on a fallen tree. The bird settled, picking at its feathers. Yet something seemed off about it, like when a person is caught staring and suddenly looks away.

Indra finished her ring counting: "Nineteen. So if this tree fell nineteen years after the fire, that means it was . . ."

"Thirty years ago," said Arlo. "That's when my uncle was at camp."

"Along with Yellow Patrol." Indra smiled, clearly excited. "Whatever happened here, they would have seen it. They would know."

"We're pretty close to the water," said Arlo. "This could be Summerland. It could be buried underneath all these trees."

"Do you have the photo?"

Arlo pulled it out, flattening it at the crease where he'd folded it. The photograph showed the six Rangers in front of the sign for the Summerland campsite. Around them were trees—none of which were standing now.

Indra pointed to one of the boys. He was crouched on a small boulder. "That rock would still be here. We just need to find it."

They spent the next ten minutes carefully judging every rock on the hillside. More than once, Arlo noticed the crow keeping an eye on him. Then Indra yelled out, "Here!"

He hurried over. Indra had found a lichen-covered rock with a cleft down the middle. It matched the photograph perfectly. "Why don't you get up there, and let me see if it lines up," he said.

With Indra kneeling on the rock, Arlo tried to imagine where the photographer would have taken the shot. Once he'd determined the right angle, he visualized where the other boys would be standing, and where the campsite sign would be.

Sure enough, right where he expected, he found the remains of a wooden post. Indra hopped down to help search through the fallen logs and debris.

Under a thick layer of pine needles, Arlo found the edge of a board. He turned it over, scraping away the dirt. The paint had long faded, but the engraved letters were still clear:

SUMMERLAND

33
KEEPER OF THE OLD AND NEW

OVER THE PREVIOUS SIX MONTHS, Arlo had come to appreciate Julie Delgado's many fine qualities as a Ranger. She had a great memory—not just for numbers and facts, but also jokes. She could sing harmony on any campfire song.

And of course, her talents in flag semaphore were unparalleled.

But Julie didn't seem to understand the occasional necessity of keeping one's voice down.

"Wait! There's a secret campsite on the far side of the lake!?" asked Julie, entirely too loudly.

Arlo and Indra shushed her. There were at least a dozen other Rangers within earshot, including most of Red Patrol.

"Yes," whispered Indra. "And we don't want other people knowing about it."

Arlo studied the nearby crowd. If anyone was eavesdropping,

it wasn't obvious. They were all busy with their own conversations, or focused on the stage at the front of the amphitheater. The last of the companies had just arrived.

It was Skit Night, an annual camp tradition in which all the companies competed to put on the funniest performance as judged by the counselors. Green Patrol had easily beaten the other Pine Mountain patrols at the previous campout, and would be representing the company for the championship. Arlo felt certain they'd win. They had costumes and props, songs and choreography.

Arlo secretly envied Green Patrol. The most they had to worry about was forgetting a line of dialogue, not mysterious spirits and shape-shifting villains. He could understand why Indra might want to join them. She wanted to win, and they always won.

Thomas leaned in, keeping his voice at an appropriate volume. "So how did you all find the campsite?"

Indra quickly recounted uncovering the hidden map in the supply room, the marsh trail and the warning sign.

Wu shook his head. "If someone spotted you, we could all get sent home. Trespassing is a big deal."

"We weren't trespassing!" insisted Indra. "This isn't like what happened with Red Patrol when they went onto Walker Ranch." Arlo had heard the story: A few years earlier, some boys from Red Patrol had snuck onto a property east of Redfeather, a glamorous camping resort where millionaires pretended they were lumberjacks. The county sheriff was called, and the whole patrol had to apologize.

"Where we went is still technically part of the camp," said Indra. "And there's nothing in the rules that says we can't go there."

"Except for the giant warning sign," said Wu.

"A sign is not a rule," said Indra. "It's a suggestion."

"Right. And a stop sign is a 'stop suggestion.'"

Julie shook her head. "This isn't like you, Indra. You're always the one who wants to do everything by the book. Like with the duty roster."

"It sounds more like a Wu thing," said Jonas. "No offense."

Wu shrugged it off. "Look, as patrol leader, I have to think of more than just myself."

Indra grimaced, but held her tongue.

As the last company filed in, Jellybeans took the microphone. "First up, we have Green Patrol from Pine Mountain Company." The other patrols cheered as Green made its way to the stage.

Indra tried to put the issue of the warning sign to rest. "Look, I understand everyone's concern. The point is, no one saw us."

But maybe someone did see us, thought Arlo. They were dealing with a shape-shifter, so there was no way to be certain they were really alone.

And whoever that person was, there was a good chance they were there tonight, somewhere in the audience. Arlo scanned the faces, looking for suspects.

Russell Stokes was an obvious choice for villain. He seemed to go out of his way to be a jerk. Yet Arlo felt pretty certain Russell could be ruled out in this case. For starters, he had actually been a co-conspirator in finding the photo of Summerland. Plus, Arlo knew about the grisp. Russell wouldn't do anything to risk his secret being exposed.

Arlo was also confident Russell Stokes didn't have the ability to control crows.

Resuming his inspection of the crowd, Arlo focused on some of the other Rangers in his classes, including Stevens, Sophia and Farhad. In detective stories—like the Agatha Christie mysteries he'd started reading at school—the villain was always the person you least suspected. So Arlo tried to imagine one of them as the crow manipulator and possible doppelgänger.

The problem with this theory was that for a scheming villain, each seemed wildly uninterested in Arlo. He'd barely spoken to any of them.

The ideal candidate would be someone close, someone Arlo trusted, even if they didn't know each other well.

Arlo's gaze drifted to a bench at the side of the stage, where five camp counselors were serving as judges. One of them was looking directly at him.

Darnell.

Arlo stared right back. Could Darnell actually see him? It was dark, and he was pretty far away. Darnell might just be looking in his general direction.

Either way, Darnell turned back to the stage as Cassandra from Green Patrol took the microphone. "Our story begins at the edge of Redfeather Lake," she said. "Where two young Rangers have just made an amazing discovery."

The skit told the story of Ekafos. Green Patrol had expanded on the tale with the addition of a rival dinosaur, a witch and a singing meteorite.

Arlo kept his focus on Darnell, reconsidering all of their previous interactions.

On the first day of class, Big Breezy had refused Arlo's offering until after Darnell had left the mountaintop. Maybe the spirit knew that Darnell couldn't be trusted.

Later, at the Nature Center office, Arlo had witnessed Darnell controlling a fly. "Shifting," he'd called it. That fact alone put Darnell at the top of the suspect list. Of everyone at Redfeather, he was the only one Arlo knew for certain could use animals this way.

Finally, there was *Culman's Bestiary*. The page with the entry for *Doppelgänger* had been ripped out of the book. It suddenly seemed no coincidence that the only copy was in Darnell's file cabinet. He was the doppelgänger, and didn't want anyone knowing how to stop him.

Everyone around Arlo began laughing. He'd missed a joke.

As expected, Green Patrol won Skit Night. To celebrate, the whole company joined them for homemade ice cream back at their campsite. Arlo took a shift hand-cranking one of the mixers, feeling the chill radiating from the wooden bucket of ice and salt.

When his arm got tired, he handed it off to Thomas.

"How's camp so far, Finch?" Arlo turned to find himself face-to-face with Diana Velasquez. She was halfway through a cone of vanilla ice cream, catching a drip before it fell. "You enjoying yourself?"

"Yeah. Sure. All good." Diana made him nervous. She was too calm, too mature. She seemed much older than sixteen.

"I hear you missed class today. Elementary Spirits?"

Did Darnell tell her? Or Wu? Or Julie? Arlo tried not to panic. "I was out hiking. With Indra."

"You seem to spend a lot of time with her."

"We're friends." He said it a little too quickly, too defensively.

"Good. It's important to have friends. And to go exploring. Believe me, I skipped some classes my first year at camp, too."

"Really?" That surprised Arlo. Diana had always struck him as a rule follower.

"Look where we are. It's beautiful here. Sometimes you see a trail and you just have to take it."

Does she mean the trail to Summerland? Does she know?

"How are you doing on your Vow?" she asked.

Arlo was confused. "I already memorized it. I had to, for Squirrel."

"But do you understand it any better? It's not just about knowing the words. It's knowing how to live it."

Arlo forced himself to look Diana in the eye. She was easily a foot taller than him. "I try to be loyal and brave and kind and true," he said. "Both honest and, you know, like with good aim. Morally." Was that what she was looking for?

Diana smiled. "The Vow is eight lines long. You can't stop at the first one."

"Right. Of course." Arlo kept reciting: "Keeper of the Old and New . . ."

"What does that mean?"

Arlo was embarrassed that he hadn't thought much about it. Basically ever. "Well, to keep something is to hold on to it. Like, not waste it."

Diana finished her ice cream cone. She held up a finger to pause while she swallowed. "*To keep* something can also mean to protect it. Defend it. So you're vowing to defend the old and the new."

"Okay."

"How do you do that?"

"I don't know," admitted Arlo.

Diana put a hand on his shoulder. It was the first time she'd ever touched him. "My advice is, if you're going to miss class, spend that time trying to figure out your Vow. It's the most important thing you have as a Ranger. It's your map and your compass. Without it, you're lost."

Back at Firebird, Arlo looked for Indra. He hadn't had a chance to talk with her about his Darnell theory. Her tent's flaps were open. Both cots, empty.

"She was looking for you," said Julie, returning with her toothbrush. "I think she went down to the lake. She had her binoculars."

Arlo half ran down the mountain. In the moonlight, all the rocks and trees seemed to be draped with glowing dust. Arlo felt nimble, like a deer or a rabbit, every footstep landing true. He quickly reached the lake, barely winded.

The full moon was giant, a perfect circle just over the horizon. Its light shimmered on the water, forming a silvery path across the lake.

In every ripple, Arlo saw patterns. They weren't fixed like Indra's Pinereading etchings. Rather, they were constantly shifting and combining, like silent music.

Arlo felt goose bumps.

Then he saw a flare of light by the water's edge. A snaplight.

It was Indra.

He hurried over to her. "What are you doing out here?" he asked. "You missed ice cream."

She held up her binoculars. "I wanted to look at the moon, but I found something else."

"What, more Ekafos footprints?" joked Arlo.

Indra pointed to the far side of the lake. Arlo squinted, not sure what he was supposed to be looking at. Despite the full moon, the distant shore was almost totally black beyond the water's edge, a curtain of shadowy trees.

"I don't see anything," he said. "It's too dark."

"But not completely dark," said Indra.

She handed him the binoculars. As Arlo peered through them, he suddenly saw what she was talking about: flickering points of amber light in the darkness. Campfires, maybe. Or lanterns.

"That's where we were this afternoon," she said. "There shouldn't be anybody over there."

Arlo wondered if the lights could be wisps or some other type of supernatural spirit. He tried to sharpen the focus, but he couldn't make out any additional details. Then he spotted three small flares shooting up out of the forest. They were unmistakably snaplights. *Rangers.*

He lowered the binoculars, looking at Indra. "Someone's in Summerland," he said. "We need to find out who."

34
THE LAKE OF THE MOON

A CANOE. They both agreed it was their best option.

On foot, it had taken nearly an hour to get to Summerland, and that was in daylight. Crossing the marsh at night would be much more difficult.

But in a canoe, they could go directly across the water. It would take fifteen minutes at most.

"They'll see us coming, though," said Arlo.

"Maybe," said Indra. "But they'd see us coming on the trail, too. And we don't know who *they* are. It could be Red Patrol, or Rangers from one of the other companies. Anyone could have overheard Julie. The good thing is that whoever they are, they're not supposed to be there, either. Worst that happens is they see us coming and hide."

Arlo could think of many worse outcomes from this plan, including drowning in the lake. But he agreed that a canoe was a better choice than trying to hike around the perimeter in the dark.

Still, he needed to be certain he was really talking with Indra. "Before we go, we need to make sure neither of us is actually the impostor."

"You're right. How should we do it?"

Arlo suddenly recognized the flaw in the plan: if he said "Rocky Road" first, that only proved that he was Arlo. She could still be the impostor. But if Indra said it first, there was no way for her to be certain that he was Arlo. The only solution was to give it at the same time. "We both say the code word on three."

"What code word?" she asked.

"Remember what we talked about at the sinks?"

"No. When?"

"A couple of nights ago. I told you my favorite flavor of ice cream." Arlo tried to blank his mind, just in case the doppelgänger was telepathic.

Indra seemed genuinely confused. "I don't remember any of this."

"It was your idea." Arlo took a step back.

"Arlo, it wasn't me. Are you sure it wasn't him?"

Arlo thought back to that night at the sinks. He'd been brushing his teeth when Indra came up to him. They'd talked about Wu. Indra had suggested picking a code word. Then Arlo had said he was going to look for a *Culman's Bestiary* at the Nature Center. *That's why the page was ripped out,* he realized. *Because I said I was going to look there.*

The only way to be certain who somebody was was to ask a question the impostor wouldn't be able to answer. "We should each say something he couldn't possibly know."

Indra went first: "Merilee Myers has a crush on you."

Arlo was aghast. "No she doesn't!"

"Of course she does," said Indra. "She's always staring at you. And she basically admitted it one day after gym class. Now you tell me something."

Arlo racked his brain for something that wouldn't have come up in conversation at camp. He thought about school, Rangers, their town. Then he found it: "Your dad makes great peanut butter cookies."

They were unquestionably fantastic, just the right combination of crispy and chewy and crumbly. He was suddenly hungry for peanut butter, the one food specifically banned at Camp Redfeather because of the danger of howlers. Their identities confirmed, they headed to the Lake Center, ducking under the rope with the sign that read KEEP OUT! AREA CLOSED! They'd been ignoring a lot of signs that day, Arlo realized.

The shed holding the life jackets had been left unlocked, and the canoes were all in their racks. "None of them are missing," pointed out Indra. "However they got over there, they didn't use a canoe."

Arlo and Indra selected one, carefully and quietly lifting it off its berth. They carried it down to the water and climbed in. Arlo took the bow, paddling as Indra pushed off.

Over the previous week, they'd finally figured out their

rhythm. They no longer squabbled or struggled to keep moving in a straight line. From the back of the boat, Indra made corrections without interrupting their flow.

The moonlight on the water was dazzling, so bright that Arlo needed to squint. The patterns he'd noticed from the shore were even more evident now, ribbons of light continuously joining and dividing. The blade of his paddle seemed to be dipping in and out of a liquid mirror.

They were making good progress, nearly halfway to the far side when . . . *thump!* The keel hit something beneath the water.

"What was that?" asked Indra, resting her paddle.

Arlo was just as puzzled. They were too far from the shore to have hit a rock.

"Could have been a stick floating in the water," he said. "Maybe we just didn't see it."

Indra was unconvinced. "I guess."

They resumed paddling. If they kept at this pace, Arlo suspected they could reach the shore in five more minutes.

THUMP!

This time, they didn't just hear it. The whole canoe shook, a vibration traveling through the aluminum frame.

"Okay, that wasn't a stick," said Arlo.

He turned to look back at Indra, who was similarly stumped. Then he noticed something odd: "Indra. Where did the dock go?"

He pointed. She turned.

The Lake Center and dock should have been easily visible in

the moonlight. But there were no structures at the water's edge, just cattails.

"Did we get turned around?" she asked. That seemed impossible. They'd been paddling in a straight line. Besides, Giant's Fist was right where it was supposed to be.

Indra set down her paddle to use her binoculars. "The Trading Post is gone, too. And the road, I think."

"How is that possible?"

"I don't know."

They sat silent for a few moments. Water lapped against the canoe. A strange bird trilled in the distance. Arlo was certain he'd never heard it before, which seemed odd after all these days at camp.

They both had the same thought at the same time. Indra said it aloud: "Arlo, are we in the Long Woods?"

Just then, a dragonfly landed on the keel of the canoe. Its double wings stretched out in an elongated *X*, their translucent panes catching the light. It seemed perfectly ordinary except for its size: *it was nearly two feet long.* Its eyes, surrounded by spiky hairs, were as big as ping-pong balls.

Indra and Arlo shared a silent look: *Do you see that?*

For its part, the dragonfly paid them no mind, content to have a place to rest its wings.

"I think I've seen one of these before," whispered Arlo.

"Where? The Amazon?"

"In Chicago. At the natural history museum."

"Then it's not from the Long Woods. That's good."

Not *good*, exactly: "It's from the Paleozoic era. It should be extinct."

Indra took a moment to make sure she was hearing him correctly. "You're saying this came from the past?"

"Either that, or we're *in* the past."

All around them, moonlight was sparkling on the water. He had seen the patterns and dismissed them as random. But there was clearly magic happening here. Maybe he had accidentally followed a trail, just as he would through the forest.

If the Long Woods went everywhere, where did this lake go? *Everywhen?*

Indra looked up at the night sky. "I wish I knew the stars better. It might give us some clue where we are. *When* we are."

THUMP! The canoe rocked. The dragonfly flew off.

Arlo very carefully stood up to get a better look. That's when he saw the ripple. A massive creature had swum under the canoe, the ridges of its back scraping the keel. As the beast turned, its tail whipped around.

Indra stood as well, trying to make out the shape in the water. It was swimming directly towards them, its head and neck rising twenty feet out of the water. Its jaws cracked open, revealing needle-like teeth as it roared, backlit by the moon.

"Arlo, is that . . ."

Ekafos. The legendary monster of Redfeather Lake.

This creature seemed ancient, but it wasn't a dinosaur. Arlo was certain of that.

On school trips to museums, he'd seen dinosaur skeletons this size. They looked like giant lizards. Or crocodiles. Or birds. They had feet or flippers or wings.

This was different.

Ekafos was a sea serpent, an eel scaled up to massive proportions. It held its head out of the water by constantly swirling its body. Arlo might have believed it to be an undiscovered Jurassic creature except for the sounds: the beast's scales *clink*ed and *clank*ed as water dripped through them. It sounded like wind chimes on an icy-cold day. But there was a pattern to the notes. A melody.

"It's from the Long Woods, isn't it?" asked Indra.

"Or somewhere," said Arlo. The creature had an otherworldly shimmer to it that reminded him of the grisp and Cooper. *Is it a spirit?* he wondered.

Ekafos seemed to be studying them, perhaps trying to figure out if their canoe was one creature or three.

Water lapped against the aluminum. Strange birds flew overhead.

Still Ekafos watched and waited.

"What do we do?" whispered Indra.

"I don't know."

"We could paddle back. Try to get away."

"Okay. You start."

Indra carefully sat down and began gently backstroking. Arlo clenched his paddle like a club. He would only have one swing.

Suddenly, Ekafos lunged for them.

Arlo swung with all his might. The blade of the paddle hit

the side of the creature's head. The beast turned and snapped, taking a bite out of the paddle. Indra jabbed at it, striking its jaw.

The beast crashed down on the edge of the canoe. Arlo tumbled out.

The cold water was a shock. Stars spun around him. He grabbed the paddle tight, ready to swing again, but there was nothing to hit.

The life jacket pressed against his ears. He couldn't look around him. "Indra!" he yelled, swallowing some lake water.

"Arlo!" Her voice was strangely muted. It took Arlo a moment to realize where she had to be.

The canoe was upside down. She was underneath.

Arlo ducked his head under the edge of the canoe, surfacing in the air pocket beneath it. It was echoey and dark, just a little moonlight rising up from the water. Indra was clinging to the thwarts, the metal crossbars of the canoe.

"Are you okay?" asked Indra.

"Yeah, you?"

"We have to flip the canoe."

It wouldn't be easy. Just the day before, they had learned how to right a swamped canoe in class. In daylight, with perfect conditions and no lake monsters, it had taken seven tries and left them both exhausted.

Now, in the dark, with an ancient beast after them? This was way beyond what Trix had taught them.

"You call it," he said. "I'll follow you."

Indra took a few deep breaths. "On three. One. Two. Three!"

They both kicked with all their might, lifting the canoe up out of the water and rolling it to the side. Maybe it was the adrenaline, but it was by far their most successful flip. The boat landed right side up with only a few inches of water in it.

Arlo moved around to the far side of the canoe. With a nod, they climbed in at the same time, matching their motions so it wouldn't flip again.

Once inside, they quickly looked around, trying to spot Ekafos. The surface of the lake was still except for the ripples around the canoe. Either the beast was back underwater, or it had vanished altogether.

Indra quickly retrieved her paddle, but Arlo's was floating just beyond reach. He leaned as far as he dared. His arm strained. His fingertips touched the very edge of the paddle—only to nudge it further away.

He repositioned himself. He'd have to lean just a little . . . bit . . . more.

"I've almost got it," he said.

This time, he got two fingers on the paddle. He carefully started to pull it in.

Suddenly, a jolt rocked the canoe. Arlo flew headfirst back into the water.

"Arlo!" shouted Indra.

Arlo caught a glimpse of the canoe as he was sucked under, caught in a riptide. Ekafos was swimming past him. Arlo was spinning, dragged through the water in the mighty creature's wake.

He tried to swim, to fight against the water, but he wasn't even sure which way was up. So he mostly tried to conserve what breath he had left. To stay conscious as long as he could.

Suddenly, the motion stopped. He'd stopped. He saw moonlight above him and swam towards it.

Arlo surfaced and gasped for breath. His heart was pounding. His arms were shaking. He wiped his eyes. Blew the water out of his nose. He could taste the lake in his mouth. He'd probably swallowed a lot.

He floated in his life jacket, staring at the sky. A cloud was drifting in front of the moon. The night was no longer sparkling. It was just dark.

Arlo couldn't see the canoe anywhere. "Indra?" he called.

There was no answer. The lake was empty, and still. But the night wasn't completely quiet. He could hear singing. Distant campfire songs.

There was other music, too: rock. Thin and tinny, like it was coming from a pair of headphones. It was close.

Arlo turned to look back at the shore. A flashlight blinded him.

"You okay?" asked a boy's voice.

Arlo squinted, trying to make out the boy's face. He could only tell that the kid was wearing a uniform. A neckerchief. A Ranger.

"I'm fine," said Arlo. "I think."

He swam a few yards, then stood and began walking as the water got shallow. "Do you see a canoe? My friend is out there."

The Ranger swept his flashlight across the water. There was nothing but water.

As the cloud drifted away from the moon, Arlo got a better look at him. The kid was around thirteen, with messy red-blond hair and scraggly whiskers.

Arlo recognized him immediately. He had seen this kid before in photos.

It was his Uncle Wade.

35
YELLOW PATROL

TEENAGE WADE BELLMAN was wearing old-style headphones, the kind with two small disks covered with foam and connected by a thin metal headband. A wire ran down to a cassette player the size of a paperback book.

Arlo was pretty sure it was called a Walkman. He'd seen one on the shelf in the basement of their house. *It might be that actual Walkman,* he thought.

Wade clicked a button and the music stopped. He pulled down his headphones, resting them on his yellow neckerchief.

"What were you doing in the lake?" he asked.

Arlo pointed at the water while trying to think of an excuse. "I fell out of the canoe."

"And your buddies, they ditched you?"

"I guess."

"Sucks. What camp are you in?"

"Firebird."

Wade whistled. "On the far side of the lake? Man. You got a hike ahead of you." He paused, considering something. "You know, some guys and I were talking about going out to Giant's Fist. Maybe we could take you across. Save you some time."

"Okay. Thanks."

Arlo tried not to stare too hard at Wade, but he couldn't help but imagine how this teenage face had aged into his forty-something uncle. Even in the moonlight, Arlo could see that Wade had a lot of acne. That would all be covered by the beard, of course. But the basic shape of this boy's head, his eyes, his nose—that was the Uncle Wade he knew.

Wade seemed to misinterpret Arlo's staring. He took off the headphones and Walkman, shoving them into a daypack. *He's not supposed to have electronics at camp,* Arlo realized. *Just like we can't have phones or computers.*

"So yeah, the thing is, I have a medical condition," said Wade. "I get kind of crazy when it's quiet. My thoughts get too loud. So the music helps me out. Lets me focus. It's a real thing. I'm not making it up at all."

Arlo pictured his uncle in his workshop. He always had his headphones on, music blaring.

"I won't say anything," said Arlo.

Wade smiled. "Cool. Didn't peg you as a narc." Wade zipped up his pack. "My camp's right up here. I'll get you a towel." He walked a few steps, then turned back. "Hey. My name's Bellman, by the way."

"Finch," said Arlo.

"*Finch* like a bird?" Arlo nodded. "That's cool. Good to meet you, Finch."

Arlo felt a shudder as they walked past the Summerland sign. He and Indra had stood there just hours earlier. *And thirty years later,* he realized.

There wasn't time to puzzle over how he had arrived at exactly this moment to meet Wade. But he couldn't explain quite how he traveled through the Long Woods, either, yet he'd consistently been able to find his way around. *Time is just another dimension,* his dad had said once while explaining some scientific concept. *Time keeps everything from happening at once.*

The Summerland campsite was much as Arlo had expected. The fire ring and dining area were at the lowest point, with tent platforms arranged along a path up the hillside. The difference was the trees; they were all still standing.

Whatever calamity was to befall Summerland hadn't happened yet.

Four boys were at the picnic table playing Dungeons & Dragons by the light of a Coleman lantern. "A thief-acrobat doesn't take damage from falling," protested one kid with orthodontic headgear.

"Fine," said the Dungeon Master. "You fall onto spikes. Rusty spikes covered with poison. Take eleven points of damage."

Headgear grumbled and penciled it in on his character sheet.

Wade stopped at the table, pointing. "Are those my dice?"

"Mine are jinxed," said Headgear. "I keep rolling ones."

"Well, don't jinx mine!" Wade plucked five translucent green dice out of a pile in front of the boy. One slipped between the boards of the table, landing in the dirt.

Arlo kneeled down to get it. He hadn't seen dice of this shape before. Each face was a pentagon, like a Ranger badge. The numbers counted up to twelve.

He handed it over to Wade. "What is that one for?"

"A d12? Not much. Longsword damage against a large creature."

"Also barbarian hit dice," added Headgear.

"Enough with the *Unearthed Arcana*, Cunningham! Not everyone has the new book!" *Cunningham—like Connor and Christian,* thought Arlo. Two of the boys at the table were wearing yellow neckerchiefs like Wade's, but Arlo had also spotted green and red.

"How many patrols are in your company?" he asked.

"Four," said Wade. "No, wait, five. We just added Yellow. We got a bunch of new Rangers in the spring, so they split up the patrols. I used to be in Green. Here, let me show you something cool."

He stopped at a large stockpot that was resting on a camp table. He carefully removed the heavy rock holding down the lid. Inside were a few gallons of still water.

"Watch this," said Wade.

He set a piece of bark on the water. It floated, then began to slowly move in a clockwise circle, faster and faster until a small whirlpool formed. Water started to creep up the sides of the pot.

Wade slammed the lid back on, setting the heavy rock back in place to hold it down. "Know what that is?"

"A water spirit?" guessed Arlo.

"Yup! We caught it a few days ago."

"You're not supposed to catch them, though." Arlo had learned that the first day of Elementary Spirits. They didn't like being outside of their natural habitats.

Wade was already on the move. "We're not gonna hurt it. It's just cool to study."

They had arrived at what was evidently Wade's tent. Two towels were hanging on side rails. Wade sniffed them both before handing one to Arlo.

The tent flap pushed open. "Bellman! Are we going or not?"

A boy with thick dark hair stepped out. Arlo recognized him as Mitch the mechanic, only now he was thirteen or fourteen. His voice was higher than Arlo had expected.

"Let's do this," said Wade. "Jansen, this is Finch. He's over in Firebird. I said we'd drop him off."

Mitch looked him over. "What company are you with?"

"Cheyenne," Arlo lied. If they read his neckerchief, they would see it was Pine Mountain, but at the moment it was hidden underneath his life jacket.

"I heard you guys have a girl in your company," said Mitch.

"That's Laramie," said Wade.

"Same difference. Still Wyoming." Mitch headed behind the

tent. Wade followed him. "How crazy would it be to have a girl in your patrol? You couldn't pee outside or crack jokes or play pranks on each other."

Indra and Julie do all those things, thought Arlo. "Nothing would really change," he said. "Nothing important."

"Doesn't matter. They're never going to let girls in," said Wade. "Not officially. That's why they have Girl Rangers, so they can do girl stuff while we do boy stuff."

Wade shined his flashlight on a small inflatable raft leaning up against a tree. It looked to be cheap vinyl, not at all like the professional ones Arlo had seen in photos of whitewater rafting.

"Is that the camp's, or your patrol's?" asked Arlo.

"It's mine," said Mitch, untying it from the tree. "I earned it delivering newspapers back home. It's a two-man, but you're little, so it should be fine."

Mitch and Wade hoisted the raft, heading for the lake. Arlo didn't immediately follow them.

"You coming?" asked Wade.

Arlo was skeptical about getting in such a flimsy boat. But whatever force had brought him here was clearly connected to the lake. That was probably the way back to his own time.

"Yeah. Sorry." He caught up with them, picking up the braided rope that was dragging behind it.

Some of the D&D players at the picnic table looked over as they passed, but no one said anything. The trio was almost at the water when a voice called out from behind them: "Hey! You all got room for one more?"

They looked back to find a single Ranger running down the path towards them. Wade aimed the flashlight at him.

Arlo reflexively grabbed the rope tighter, trying to process exactly what he was seeing and how he should respond. He tried to imagine what expression his face was making. Shock? Confusion? Absolute bewilderment?

The approaching boy was small and wiry, with sandy blond hair. He'd seen this Ranger every day for a week.

It was Thomas.

36
A DANGEROUS CROSSING

THE BOY OFFERED him a handshake. "I'm Thomas."

"Finch," said Arlo.

With the exception of his yellow neckerchief, the kid squeezed across from Arlo in the tiny raft was the exact same one who had joined his patrol the previous week.

He had the same crooked smile, same freckles, same twang. It didn't just resemble Thomas; as far as Arlo could tell, it *was* him.

Which was impossible, of course.

But impossible things seemed to be occurring with great regularity, so Arlo focused on figuring out *what* was happening, not *how*. He wouldn't jump to conclusions. He'd watch. He'd listen. He'd figure it out.

Wade pushed them off from the shore. Some water sloshed over the edge of the raft as he jumped in. The vinyl squeaked and shuddered but held together, the waterline just a few inches below the top.

"We're good!" said Wade.

Are we? Arlo wondered. They were in a flimsy boat with a possible doppelgänger on a lake that was home to a monster. That seemed anything but good.

At the front of the raft, Mitch began rowing. Unlike a canoe, this was a one-man job. Arlo had nothing to do but think.

Thomas was staring at the moon, a few fingers dragging idly in the water. If he had a sinister agenda, he was taking his time.

"We got nothing like this back home," he said.

"Where's that?" asked Arlo, pretending not to know.

"Texas. Near Laredo. Don't get me wrong; it's pretty. But it's all pretty in the same way, any direction you look. This here is something else."

"Thomas got assigned to our patrol the first day," explained Wade. "He's the only one from his company who's up here."

Arlo looked back at Thomas. "Is this your first time out of state?"

"Heck, it's nearly my first time out of Webb County. Before this, the closest I'd come to climbing a mountain was stairs."

Arlo had smiled the first time Thomas made that joke. *Or is this the first time?* he wondered. Time travel made it challenging to sort events chronologically.

"Is Thomas your first name or last name?" asked Arlo.

"Last name," he answered. "My first name's kind of

embarrassing. It was my daddy's, and his daddy's, but they didn't use it either. So who knows why they gave it to me."

"Is it Alva?" asked Arlo. He wanted to see Thomas's reaction.

Surprised. Curious. But totally appropriate. "How did you know?" Thomas asked.

"I must have seen it on a list or something."

Thomas nodded. He seemed to accept the excuse. "We're not in any classes together, are we?"

"I don't think so." Then Arlo added: "Why? Do I look familiar?"

"Nah, it's just that up here at camp there are so many new faces."

So why are you wearing this one? wondered Arlo.

Being the new kid in the patrol would certainly be a great cover. As the newcomer, Thomas could freely invent his history, and ask questions about anything. He'd done a great job of becoming friends with everyone in Blue Patrol, always cheerful and happy to help. He had stayed out of arguments, only interceding as peacemaker at the end.

Even when Thomas had proposed Wu for patrol leader, he did it subtly, never making himself seem like the bad guy.

Arlo couldn't help but admire how well Thomas had pulled it off. They'd all fallen for him.

But was this Hadryn? And if so, what was his agenda? Why

infiltrate a Ranger patrol at a camp in the mountains of Colorado? He had to be after something.

"Hey, Finch," said Mitch. "Okay if we go to Giant's Fist first? We'll drop you off after."

"That's fine," said Arlo.

He turned to look at the shadowy rocks rising out of the lake. *Giant's Fist.* That was where the impostor had posed as Wu. On that afternoon, he had seemed intent upon looking for something hidden there. He'd been frustrated when he couldn't find it.

But what was it? What was he after?

Arlo glanced back over at Thomas. *Does he even know who I am?* Once again, time travel was a complicating factor. Arlo had met Thomas, but there was no guarantee the reverse was true. From Thomas's point of view, this might be the first time they'd encountered each other.

Which led Arlo to a new possibility: What if this was the *real* Thomas, and the one with Blue Patrol was the impostor? Perhaps this kid in the raft wasn't a villain, but a future victim.

Arlo was almost certain that the Thomas back at Blue Patrol was not who he claimed to be. That meant his friends were in danger, and he had no way to warn them.

"Guys," said Wade. "Over here."

Wade had his camera out, an inch-thick rectangle of black plastic. He didn't count to three. He just clicked. The flash was blinding.

"Bellman, c'mon!" shouted Mitch. "Warn us next time."

Arlo squeezed his eyes shut, waiting for the glowing halo to fade. He listened to the water and the oars.

He suddenly thought of Indra.

For all he knew, she was still on the lake with Ekafos. In the confusion of meeting young Wade and young Mitch, of traveling thirty years back in time and encountering Thomas, Arlo had forgotten that his friend was still out there somewhere.

37

INDRA

INDRA STEADIED THE CANOE as Arlo reached for his paddle in the water.

"I've almost got it," he said.

She watched as he put two fingers on the handle.

Just then, the front of the canoe flew up out of the water, hit from below. Indra held onto the gunwale, but Arlo toppled over the edge. "Arlo!" she shouted.

The canoe slammed back down. Keeping low, Indra rushed to the center, ready to pull him back in. But he wasn't there, just his paddle.

She yelled for him again.

No answer.

Indra knew exactly where he should be. With his life jacket, Arlo couldn't stay underwater long. *Unless Ekafos got him,* she thought. She pictured Arlo's leg caught in the monster's jaws as he was dragged away to the depths.

No. I would have seen something, she thought. *A splash. A ripple.* He had to still be there.

Indra fought the instinct to dive in. After all, what could she do in the water? At least in the canoe she could see in all directions.

At least in the canoe, she could rescue him.

Indra twisted to look across the lake, scanning the ripples for any sign of Ekafos. Then, a shift. A sudden hush. Something was happening.

She looked to the east, where puffy clouds were drifting across the horizon. The light on the water—a silvery path—was vanishing as the moon was swallowed up.

A breeze. A chill. Indra felt goose bumps rise. She wasn't sure what it all meant, but she was sure it mattered. "Arlo!" she shouted again.

Indra watched as the clouds blotted out the moon completely. The lake was now just a flat black plane, a featureless void.

Water dripped in her eyes. She ignored it.

Her fingertips started to prune. She ignored it.

She kept her eyes focused on the water, waiting for Arlo to surface. As the spike of adrenaline faded, her heart rate gradually slowed. But what it left behind was worse: a creeping darkness. A sinking worry. It felt like she was poisoned.

You're panicking, she thought. *Stop it. Breathe.*

She forced herself to take a deep breath, exhaling slowly. Her mom taught patients to do breathing exercises for anxiety. *Four counts inhale. Four counts hold. Four counts exhale.*

She rested her paddle. She listened.

There. Under the wind, a faint hum. Mechanical. *An engine.*

Tracking the sound, Indra did fan strokes to turn the boat.

On the far shore, she spotted the headlights of a pickup truck driving on the road. She followed it to the Trading Post. The Lake Center. The dock.

She was back in the present day. But where was Arlo?

Or more importantly, *when*?

38
CONTRABAND

ONCE THE RAFT WAS securely tied, Mitch led the way up the palm of Giant's Fist. "C'mon. It's supposed to be right up here."

Mitch said he had heard about the hidden cave from some friends of his older brother's. "They used to come out here and drink beer. This one night, they didn't tie up their canoe tight enough and it blew away. They had to swim back to shore in the morning."

The footholds were harder to find in the dark. Arlo was the last one up. He wanted to keep Thomas in his sights.

The cave was just how Arlo remembered it, with the exception of the back wall. Where there had been a chalky *A* scratched into the stone, it was now bare.

Wade unloaded snacks from his backpack: pretzels, teriyaki jerky and two bright red cans of soda, a brand Arlo didn't recognize. "It has all the sugar and twice the caffeine," Wade said. "It's not even legal to sell in fifteen states."

He popped the top and handed it to Arlo. It was warm and, honestly, just tasted like cola.

Wade had one last surprise in his daypack: a giant canister of Lysol spray.

"Why do you have that?" asked Mitch.

Wade gave a devious smile, then twisted the can. It slid apart to reveal a secret compartment holding a foil-wrapped inner package. None of them could believe it.

"That's like James Bond!" said Thomas.

Mitch examined the two-piece canister, impressed. "You made this yourself?"

"It works, too! It still sprays." Wade demonstrated, sending a sweet-smelling mist out into the air. "When they did bag inspection, no one gave it a second thought." Arlo smiled to himself. Even teenage Wade had his uncle's combination of artistic skills and aversion to rules.

"So what's that inside?" asked Thomas.

Wade peeled back the foil to reveal a glass jar with a familiar red-blue-and-green label: Jif. *Peanut butter.*

"What about howlers?" asked Mitch.

"We're safe out here," said Wade. "Howlers can't swim."

"You're sure about that?"

"I looked it up in *Culman's.* They can't swim." He started to twist the lid.

"Wait, wait!" said Mitch, grabbing Wade's arm. "Did the book say they *can't swim*, or it *didn't* say they *can*?"

"Same difference." Wade opened the jar. He dipped a finger in to scoop out a giant wad of peanut butter and popped it in his mouth, washing it down with soda.

He held out the jar. No one wanted to touch it. Wade finished swallowing, then said: "Look, at this point, either the howlers are coming or they're not. You might as well have some."

The other three traded looks. Mitch was the first to take the jar, taking two fingerfuls. He handed it to Thomas, who sampled a smaller amount. Arlo took it from him, scooping out a tablespoon's worth.

He sniffed it before he ate it. The tiny peanut molecules connected with all the sensors in his nose, creating a rush that went through his whole body. By the time he tasted it, he was fully primed. That first taste of peanut butter was like fireworks and Christmas and climbing between warm flannel sheets on a cold night.

Wade propped his headphones on his pack and cranked up the volume on his Walkman. The pounding guitars and drums sounded cartoonishly thin on the tiny speakers. Between bites, Mitch checked the Walkman. "What is that?"

"Black Flag," said Wade.

"Like the bug spray?" asked Thomas.

"Kinda sounds like the Ramones."

Wade was outraged. "It's nothing like the Ramones! Ramones are pop. They're the Beach Boys. Black Flag is true punk."

"Whatever," said Mitch. "I like Van Halen."

"Of course you like Van Halen. They're literally the Beach Boys with leather pants."

Mitch seemed to enjoy needling Wade. "So, what, everything you don't like is the Beach Boys?"

"Yes," said Wade. "The Beach Boys is everything I don't like. It's this commercial idea that everything should be safe and happy and the worst that happens is you borrow your dad's car without asking. There's no need to worry because everything is great. Don't ask any questions! Don't challenge authority! Meanwhile, the government is corrupt and all our choices are made for us by giant corporations who only let us pick between Coke and Pepsi. The Beach Boys are the embodiment of mediocrity and surrender."

Mitch and Thomas were surprised by Wade's tirade, but Arlo had heard similar rants from his uncle almost every day.

Wade picked up a stone and turned to the back wall. He tried to scratch a line, but it wasn't leaving a mark. He searched for a better rock.

"I've got something," said Arlo. He fished in his pocket to retrieve the fossilized seashell he'd found on the mountaintop. He handed it to Wade, who held it over the flashlight to examine it.

"There used to be an ocean that covered all of this," said Arlo. "I found that a few days ago." *And thirty years from now.*

Wade took the shell and scratched it on the rock to draw an *A*. He went back over the lines a few times to make them clearer.

"What's that for?" asked Arlo.

"*Anarchy*," said Wade. "Punk rock."

Wade tried to draw a circle around the *A*, but the shell crumbled.

A few days earlier, Arlo had wondered who had drawn the *A* on the wall. Now he knew. It was Wade, thirty years earlier, using the seashell Arlo had given him.

Arlo wasn't just a spectator in the past. He was changing it.

Had he always changed it? Was he always meant to be here?

They spent the next twenty minutes talking about movies and TV shows. Arlo had only seen a few of them, but he recognized some of the titles. Mitch's family had cable, which Wade dismissed as a passing fad. "Why do you need thirty channels? You can only watch one thing at a time."

Looking at Wade, Arlo noticed something strange about the *A* he'd drawn on the wall. It seemed to be hovering an inch off the surface. Arlo wondered if it was a trick of the light, so he reached over to touch it.

His fingers went through the stone.

Again he thought he was just seeing it wrong, so he moved over closer. This time, it was clear that this was no optical illusion. His entire hand reached right through the wall. It was still there—he could see it, just not touch it. It was much like the experience of the slipknaught, only this time, he was solid and the wall wasn't.

Thomas was the first to notice Arlo's experiments. "What are you doing?"

"Something's weird with this wall." Arlo looked back towards the cave entrance. The moon had just risen over the thumb of Giant's Fist and was shining directly on the back wall. Maybe that was why the wall had changed.

The other boys turned to watch as Arlo reached further. He connected with something solid. Stone, and cut square with a flat top. Beyond that was another one, set further back.

"I think there are steps." He knew that didn't really make sense to the others. "Can you reach in?" he asked Wade.

Wade tentatively lifted his hand to the wall and looked surprised when it passed right through. "It's like a hologram," he said.

Arlo crawled forward. As his head entered the space where the rock should be, everything went dark. But pushing further, he found himself in a dimly lit space.

Eight rough-hewn stone steps led up to a deep purple sky filled with sparkling stars. He could hear little bits of music, just tinkling notes fluttering past like bird songs.

Arlo blinked twice to make sure his eyes were working, then ducked back into the cave where Wade, Mitch and Thomas were staring in bewilderment.

"Guys, you gotta see this."

At the top of the steps, a narrow path ran left along the face of a solid stone wall. It was just wide enough to walk on, with its edges rounded and crumbling.

All around was a dark violet void. It reminded Arlo of visiting the planetarium on a school trip, except it wasn't just the ceiling that was full of stars. Peering over the edge of the path, the "sky" continued below, infinite in all directions. Phrases of music drifted past. Under that, a steady drone.

"Where are we?" asked Mitch. "Are we in space?"

"Of course not," said Wade. "We still got air and gravity. If this was space, we'd be dead already. My guess would be this is some kind of pocket dimension, a bubble in space-time." Arlo admired how Wade managed to sound completely confident when he clearly had no more information than those around him.

"We should go back," said Thomas. The boys looked over. "What if the bubble pops?" Thomas seemed genuinely frightened. *That, or he's a really good actor,* thought Arlo.

Wade shrugged. "Sure, that could happen. But this all seems super old. Why would it suddenly pop now?" He pointed left. "Looks like this goes around the corner. We should check it out."

He began walking. Arlo followed him, then Mitch. Thomas lagged behind, but eventually caught up.

Arlo stayed close to the wall. He was no fan of heights, but this was especially unnerving. If he fell, it wasn't clear where he'd fall to, or if he'd ever hit bottom.

The path took a sharp left around the corner, where it started to slope downward. Arlo's sneaker slid in some loose gravel, but he caught himself. His heart was in his throat. "Careful!" he called back to Mitch and Thomas, but also to remind himself.

The path turned left again. As Arlo came around, he nearly bumped into Wade, who had stopped short. It took Arlo a moment to realize why.

Below them, a stone statue was floating in purple twilight, its right arm stretched defiantly above it. Its scale was unfathomably large. A skyscraper? An aircraft carrier? With nothing around it for a frame of reference, Arlo could only use his own height for comparison.

If this statue was a man, he and Wade were the size of ants. They were standing on the crease between two of its curled fingers, the fist at the end of the outstretched arm.

They were still on Giant's Fist. Only now they could see the rest of it.

Mitch let out a "Whoa." Thomas didn't say anything.

In its proportions, the giant looked vaguely human, but its face lacked normal features. A pentagonal indentation took the place of its eyes and nose. It seemed to have no mouth.

"Is it dead?" asked Mitch. "Or do you think it's just a statue?"

"Could be a titan," said Wade. "Some kind of celestial god."

"Let's keep going," said Arlo. The path continued down to the palm. It seemed to be the same stone fist as in Redfeather Lake, only less weathered. For the second time in an hour, Arlo found himself climbing it, headed for the hidden cave. But now he was asking himself very different questions: *Had this always happened? And if so, why hadn't Wade and Mitch said anything about it?*

Arlo lost his footing and slid down the rocky slope. Wade and Mitch caught him before he hit the smoothest part of the palm.

"You all right?" asked Wade.

"I'm fine." He was, although he had scraped up his elbow pretty badly. He gradually made his way back up to a more secure perch. He was bleeding enough that drops were falling pretty steadily onto the rocks.

"We should go back," said Thomas.

"I'll be okay. I just need a sec." Arlo brushed the grit out of the wound. The blood on his fingers was bright red. He stared at it.

Wade pulled off his neckerchief, wrapping it around Arlo's elbow and tying it in a square knot to form a makeshift bandage.

A Ranger's gonna bleed from time to time. That's life on the mountain. Uncle Wade had said that when Arlo asked about the bloodstains on the yellow neckerchief.

It's my blood, Arlo realized. *It's always been my blood.*

"Can you climb?" asked Wade.

This close, Arlo could really see his uncle's eyes. He was the same person, despite thirty years' difference.

Arlo nodded. "I'm good."

39
IN THE ASHES

GIANT'S FIST WAS two places, distinct but connected.

The first was a rocky island in the middle of Redfeather Lake. It had cracks and lichen and the remnants of birds' nests. Near the top of it, between the index and middle fingers, was a hidden cave with a ceiling so low you had to stoop.

The second Giant's Fist floated in a cosmic void, still connected to the arm of a titanic stone statue. It was pristine—no cracks or lichen or brittle twigs—but it had a small space hidden within its grasp. Veins of silver and gold snaked across its walls. As Arlo ran his hand over them, he wondered if they were literally the veins of the giant. Assuming it was ever alive, maybe it had had molten metal instead of blood.

In the center of this space stood a fire ring filled with ashes. Wade held his hand over them to check if they were hot, then poked his finger into them. The ashes began draining out through hidden slots, like sand slipping through an hourglass.

The boys exchanged panicked glances. Was this good? Bad? Should they run?

There wasn't time to decide. Within five seconds, the ashes were gone, revealing an object twelve inches long and an inch wide. Half of it was a dark metal bar with an intricate engraving depicting animals and leaves and the phases of the moon. The other half was a blade, three sharp planes intersecting at a point.

Arlo had never seen a knife like this. It felt primal. Ceremonial.

"What do you think it is?" asked Mitch.

"You mean other than a knife?" asked Arlo.

Mitch looked at Arlo, confused. So did Wade, who asked, "Why do you say it's a knife?"

Now Arlo was confused. He wondered if he had somehow forgotten the words for things, or if there was some other object they were all staring at.

Wade reached in and picked it up. "It's pretty heavy." He handled it roughly, without any of the caution one would take with a sharp object. As he examined the engraving, the blade poked right through his hand—but caused no damage. No blood, no wound.

Wade hadn't even seemed to notice it happened.

The blade was insubstantial. It could pass through things without touching them. It was also apparently invisible to everyone but Arlo.

"Is it like a switchblade or something?" asked Wade.

"The blade's already there. You just don't see it." Arlo held out his hand. Wade gave him the knife.

The moment the handle touched his skin, Arlo heard a deafening blast of music. He was so startled he dropped the knife in the fire ring. It clattered, then everything was quiet again.

"What happened?" asked Thomas.

"You didn't hear that? The music?"

The boys shook their heads. Arlo kneeled down over the knife. Bracing himself, he touched the handle with one finger.

This time, the music was just as loud, but not as jarring. As he listened, he began to recognize the same melodies he'd heard earlier, only at a much higher volume. Where before he'd heard fragments, he was now hearing everything. It was chaos, a hundred songs playing at once, but it wasn't painful. Just noisy.

Arlo picked up the knife, examining the blade. It looked to be made of smoked glass. He tried to tap it, but his finger went right through it.

"Wait—so you're saying there's a blade there?" asked Wade. It was hard to hear him over the music; he wasn't raising his voice. "Why would you see it if we can't?"

"Because I can see things sometimes. Stuff in the spirit world." Arlo thought back to his first afternoon in Pine Mountain, when he'd seen Cooper the ghost dog. Uncle Wade was the first person he'd told.

"It's because of your weird eyes, isn't it?"

"I guess." He wasn't offended. That was just how Wade talked.

Thomas reached out his hand. "Can I hold it?"

"No," said Arlo. "I don't think it's safe."

Thomas was confused. "Then why is it safe for you to have it?"

"I'm not sure it is."

On a hunch, Arlo made his way to the opening to look out. What he saw gave him goose bumps.

The void was swirling with thousands of spirits. Some had the shapes of animals—birds, lions, deer—but most were floating fields of light that twisted and shimmered against the darkness. Arlo had never seen the northern lights, but he imagined they must be something like this. Except these lights were so close he could touch them. He reached out with his free hand, watching as a sparkling swath of energy moved through his fingers. He could feel its vibration, its melody.

"What is it?" asked Wade. "What do you see?"

"Spirits," said Arlo. "They're everywhere."

And then he saw it. *Ekafos.*

The sea serpent was by far the largest spirit, twisting and coiling as it floated in the void. It had the same basic shape as what Arlo had seen in the lake, but this was its true form. This was its home.

It stared at him. The creature had no way to directly communicate, but Arlo could tell it was intelligent. *It meant for me to come,* he realized. *It knocked me into the lake so it could bring me here.* Ekafos hadn't been trying to attack Arlo, but rather giving him a shove.

Arlo held out the knife, gesturing to himself. *This is for me?*

Ekafos swirled in a corkscrew. Arlo wasn't sure what it meant.

Then, a new sound: a boom. A crack. Loud but distant.

The spirits reacted, rushing away. The ones with animal forms scurried for places to hide, tucking into the nooks of the giant's body.

More cracks. More booms. It wasn't thunder, but something like it.

Arlo looked back at the boys. "We should go."

The return trip was straightforward. Arlo hugged the wall until he reached the stone steps. Once back inside the first cave, he immediately headed for the entrance looking out over Redfeather Lake.

A storm had risen. It wasn't raining yet, but the wind was strong enough to sting his eyes. The boys watched as their vinyl raft flew up out of the water, spinning on the rope like a kite before breaking away.

"No, no, no!" shouted Mitch.

"How are we gonna get back?" asked Thomas.

Wade was staring straight up. "Guys!"

Squinting, Arlo followed his gaze.

The night sky was fractured, cracks forming between the constellations. It was as if the heavens were made of glass, which was now shattering in slow motion.

From the spaces between the stars, shadowy tentacles reached down. They twisted like cyclones, snaking their way to the ground. Light glowed within the tips of the funnels.

"What is that?" asked Wade. "What's happening?"

Arlo was almost certain he knew the answer.

"It's the Eldritch."

40
ESCAPE

SHOCK AND AWE. That's what they called it.

Three years earlier, the FBI had raided Arlo's house in Philadelphia. It was just after dawn. Arlo awoke to the front door being smashed open. A man in black combat gear was standing outside his bedroom window, holding a rifle. In her room, Jaycee screamed. Their mom yelled for them to stay calm. Suddenly, there were men moving down the hall, checking room by room. Arlo knew what they were looking for: Arlo's dad. But he was already on a plane to China.

Standing atop Giant's Fist, Arlo recognized the same strategy being used as smoky tendrils from the sky delivered glowing lights around the perimeter of the lake. They were being surrounded by an overwhelming force. Shock and awe.

Wade took a photo. The flash fired.

"Bellman!" shouted Mitch. "Great. Now they know someone's out here."

"I think they already knew," said Arlo. "They were waiting. That's how they got here so fast."

The final tentacle placed its light, snaking back up to the sky. Now the lights began to move. They floated across the lake, heading for Giant's Fist.

"They're coming!" said Thomas.

"What do they want?" asked Wade.

Arlo held up the knife. "This. Or me. Or both."

"So give it to them," said Mitch. "Maybe they'll go away."

Wade disagreed. "No, if they want it, we have to hold on to it. It's our only leverage."

"We can hide," said Thomas. "We can go back into the cave, or that place where we just were."

"For how long?" asked Wade. "We could get stuck there."

Arlo looked to the lake's edge. The lanterns and campfires of Summerland were barely visible. "If we can get to shore, I might be able to find a way into the Long Woods. We'd be safe there. Well, *safer.*"

That was presuming Hadryn was telling the truth about the Eldritch not being able to enter the Long Woods.

"How do we get to shore?" asked Mitch. "The raft's gone and it's too far to swim."

Arlo didn't have an answer. All around, the lights were getting closer.

Wade shoved his camera back in his daypack. "Guys, we gotta make a choice."

"Finch, give them the knife," said Mitch.

"We do that and they could still kill us," said Wade.

Arlo looked at the knife in his hand.

When the FBI had raided the house in Philadelphia, they were looking for more than just Arlo's father. They wanted his notes, his phone and especially his computer so they could figure out how his new cryptography system worked. They didn't know exactly what it could do, but they knew they needed to control it.

The Eldritch are afraid of this knife, Arlo realized. *They're afraid of what it can do.* Rielle had warned him that he'd found a weapon. Was this that weapon?

The lights were getting close enough that he could finally see the figures clearly. That's when he realized he'd made a fundamentally incorrect assumption.

Arlo Finch had always pictured the Eldritch as more or less human.

They weren't.

"They're giants."

The Eldritch were easily three times larger than full-grown men. But unlike the cave-dwelling brutes of fairy tales, the Eldritch were lean and elegantly dressed. Some wore long robes that clung tightly to their bodies, while others had tunics and trousers with metal plating. *Not uniforms,* Arlo noted. *They're all different.* Their faces were concealed behind helmets or masks.

In comic books, Superman hovered with his toes pointed, one

leg slightly more bent than the other. That's how the Eldritch were posed, each floating a few inches above the water. The power to do this seemed to come from the glowing staff each held.

There were twenty of these giants at least, and they would be there in a matter of seconds. Arlo looked for any way out. He considered jumping off the edge into the water, though he wasn't sure he could clear the rocks.

Then he saw it: an immense cloud of sparkling fog crashing down from the mountaintop. Its front edge rolled back on itself, forming a churning wall.

Arlo had encountered this spirit before, but it wasn't until this moment, with the knife in his hand, that he could finally see its true form.

It was Big Breezy. And she was angry.

The wind slammed into the Eldritch. Half of them fell into the lake, while the other half veered away, hoping to avoid her wrath.

"What's happening?!" asked Wade. The other boys couldn't see Breezy. They only saw the Eldritch getting tossed around.

Something was happening down in the lake as well. The water was rippling in strange ways. Arlo could see shapes rising beneath the surface. More spirits. They seemed to be lining up.

"We have to go!" Arlo bit the knife's handle between his teeth as he climbed down. Wade and Mitch followed him, but Thomas ducked back into the cave.

"Thomas! Come on!" shouted Mitch. He started to climb back up after him.

Arlo grabbed Mitch. "No! Leave him!"

"Why?"

"You can't trust him," said Arlo. "He's not who you think he is."

Mitch pushed Arlo off. "Thomas is in my patrol. I just met you tonight." Mitch continued climbing back up.

"What are we doing, Finch?" asked Wade. "We gonna swim for it?"

Arlo looked back at the lake, where the water was still rippling in unusual ways. "No. We're running."

Putting the knife in his pocket, he crouched down and slid off the edge of Giant's Fist. Rather than landing in the lake, he landed on top of it. His sneakers were standing in half an inch of water. Below that, it was solid—not ice, but solid water, held together by the spirits.

"How are you doing that?" asked Wade.

"I'm not! Hurry!" Overhead, some of the Eldritch had started circling back. Others were pulling themselves out of the water.

Wade hesitated, then finally just jumped. He landed awkwardly, but was able to push himself back up to his feet. He seemed too nervous to risk taking a step.

"C'mon!" shouted Arlo. He began running for the shore, with Wade following. The lake seemed to be solid only right under their feet. Arlo tried to keep running in a straight line so the spirits could anticipate where they were headed.

Out of the corner of his eye, he spotted an Eldritch swooping down. Without stopping, Arlo threw a snaplight back at it. It didn't come particularly close, but a few seconds later, a blast of wind knocked the Eldritch back.

Breezy was watching. She had their back.

Summerland was just ahead. Arlo could see Rangers gathering at the shore, all staring at the sky and the Eldritch in amazement. Headgear Cunningham was the first to spot Arlo and Wade running across the water. "It's Bellman!"

"Get back!" shouted Arlo. "Get away from the shore!"

It was pointless, like warning someone not to watch fire-works.

Reaching the water's edge, Arlo slipped in the mud. Wade helped him get up. They turned to look back.

The Eldritch were still over the lake. They seemed to have abandoned their pursuit at the moment. Long, whiplike strands of glowing energy extended from their staffs. One by one, they lashed at an unseen object.

"What are they doing?" asked Wade.

Arlo pulled the knife from his pocket. The moment it was in his hand, he could see that the Eldritch were encircling Big Breezy. She was so massive, so strong, that she dragged some of them around. But the lashes kept coming.

"They're trying to grab the wind," said Arlo. He knew that made no sense to Wade.

"We gotta keep running. You said you can get us into the Long Woods?"

"Maybe. But I don't have my compass."

Wade took off his daypack, then rooted around inside. He

pulled out a worn metal Ranger's compass. "Here. Take mine." He pressed it into Arlo's hand.

It was the same compass Arlo had always used, the one Uncle Wade had given him.

"Let's go!" said Wade. He began running up the hillside into Summerland, which by this point was abandoned. All the Rangers in Yellow Patrol were at the edge of the lake, watching the action.

Arlo looked back at Big Breezy.

Wherever two of the Eldritch lashes overlapped, the air shimmered and contracted. Breezy was being constrained. Bound. As she dragged the Eldritch closer to shore, Rangers began to flee. It was clear something bad was happening.

"Run! Run!" shouted Headgear. He took his own advice, following the edge of the lake to get away from the Eldritch.

"Finch! C'mon!" shouted Wade.

More and more Eldritch lashes encirled Breezy. She fought back, twisting and bucking, but it was clear they had the upper hand. The glowing tendrils entangled her. Caged her. Arlo could still see her swirling rage, but she couldn't break free. Like a deflating blimp, she slowly crashed into the rocks along the shore.

The net holding Breezy grew tighter. She was shrinking—or rather being compacted.

One of the Eldritch floated closer, holding out a device shaped like a lantern. Arlo guessed it was designed to hold her.

Arlo stared at the knife in his hand. He didn't know if it would work. But he knew he had to try. He began running back to the water's edge.

Wade shouted: "Finch! What are you doing?!"

A newly arrived Eldritch lashed at him. Arlo swung the knife. The blade sliced cleanly through the tendril, lopping it off.

This blade cuts their cords, Arlo realized.

He arrived at the rocks, where Breezy was bound. The glowing strands crackled with energy. He slashed at the closest one. The knife cut right through it, the free ends sizzling as they retracted. Arlo kept at it, cutting cord after cord, until he saw some of them snapping on their own as Breezy struggled against them.

He backed away. More and more strands were breaking.

Wade was staring from the hillside. "Get down!" Arlo yelled before diving to the ground himself.

Arlo didn't see Breezy break free, but he felt it.

It was an explosion, a detonation the force of a hundred tornados unleashed at once. His face pressed into the wet earth, Arlo struggled to breathe. All the air had been sucked away, channeled into Breezy's rage.

Arlo heard trees exploding around him. Others toppled, ripped from their roots. Dirt and debris rained down on his back.

And then it was quiet.

Arlo risked opening one eye, then the other. He pushed himself up to his elbows.

Summerland was destroyed, blasted to pieces. Some trees were still slowly falling, crashing through other branches as they came down. Near the boulders, the signposts were still standing, but the sign itself was gone.

This is what happened to Summerland, Arlo realized. *I did this.*

In the distance, Wade stood up, bewildered. He was the only other Ranger in sight. Everyone else had cleared out during the battle. *That's why so few of them were hurt,* Arlo thought.

And then the world went green.

The emerald light seemed to come from everywhere, a vibrating radiance. Arlo stared at his hands, marveling at how bright his fingernails were.

There was sound, too. A gentle rush like rain. It was calming. He felt his heart rate slowing.

He thought back to that morning in Philadelphia when the FBI showed up looking for his father. The front door had been smashed open.

Or had it? Maybe there was a knock at the door.

He had looked out the window and seen a man in riot gear.

Or had he? He looked again and there was no one there.

Jaycee hadn't screamed. His mother hadn't yelled to stay calm.

Because there had been no reason to be worried. Nothing had happened.

Arlo felt this memory unwinding, fading away like a dream. He struggled to hold on to it.

It's the Eldritch, he realized. *They're doing this. They're making us forget what happened.*

He hurried over to Wade, who was zipping up his daypack.

"Man, did you see that?" Wade asked. "We're lucky the tornado didn't kill us."

Arlo took him by the arm. "We have to go. Now!"

"Yeah. Right!" Wade walked with Arlo, then stopped short. "Where are we going again?"

"The Long Woods."

"Cool! Very cool." Then Wade smiled sheepishly and asked, "Also, who are you?"

Arlo felt his heart sinking, but he forced a smile. "My name's Finch."

Wade offered his hand. "Bellman. Good to meet you."

41

A RESCUE MISSION

"WHAT DO YOU MEAN GONE?" asked Wu.

It was nearly midnight, and the five remaining members of Blue Patrol were gathered around the picnic table. Indra had just roused them from their tents.

"Is Arlo lost?" asked Julie, stifling a yawn.

"Dead?" asked Jonas.

"No! At least, I don't think so," said Indra.

"Well, where is he?" asked Thomas.

"I don't know."

"If someone goes missing, we have to tell the marshal," said Wu. "She'll tell the Warden, then they can start a search party."

"They won't find him!" Indra cut to the chase: "Arlo's not anywhere, at least not anywhere *now*. I think he's trapped in the past."

Over the next ten minutes, Indra told them everything: the lake, the monster, the lost campsite. As she spoke, she realized just how much she and Arlo had been keeping from the rest of the patrol.

"Why are people always trying to kill Arlo?" asked Julie. "He's nice."

"It's because of his eyes," said Jonas. "He's a *tooble*, whatever that means. Remember the hag called him that?"

"What hag?" asked Thomas.

There wasn't time to explain everything that had happened in the Valley of Fire. Wu gave Thomas the briefest summary: "Last winter, there was this witch in the Long Woods who came after Arlo. She nearly killed all of us, but then we got out."

"Hold up," said Thomas. "You're saying that you all have been in the Long Woods, and fought a witch, and survived?"

"Thanks to Arlo," said Julie. "He can find his way through the Long Woods."

Jonas looked at Indra. "Is that where he is now, the Woods?"

"I don't think so. I'm pretty sure we were in the normal world, just in the past. Except Ekafos, the sea monster, he's definitely supernatural. I think it's related to the moon—or the moonlight. The moment the clouds came, he was gone. I was back here. Back now."

"But why not Arlo?" asked Wu. "If you came back, why didn't he?"

Indra wasn't sure. "I was in the canoe. He was in the water. Maybe that's the difference."

Wu began pacing, piecing together a theory: "Okay. Let's say the moonlight does something to the lake. Like it's charging it. Electrifying it."

"Tonight's a full moon," pointed out Jonas.

"Right," said Wu. "Maybe it only works during the full moon, or special moons, or whatever. But as long as you have that moonlight on that lake, time doesn't work the same. Everything gets jumbled up. You get sea monsters and giant dragonflies." His eyes grew wide. "Maybe the lake isn't really a lake. What if it's some kind of magical sea? A Sea of Time!"

"Arlo is stuck in the Sea of Time?" asked Julie.

"Don't call it that," said Indra. "Wu just made that up right now."

But Wu was enamored with the new name. "Arlo is *shipwrecked* in the Sea of Time. A castaway!"

"There's no Sea of Time!" insisted Indra. "If anything, it's the Lake of the Moon."

"Oh, I like that better," said Julie. "It's more mysterious."

Jonas wasn't a fan. "Sea of Time is cooler."

"We could vote," suggested Wu.

Thomas interceded. "Guys, it doesn't matter what we call it. Arlo is lost. Stuck. We need to find a way to get to him. Now, you all say you've done stuff like this before. How'd you do it then?"

"We had Connor," said Julie.

Indra, Wu and Jonas silently nodded. She was right. The difference was Connor.

"Look, Connor seems great, but he's gone. So you all got to

step up. You got to put aside all the little things and figure out how you all can work together."

Everyone was quiet for a long moment, reluctant to make eye contact with each other.

Finally, Jonas spoke. "Is there anyone we can ask? Like Warden Mpasu?"

"Indra said Arlo didn't trust anyone," pointed out Thomas. "We go to someone, and they could turn out to be the doppelgänger or whatever it is."

"How about a book?" suggested Julie. "You guys are always looking in books."

"There's a *Culman's Bestiary* in the Nature Center," said Indra. "But I don't think we're dealing with a monster, at least not mostly. This is something else. A natural phenomenon."

"Supernatural," corrected Jonas.

"A glitch!" said Wu, suddenly excited. "Okay, so there was a bug in *Galactic Havoc 2*, where if you went into this one part of the map, you'd fall through the floor. You don't die. You're just falling and falling forever. The lake could be like that glitch, a place where the world is kind of broken."

"But Arlo's not in a video game," said Julie.

"No, but he's *somewhere*," said Indra. "Some*when*. The lake, the sea, whatever you want to call it, it's like a hole in time. I think Wu's right."

"You do?" said Wu, surprised.

"I do. It's a good metaphor. So how do you get out of the glitch? How do you stop falling?"

"Well, you don't want to restart, because then you'd lose your progress. In *Galactic Havoc 2*, it turns out there's a keyboard command that puts you back on the map."

"How did you figure it out?" asked Thomas.

"I didn't. I looked in the online forums. Someone else had the answer."

"We don't have the internet," said Jonas.

Wu hesitated, then spoke. "Actually, we do."

Their flashlight beams serving as a spotlight, Blue Patrol crowded inside the tent as Wu unzipped his pack. He fished around inside it, finally pulling out his phone. It seemed like an artifact from the future, so out of place in a Ranger campsite.

"Wait, you smuggled a phone up here?!" asked Jonas. "That's a big deal! You could get sent home."

"I know! I'm not saying it was a good idea, but I did it. Arlo changed the passcode, but if we can figure out what it is, maybe we can find something useful."

"Try his birthday," said Indra. "Zero seven one eight."

Wu punched in the numbers. No luck.

"Try one one one one," said Jonas. "Or one two three four."

"Guys, stop!" said Julie. "This won't work! Even if we figure out the code, we're not going to google our way out of this. Whatever's happening is supernatural Ranger stuff, so that's what we need to be doing."

"She's right, you know. Quite smart, that one."

It was a man's voice, but no one could tell where it was coming from.

"What matters is not where Arlo is, but where he's headed."

The voice was coming from deeper inside the tent. Flashlights swept in all directions as a small creature leaped in through the back flaps of the tent. It darted among the shadows, finally springing up onto Arlo's cot.

It was a small red fox with gleaming eyes. It sat with its bushy tail curled around it.

"Luckily for all of us," said the fox, "I know how to get there." It seemed oddly natural for the fox to be speaking with a man's voice.

"Who are you?" asked Indra.

"Fox, of course. I'd think that quite obvious."

"But why are you here?" asked Wu.

"I've been sent to find you."

"Sent by whom?" asked Indra.

"The one and only Arlo Finch."

42
THE ANCHOR

A BUZZING STREETLAMP lit Pine Mountain's only stop sign. Moths swirled in the amber light, plinking against the glass.

Wade stared at the fluttering bugs, a slack grin on his face. He elbowed Arlo. "Do you know why they do that?"

"Because they think it's the sun?"

"No, because they think it's the *sun*," he said, giving no indication that he knew he was repeating Arlo. "Artificial light messes up their navigation."

Back at the lake, the Eldritch's magical light had messed up Wade. He was alternately giddy and surly and tired, like a preschooler who had missed his nap. It was hard to keep him focused, especially now that they'd arrived.

They were standing at the anchor in front of Pine Mountain Elementary School. A few nights earlier at the Health Center, Fox had told Arlo he would meet him next at the anchor—and this was the only anchor Arlo could recall. But there was no Fox to be found, and Arlo was starting to think he'd misunderstood him. Had Fox really meant "next time" to be now, thirty years in the past? How could Fox have known to be here?

"Hey, Finch? Why are we at school?" asked Wade. "It's summer. Also, it's dark."

"We're on a secret mission," whispered Arlo. "I need you to find me three small rocks." Wade beamed with excitement and started looking for stones. Arlo hoped the task would buy him a few minutes to focus.

Was it possible he was simply too late? The trip through the Long Woods had taken much longer than he had hoped. He'd found a path relatively quickly—Wade's compass had worked as well as ever. But Wade was a terrible traveling companion. He kept forgetting who Arlo was and why they needed to hurry. He got distracted by every exotic plant and endless vista.

They had finally arrived at a spot near the Gold Pan, a connection to the Long Woods that Arlo had discovered a few months earlier. The short walk down Main Street had taken twenty minutes, with Wade constantly stopping to rest or tie his shoes.

"Someone's coming!" hissed Wade, hiding behind a too-skinny tree.

Arlo turned to see a man emerging from the shadows of the school. He wore plaid shorts, leather boat shoes and a collared shirt with an alligator logo. But it was the mustache that Arlo recognized first.

"You'd be the one, then—the boy with the knife. I'm Fox."

"I know," said Arlo.

"Yes, I suppose we've met before, or you've met me at least. And I've already met you just now, but that won't happen for years."

Arlo had gotten used to Fox's odd sentences. "How did you know to come here?"

"I suppose it was instinct," said Fox. "It's an underappreciated talent, to know something without knowing why. It's like the wind is whispering in your ear. Is he your brother?" he asked, pointing to the poorly hidden Wade. "There's quite a resemblance."

Arlo hesitated. Fox guessed the reason. "You don't need to worry about his remembering. He's obviously been unwound. There was a bright green light, yes?"

"What was that?" asked Arlo.

"An Eldritch specialty. You see, human memories are like little knots in a string. The green light, it unwinds them. People forget what they've seen, or remember something different. The Eldritch, they used to visit your world quite a bit before there were cameras and such they couldn't untwist."

Wade slowly approached, apparently having decided Fox was not dangerous. "I found three rocks!" He handed them to Arlo.

Fox took Wade by the chin, staring into his eyes. "I'd say it's a few more hours before anything sticks." Fox turned to Arlo. "Your eyes, your *tooble-ness*, I suspect that protected you. You didn't get unraveled."

Arlo had more questions, and couldn't babysit Wade. "Why

don't you listen to your Walkman, okay?" he said to him. "I think it's in your pack." Wade began rummaging through the bag, excited. He'd forgotten all about his Walkman.

"So back at camp, the Rangers won't remember anything about what happened?"

"Not if they saw that light. But the spirits remember. In fact, they're all abuzz about what you've done. Some are calling you a champion. They'll write about you."

Pinereading, thought Arlo.

"You went back and saved the wind," said Fox. "She would have been quite a prize for the Eldritch. She was strong. They could have used her, no doubt."

"Used her for what?"

"The Eldritch are builders," said Fox. "They're like humans in that way. But where your people use oil and electricity"—he pointed to the streetlamp—"the Eldritch use spirits. Their whole society is powered by them."

Arlo thought back to the events at the water's edge. "They were trying to put Big Breezy into something. It looked like a lantern."

"More like a cage. But you cut her free. Has anyone told you about the silver strings?"

In fact, Fox himself had told Arlo about them at the Health Center. "They keep a person's body and spirit bound together."

"Exactly. But strings like that can bind other things, too. The Eldritch use them to bind spirits to their weapons, their armor, their forges . . ."

"But this knife can cut them," said Arlo.

"Exactly. It's one of the only things that can. The Eldritch want to make sure that knife stays far away from their world. They'll destroy it if they can. That's why it was hidden, to keep them from finding it."

"So what do I do now?"

"I'm afraid you don't have much *now* left. You traveled in the moonlight, correct?"

Arlo sensed there was more bad news coming. "What happens when the sun comes back up?"

"You'll be back in your own time. And the knife won't travel with you. You'll only have what you came with."

"So how do I keep the knife without keeping it?"

"That's the riddle, I suppose."

Wade banged his flashlight against his hand, trying to get it to light. "Man, the batteries are dead."

Arlo felt a spark of an idea. "Let me see that." Wade handed him the flashlight. It was shiny metal, standard-issue, the kind that took two D batteries. Arlo had seen it before, only then it was rusted.

Arlo smiled. He had a plan.

43
THE HOUSE ON GREEN PASS ROAD

FOR THIS TO WORK, Arlo would need to get to the Broken Bridge before sunrise, which was just an hour away.

He had two choices. The closest entrance into the Long Woods was back near the Gold Pan, but Arlo wasn't certain he could find the right path to the bridge from there. A much safer bet was the ravine by his house—he wouldn't even need to use the compass. Unfortunately, it was a thirty-minute walk from school. And that was without Wade.

"Wait, wait." Wade stopped, trying to get his bearings. "Where are we going again?"

"You're taking me to your house. We have to hurry. Do you think you can run?"

"Absolutely!" Wade started running, but stopped after twenty steps. He leaned over his knees, winded. Then he looked up at the sky. "Why is it so dark?"

"Because it's night. Barely. We have to hurry."

"Okay. I just need a little rest." Wade lay down at the edge of the gravel road, arms forming a pillow under his head.

Arlo turned to Fox. "He's getting worse. Does he have brain damage or something?"

"No. It's just the unwinding," said Fox. "He'll be back to normal after he sleeps."

Wade was never normal, of course. Arlo would settle for cooperative and mobile. He tried to pick him up, but Wade had gone limp.

A dusty Subaru came around the bend, its high beams on. As it slowed, Wade sat up, squinting. The car pulled up alongside them. As the passenger window rolled down, two bright-eyed Scottie dogs popped up to look out.

"Are you all right?" Arlo recognized the driver's voice immediately. It was Mrs. Fitzrandolph, the school librarian. She was thirty years younger than Arlo was used to seeing, but honestly didn't look much different.

Wade sat up. "Hi, Mrs. F.!"

"Wade Bellman! Is that you? What are you Rangers doing out here in the middle of the night?"

Wade was honestly stumped. "I don't know!"

Arlo intervened. "We were doing a night hike."

"We got so lost," said Wade. "They're taking me home."

That seemed to satisfy Mrs. Fitzrandolph. "Well, do you need a ride? I've got groceries, but I bet we can squeeze you in."

On the short drive to the house, Mrs. Fitzrandolph explained that her insomnia often had her shopping at the twenty-four-hour grocery in Cross Creek. "I use a lot of coupons as it is, so that way I'm not creating a bother for other people waiting in line."

She seemed to assume that Fox was Arlo's father. Meanwhile, her dogs stared intently at him. Maybe they sensed Fox wasn't quite human or canine, but a mix of the two.

Arlo signaled as they reached the end of the driveway. "Here's fine." He didn't want to risk waking up Wade's parents—his grandparents. He'd never met them, but from stories his mom had told him, they weren't big on surprise visitors. He thanked Mrs. Fitzrandolph for the ride and shut the door quietly.

"This is my house!" Wade exclaimed as the Subaru pulled away. "I live here!"

The house looked much better than Arlo had ever seen it. The porch was painted and level. To the left, a proper staircase ran up to the side door. A full garden grew in front of the house, surrounded by a wrought iron fence. Arlo had never realized how much he had been living in the ruins of a proper home.

Under the drone of crickets came a metallic jingle. Arlo turned to see a dog running down the driveway. It was barking with happy yips and squeals.

Wade kneeled down to greet it. It ran into his arms, licking his face. "This is Cooper! He's our dog."

Arlo scratched the soft fur behind Cooper's ear. He was real. Touchable. Alive.

The dog sniffed Arlo, licked him, and deemed him worthy of further study, nuzzling his leg. Arlo had seen Cooper a hundred times, usually at sunset. But the dog had never interacted with him. It was always a one-sided conversation.

"I want a Coke!" said Wade. "Or a Jolt! I think we still have some."

Arlo grabbed him by the arm. "Wade, we're not going in. We need to go back into the Long Woods."

"We do need to hurry," agreed Fox. Cooper was sniffing his shoes.

Wade crossed his arms, grumpy. "Fine."

As he picked up the daypack, Wade suddenly sprinted for the house. Arlo chased after him. He finally caught him at the front door, one hand on the knob.

"Listen to me," Arlo said, keeping his voice low. "This is serious. If we don't go to the Long Woods right now, if you don't come with me, a lot of people could get hurt. Not just people, but spirits, too."

"How do you hurt spirits?"

"By binding them, locking them down. The spirits? They want to be free. They want to be punk rock."

"I love punk!" said Wade.

"I know! And you love art, and animals, and disobeying rules.

So let's do this, okay? Let's be punk rock and anarchy. Let's show them how we do it."

Just then, the front door opened, revealing a sleepy nine-year-old girl in flip-flops and unicorn pajamas.

"Wade?" she said. "What are you doing here?"

Arlo stared at her, speechless. It was Celeste, his mom. Only now she was younger than he was.

44

TWO WORLDS AND THE WOODS BETWEEN THEM

YOUNG CELESTE BELLMAN was confused: "Why aren't you at camp?"

"We're gonna go save spirits for punk," said Wade. "This is my friend—" He turned to Arlo. "What's your name again?"

"Finch," Arlo said. He tried not to stare too hard at Celeste, not to mentally age her into his mother. But it was unquestionably her. She had the same soft brown eyes.

Wade rubbed a knuckle on her head as he pushed his way inside.

"Ow! Cut it out!" She batted him away.

"Wade!" whispered Arlo. "We have to go!"

"I just want a soda!" Wade hissed back. He disappeared through the swinging door into the kitchen. With Fox still back at the road with Cooper, Arlo was alone on the porch with his nine-year-old mom.

"You're not from Pine Mountain," she said. "I'd recognize you."

"I'm from Chicago," he said. It wasn't exactly a lie. "Why are you awake?"

"I heard Cooper barking." She stepped closer to look at him. "Your eyes are two different colors."

"Yeah. It's a thing." *Heterochromia iridum. You taught me the term.*

"Is it genetic?"

"Sort of, I guess? Not really sure how it happened." He looked back at Fox, who was gesturing to hurry up. They needed to get going.

Wade returned from the kitchen with a Jolt! cola and a huge handful of breakfast cereal that he mashed into his mouth.

"Where are you going?" Celeste asked.

"Duh wuhdz," mumbled Wade.

"Can I come with you?"

"Uh-uh!"

"I'll tell Mom and Dad you were here."

"Fye-nuh! Do it!"

"I'll wake them up right now. I'll scream!"

"Please don't," said Arlo. "We really have to—"

She pushed past him. "Something's wrong with Cooper."

Cooper, who had been busy scratching at a tree stump, was now barking ferociously. Just over the trees, the sky was beginning to crack open, with smoky tendrils reaching down.

"Coooooool," said Wade, still chomping on his cereal.

Celeste began to panic. "What's happening?"

A tendril touched down at the edge of the road, depositing a glowing white form. It was an Eldritch, its armor glowing in the moonlight. Cooper held his ground, barking his lungs out as the giant soldier approached.

In the distance, two additional lights touched down. Then three more. They'd soon be surrounding the house.

Fox raced to the porch. "We have to go!"

Arlo looked back at Celeste. "Just stay inside. They're not interested in you."

Celeste grabbed Wade's arm, terrified. He put his hand over hers. As much as they bickered, they were still brother and sister. "She's coming with us," said Wade.

Arlo looked at Fox. There was no time to argue. "Okay," Arlo said. "Hurry!"

Arlo led the way off the porch and past Wade's workshop—which in this era was simply a garage. A pickup truck was resting on cinder blocks, the hood propped open to work on the engine.

A strong wind was picking up. Arlo suspected it was a spirit trying to slow the Eldritch. He could hear Cooper barking, but didn't risk looking back.

"Cooper!" shouted a man's voice. "Hush up!"

Arlo guessed it was his grandfather yelling from a second-story window. No doubt he would see the Eldritch. No doubt they would make him forget he had.

Reaching the edge of the trees, Arlo waited for Celeste to catch up. "Shut your eyes!"

"What?!"

"Just do it!"

She closed her eyes. Arlo clasped a hand over them.

Suddenly, the world went emerald green. Arlo could feel his memories starting to unwind. *Did the front door actually open? Had Cooper been sleeping on the porch? Was it really Mrs. Fitzrandolph in the car?* He struggled to hold on to the moments before they slipped away.

He looked at Celeste. Some of the Eldritch light was slipping between his fingers. Then the green light passed. Normal night resumed.

"Keep moving!" shouted Fox, pushing Wade along. Wade had gotten a blast of light, but was already so scrambled it didn't seem to have much of an additional impact.

Once they were in the forest, Arlo had no trouble finding his way. Some trees had grown, others had fallen, but the basic layout hadn't changed over the last thirty years. Arlo quickly got them to the ditch, helping them climb down into it. Even the tree root handhold was in the same place.

"Grab onto it. Pull on three!" said Arlo. "One, two, three!"

Arlo, Wade, Celeste and Fox tugged on the exposed tree root. As before, the ravine shifted, pivoting in space. Ice-cold water rose to their ankles. Celeste, in flip-flops, got the worst of it.

"Sorry!" Arlo said. "I keep forgetting about that."

Wade looked back to the top of the ravine, expecting to see the Eldritch.

"We're safe," said Fox. "They can't follow us here."

"Why is that?" said Arlo.

"They can't find their way in the Long Woods, not since the day the bridge fell."

Arlo pushed aside the curtain of fluttering faerie moths, leading the group to the clearing in front of the Broken Bridge. In the blue moonlight, the massive tower looked like a monument. A gravestone.

He was back where this adventure had begun. Only now it was night, and he had new companions at his side.

"We have to whisper," he warned them.

"Why?" asked Wade, not whispering at all.

Arlo shushed him. "Because there's a troll under the bridge. So just be quiet. We have one thing to do and then we can go."

In truth, there was more than one thing to do. Arlo needed to put the knife in the flashlight and place them both under the rock for his future self to find thirty years later. But one thought kept nagging at him: Hadryn.

Hadryn wanted the knife, and Arlo had no good way to keep him from getting it.

Assuming everything went perfectly and the knife ended up in the present day, Hadryn would no doubt show up to take it. Arlo needed to prepare for that.

So he'd come up with a plan, one he hadn't even shared with Fox.

Arlo took off his Blue Patrol neckerchief, wrapping it around the knife. He then unscrewed Wade's flashlight, dumping the dead batteries back into the daypack. After one last bit of preparation, he slid the wrapped-up knife into the flashlight and twisted it back together.

Celeste kept looking back at the trees, expecting something to come charging out. "Is this really happening?" she asked. "Or is this all a dream? You can tell me."

"Nothing's gonna hurt you," said Arlo. "I promise."

She half smiled, like she wanted to believe him.

The foursome made their way along the edge of the chasm. The massive bridge tower loomed above them, backlit by the moon.

Arlo whispered to Fox, "You said the Eldritch were builders. Did they build this?"

Fox nodded. "This bridge used to connect the Realm to your world. Eldritch trappers would cross to bind spirits and haul them back to their cities."

Arlo remembered Indra speculating that heavy wheels must have worn the grooves in the roadway. *They were hauling spirits,* he thought. *Like Big Breezy.*

"What happened to the bridge?"

"The Eldritch had managed to capture this ancient spirit, the most powerful one they'd ever found. They figured it could drive their cities for a thousand years. What they didn't know was that the thing they'd caught wasn't a single spirit, but two. Twin serpents, coiled together. Ekafos and Mirnos. *Time and Space.*"

"Wait, literally time and space?" asked Arlo.

"Am I literally a fox? Yes and no and close enough for our purposes." Fox continued: "The Eldritch got the twins halfway across when they suddenly broke free. It's like what your people do with atoms. They split. Divided. The explosion didn't just destroy the bridge. It smashed everything. What settled out of it became the Long Woods. And this bridge became, well, *timeless*. Not sure you have a word for it. But it's how something can be both now and then at the same time."

They'd reached the rubble near the base of the tower. Arlo was quickly able to figure out which block he'd found the flashlight under. "I'm gonna need all your help."

Together, Fox, Wade and Celeste tipped one of the heavy stone blocks up on its edge so Arlo could slide the flashlight underneath it. With his fingers, he dug a little trench for the flashlight so it wouldn't get crushed. Then they slowly lowered the stone back down on top of it.

Arlo handed Wade his compass and daypack, along with the yellow neckerchief. The bloodstains were dry. "Thanks for this."

"You can keep it."

"No, you should have it. You can give it to me later. Also, will you do me a favor?" He held out the piece of shell from his pocket. "I need you to mark an *A* for *anarchy* on the side of the rock. Can you do that?"

"Heck, yeah," said Wade.

While he was working, Arlo pulled Fox aside. "Can you get Wade back to Redfeather? I can take Celeste back."

"Certainly," said Fox.

"One more thing: thirty years from now, on the night I cross the lake, I need you to find Blue Patrol and bring them here. They can't find their way in the Long Woods themselves."

"Will they know what to do when they get here?"

Arlo knew his friends. He knew he could count on them. "They'll figure it out."

"And when should I see you again, Mr. Finch?" asked Fox.

"Winter. In the parking lot of the church. That's where we'll meet for the first time. Then in the summer at Redfeather. I'll be in the Health Center." Arlo realized he was making very specific and difficult requests. "Will you be able to be at the right place at the right time?"

Fox smiled. "After all you've seen, you still think of places and times in such ordinary ways. It's charming, really."

The sky was starting to turn pink. It would be dawn soon.

"What happens when the sun comes up?" asked Arlo.

"You'll be back in your own time. Don't know what that will feel like. Never done it."

Arlo looked over at Wade and Celeste, who were standing near the edge of the chasm. They were the same age difference as him and Jaycee, and seemed to have little in common other than being born into the same family. But there was a resemblance, and a closeness Arlo didn't see in their adult forms.

He'd miss this version.

Then Wade cupped his hands around his mouth and yelled as loud as he could: "ECHO!"

Indeed, there was an impressive echo.

Followed by the mighty roar of a troll.

45
TOOBLE

"RUN!" SHOUTED ARLO.

Celeste didn't need any prompting. She immediately began racing back from the edge of the chasm as fast as her flip-flopped feet would carry her. Wade, meanwhile, watched in fascination as the massive troll climbed up onto the roadway of the Broken Bridge.

"What is that thing?!" he yelled back at Arlo and Fox.

"Wade! Hurry!" shouted Arlo.

"I'll get the boy," said Fox. "You take her."

"Are you sure?"

Fox was already running toward Wade. "There's not much time, Mr. Finch!"

Celeste reached Arlo. Only then did she look back, realizing that her brother wasn't with her. Wade was still at the chasm's edge, roaring back at the troll.

"Wade!" she shouted.

"Fox will get him back to camp," said Arlo. "We need to go. He'll be fine."

She reluctantly took Arlo's hand as they headed into the woods. Arlo didn't have a compass—he'd put Wade's compass back in the pack—but he was pretty sure he could find the way. They simply needed to go left at the aspen grove, then over the rise and under the fallen log.

Ahead, he saw a clearing. It didn't look quite right, but he'd never been down this path at night.

They emerged from the edge of the trees to find themselves back at the Broken Bridge. Even though they had run in a straight line, the path had circled back on itself.

The troll had just finished climbing around the outside of the tower.

Arlo hoped it hadn't noticed them in the dim light. But then it roared and charged.

Celeste screamed. Arlo half carried her back into the woods.

This time, he didn't consciously try to follow a path. He was just looking for a way out. A way through. Like prey, they darted left and right, pure instinct.

The less he thought, the simpler the choices became. Arlo began to sense what was coming up ahead, as if the forest were part of him.

He didn't risk looking back. He didn't need to. He could feel where the troll was. It was close. They wouldn't be able to outrun it. They needed to hide. But where? There weren't any boulders to duck behind. No logs to tuck themselves under.

"There!" shouted Celeste.

She pointed to a massive leafless tree. It looked like it had grown upside down, its hundred branches twisting like roots.

He gave Celeste a boost to get started, then followed behind her. He hadn't climbed many trees in his life, but this one seemed uniquely suited to the task. At every turn, there was another handhold. Like a ladder, it required no particular skill to ascend.

Once they were twenty feet off the ground, Arlo motioned for Celeste to stop. The troll was coming, smashing through the lower branches of nearby trees. He felt Celeste shaking with fear.

"It's okay," he whispered. "It's just a dream." He wished it were true.

Celeste squeezed her eyes shut.

Arlo held his breath as the troll bounded past right beside them, its stench rising off it. It seemed to hunt by sight, and was still looking for them on the ground. After a full minute, it had disappeared deeper into the forest.

"It's okay," Arlo said. "It's gone."

He helped Celeste climb down from the tree. Once they were back on the ground, Arlo tried to get his bearings. There had to be a path back to the house. He just needed to find it.

"Where are we again?" asked Celeste.

"The Long Woods. It's a magic forest."

"Like in a fairy tale."

"I guess," he said. "This is probably where the stories come from." *The Wonder makes them forget the details,* he thought, *but they remember the feeling.*

He narrowed his choices to two directions, both of which seemed equally likely ways to get back to the house. He couldn't afford to pick wrong. There wasn't much time.

Meanwhile, Celeste was examining a single green leaf hanging from a low branch. It seemed to be the only one on the entire tree. It was perfectly green, radiant in the twilight. It trembled in a light breeze.

Arlo made his decision on a route. He looked over just as Celeste reached towards the leaf. He sensed danger, but there wasn't time to shout anything.

As Celeste touched the leaf, all the green drained out of it, leaving only gossamer veins. It crumbled into dust.

Then she collapsed.

Arlo raced over to her, his first-aid training kicking in. He checked her breathing, then her pulse. Both normal. But she was unconscious.

"C'mon! Wake up!" He jostled her. "You have to wake up! Please! Mom!"

Tears welling in his eyes, he scooped his arms underneath her. He figured he could probably carry her, at least for a little bit. But it was hard to lift her. In lifesaving drills, the Ranger "victims" were always helping a little.

Celeste was limp. She was just a body. Deadweight.

Arlo choked back a sob. He felt helpless. Alone. And guilty. *She was never supposed to be here,* he thought. *I did this.*

Then Celeste sat up by herself. "What happened?" she asked. "Are you okay!?"

When she looked at him, Arlo saw that her eyes had gone emerald green. A light was swirling within them. Within a few seconds the light faded, leaving them brown again.

"Why are you crying?" she asked.

Arlo remembered what Fox had said at the Health Center. *It's definitely a forest spirit, something quite old, I'd say.* Arlo looked up at the massive tree towering over them. It had only had a single leaf. *Spirits do sometimes hitch a ride with humans, but you were definitely born with this one.*

Celeste Bellman now had a spirit riding along with her. She would carry it until Arlo was born.

"Can we go home?" she asked.

Arlo helped her up. "I'll find the way."

Ten minutes later, they were climbing the stairs of the house on Green Pass Road. Arlo was careful to skip the third step—the squeaky one that might wake his grandparents.

Very little about the inside of the house had changed. It seemed to be the same carpet, same paint, same framed photos on the wall. Celeste's room was Arlo's room. The wallpaper hadn't faded yet, the flowers still dark.

"Is this a dream?" she whispered as she climbed into bed.

"That's probably the right way to think about it." He helped her pull up the covers. Her feet were filthy, but there wasn't time to wash up. The sky outside was already starting to brighten.

Celeste switched on her flashlight. She aimed it at Arlo as he stood at the door.

"Will I see you again?" she asked.

Arlo smiled. "Definitely."

46

THE BROKEN BRIDGE, PART TWO

INDRA, WU, JONAS AND JULIE stood at the edge of the bottomless chasm, watching as Arlo Finch hurried back into the woods.

"So what happens next?" whispered Jonas.

"Arlo goes to get me and Wu," said Indra. "Then he brings them with him."

"But you're *already* here," said Julie.

"No," explained Indra. "We're *now* us. We need *then* us."

"I'm still really confused," said Jonas.

"Okay, so—this is now," said Wu, gesturing at the ground. "The far side over there? That's then."

"What do you mean, *then*?" asked Jonas. "Is it the future or the past?"

"Just *then*. It's whatever time isn't now."

"Why do you guys always talk in riddles?" asked Julie. "You're worse than that talking fox." She pointed over towards the tower, where Thomas and the small, furry fox had been instructed to hide in the shadows.

Indra tried to explain it all as best she understood it. "So, thirty years ago, Arlo hides the flashlight under that rock. Then ten days ago, he finds the bridge for the first time. He looks across and he sees us."

"And that part just happened," said Wu. "That's our now, and his ten days ago." He pointed back across the chasm to underline his point. "That's Then. This is Now."

Indra continued: "So Arlo goes off and calls me and Wu. In about half an hour, we'll come with him and see us all over here."

"Wait," said Jonas. "So the Blue Patrol you saw ten days ago, the one you never bothered telling us about . . ."

"Was the four of us standing here right now."

Julie suddenly seemed to understand. "So when Arlo comes back with Indra and Wu, that's when I do the semaphore?"

"Exactly! Arlo can't really understand it, but Wu and I can."

"You're much better than I am," said Wu. "I would have messed it up."

"No, you're pretty good, though," said Indra. "If I weren't there, you would have still figured it out. And you're the one who makes the big catch at the end. You're the hero."

Jonas tried to refocus on the mission ahead. "So Arlo comes back with the two of you, then what?"

"We point him to the right rock," said Indra. "The one with the *A* on it."

"*A* for Arlo," said Julie.

"I guess. And they get the flashlight and toss it to us. Arlo throws it past Jonas, then it lands on the bridge and Wu barely grabs it before it falls in. And then we run from the troll. We don't know what happens after that."

"But what happens if I catch the flashlight?" asked Jonas.

"You don't," said Wu. "You won't."

"But what if I do? Or what if I trip and fall over the edge? I mean, you're talking like all of this is set in stone, and it can't be. Because I could still do anything."

"He's right," said Indra. "I mean, let's say the past is set. Whatever happened, happened. But this moment, the one we're in right now, this isn't the past."

"It sort of is, though," said Wu. "Think about it. You and I saw what happened. To us, this is part of the past. We're going to end up doing the exact same things."

"But why?" said Indra. "There's nothing forcing us to. We still have free will."

Julie groaned. "This is making my brain hurt. Just tell me what to do."

"I agree," said Jonas. "Let's just do whatever we did before. I don't want to break the universe. I just want to make things right."

Twenty-two minutes later, Arlo Finch returned to the far side of the chasm, accompanied by Wu and Indra. Using improvised semaphore flags, Julie instructed them to stay quiet and look for the stone block with an *A*.

Just as had happened before, the trio on the far side recovered the flashlight and carefully made their way onto the Broken Bridge. But as Blue Patrol approached their end, Wu called them in for a huddle.

"I think we should take different positions," said Wu. "We know Arlo's going to throw it too far, so we should put Jonas further back to catch it."

"But that's your job," said Indra. "You catch it."

"That was luck. I barely caught it. Look, we know where it's going. We should just put our best catcher there."

"I'll go wherever you want me," said Jonas.

Indra took Wu by the arm. "Are you just worried you're going to mess up?"

"Kind of. I mean, it's a lot of pressure. As long as we catch it, it doesn't matter if it's me or someone else."

"But maybe it does," said Indra. "If you hadn't seen yourself catching it that day, maybe you wouldn't have run for patrol leader. Everything might be different."

"I think you can do it," said Julie. "You're not totally awful at catching. There are people worse."

Wu relented. "All right. We'll stick with the plan."

The patrol split up and took their positions. After a test throw with a rock, Arlo Finch threw the rusted flashlight across the gap.

Exactly as it had before, the flashlight flew over Jonas's head. Julie squeezed her eyes shut. This time, though, Indra had repositioned herself. She had a perfect opportunity to catch it. But at the last moment, she didn't reach for it. She let it *clang* on the stones.

Wu dived for it. But perhaps because he had assumed Indra would catch it, he was a little too late.

His hand grazed the flashlight, redirecting it.

The flashlight continued skidding. Rolling.

It was four inches from the edge. Three. Two.

Wu scrambled after it.

One.

The flashlight tipped over the far side. Indra gasped.

Wu made a final desperate lunge for it. But it was clearly too late.

After all this preparation—or perhaps *because of* the preparation—they had failed. Indra traded disbelieving looks with Jonas and Julie. Wu lay on his belly, staring down into the bottomless chasm.

Then he rolled over onto his back, holding up the rusted flashlight in victory. He'd snagged it at the very last moment.

Blue Patrol gave a silent cheer. Henry Wu had done it. Again.

47
A LONG TIME COMING

ARLO FINCH WATCHED all of this from the edge of the forest.

After leaving Celeste, he had returned to the bridge just as the first rays of dawn broke over the horizon. Night was gone, and with it, the magic of the moonlit lake. As the light bloomed, Arlo had felt time shifting.

Without moving, he had returned to his own time.

Tucked into a hiding spot under the gnarled roots of a tree, he had waited for Blue Patrol to arrive. After an hour, he had spotted them emerging from the forest behind Fox: Indra, Wu, Jonas and Julie.

And Thomas. He'd come too. Arlo had been expecting him. Preparing.

It was strange to be simply an observer, to witness how his friends interacted without him. They were far enough away that Arlo couldn't hear most of what they were saying, but from their interactions it was clear that Wu and Indra were getting along better. They weren't just talking. They seemed to be actually listening to each other for a change.

Thomas and Fox had found their own hiding places in the shadows by the bridge tower. It made sense for Thomas to keep out of sight; he hadn't been part of the patrol when Arlo had first seen them. *Did Wu and Indra tell him to stay hidden?* wondered Arlo. *Or did he suggest it?*

Eventually, Arlo had spotted himself on the far side of the chasm. He was surprised by how small he looked. In mirrors, he always saw himself close up. But at this distance, it was clear he was truly just a smallish twelve-year-old boy.

He could forgive that kid for his mistakes.

This other Arlo—Past Arlo—had left, then returned with Wu and Indra. There were signals and discussions and a flashlight found under a stone. Everything happened exactly as it had before. It was like watching a play from a new angle.

And then came the toss. At the last moment, Wu snagged the flashlight and held it up in triumph. Arlo smiled as Blue Patrol cheered. He wanted to celebrate with them, but he needed to keep his eye on Thomas. This was the part of the play he'd never seen before.

As Wu unscrewed the flashlight, Arlo watched Thomas creeping in a little closer.

Jonas discarded the empty flashlight. It fell into the chasm.

On the far side of the bridge, Past Arlo shouted at the top of his lungs: "TELL ME WHAT IT IS!"

It's the knife you put there, thought Arlo. *It's all part of the plan.*

He just hoped the plan worked.

A pause, then deep howls rose from both sides of the canyon. Arlo had now heard it three times, but it still sent a shiver through him. The trolls had been awakened by the shout.

"Run!" yelled Indra and Wu.

Blue Patrol raced for the tower arch. So did Arlo. He needed to reach them before Thomas could convince them to give him the knife.

He was certain he had never run so fast, not even when running away from the troll the first time. He didn't hold anything back.

The patrol had just now emerged from the tower, their backs to him. But where was Thomas? He couldn't see where he had gone.

"Indra! Wu!" he shouted. They turned. So did Jonas and Julie. "Don't give it to Thomas!"

But Arlo could see their hands were empty. Was he too late? As he got closer, it became clear why his friends had been so quick to hand over the knife. They hadn't given it to Thomas.

They had given it to Arlo Finch.

That's who was standing there. He had mimicked Arlo perfectly, right down to his mismatched eyes. He was holding the knife, still wrapped in Arlo's blue neckerchief.

Arlo stopped short.

The patrol spread out, suddenly not sure which Arlo was

which. They looked identical, or very nearly; the impostor was wearing Thomas's uniform, complete with blue neckerchief.

On both sides of the chasm, identical trolls began howling at each other.

But here in the shadow of the broken tower, identical Arlos were staring each other down.

"I'm confused," said Julie.

So was Jonas. "Where's Thomas?"

"You have what you want," said Arlo to the impostor wearing his face. "Let them go."

The false Arlo smiled. "You have no idea what I want." He pushed past the others, slowly approaching Arlo.

Arlo held his ground, calling over to Fox at the edge of the forest, "Get the others out of here."

"Yes, little fox," said the false Arlo. "Run along home. This is between old friends." He grabbed Arlo by the arm and threw something on the ground. With a puff of black smoke, they were gone.

Arlo was dizzy. Nauseous. He felt like he was falling in all directions. Eventually, he righted himself. He could see treetops. Clouds.

"*Smokejumping*," said a man's voice. "You won't find that in the Ranger Field Book."

It was Hadryn. He knew the voice.

Arlo could feel dirt. Pine needles. Birds were chirping.

"I found a woman in Nepal," said the man. "She didn't want to teach me, but I convinced her. Everyone has a price. Something they want, or something they're not willing to lose. In her case, it was her grandson."

The sun was shining, but Arlo couldn't shield his eyes. Thorny vines were wrapping themselves around his wrists and legs. The more he struggled, the tighter they got.

"And that? *Vinesnare.* They'll teach you that in Bear, a simple version at least. If you ever make it that far."

They were on a mountaintop. Arlo could see Redfeather Lake far below them. Hadryn was halfway changed into adult-sized clothes, the same outfit he'd worn when they first met at the Gold Pan diner.

"Yell if you want. They won't hear you," said Hadryn. "No one's gonna find us up here. Not with these wards. We're invisible to the world. You could fly a helicopter overhead and you'd just see mountains."

This seemed to be where Hadryn lived. There was a tent, along with a table and canopy. Dozens of books spilled out of heavy crates. All around the perimeter stood stones with elaborate engravings. *The wards,* Arlo thought.

Hadryn kneeled down in front of Arlo. A smoky quartz crystal dangled from a leather cord, less a necklace than a talisman. "Have you figured out who I am? What I am?"

"You're a doppelgänger," said Arlo.

He smiled. "Wrong. But I did kill a doppelgänger. I ate its heart. That's why I can do this."

Hadryn's face changed. His body shifted, but his clothes remained the same. In only a few seconds, he transformed to look exactly like Wu. He even spoke with Wu's voice. "That's why I ripped those pages out of *Culman's Bestiary.* If you'd read them, you'd see it says very clearly that the doppelgänger's heart is the key to its abilities. You'd also learn its limitations."

He transformed into Thomas. "Becoming someone else takes a lot of concentration. One slipup and bam, it's over. It's much easier to just be my younger self. I can even sleep with this face. And to be honest, it's nice being a kid again."

Arlo looked him in the eye. "Who are you really?"

"Alva Hadryn Thomas from Texas. Exactly who I said I was when I met you thirty years ago."

"What happened to you?"

Thomas tapped Arlo on the chest. "*You* happened to me, Arlo Finch." He stood up, grabbing a T-shirt. As he slid it over his head, he reassumed Hadryn's form and voice. "Thirty years ago, we barely met, right, you and me? We spent, what, an hour together? That trip with Wade and Mitch in the raft to Giant's Fist. That whole time, you were staring at me like I was a monster. Then up in the cave, suddenly you can see stairs that no one else can.

"That's when I first realized you weren't like other Rangers, Finch. You were special. And then you find the knife, and suddenly the Eldritch are coming out of the sky. You have the spirits themselves on your side. You could literally walk on water!

You were only a Squirrel, but you could do things no other Ranger could do. I wanted to be like you."

"How do you remember all this?" asked Arlo. "No one else does. The Eldritch light should have erased it all."

"You left me behind, remember? I was on Giant's Fist with Mitch. He stayed outside to watch the action, but I decided it was safer to tuck back into the cave. I climbed those steps into that nowhere place . . ."

Arlo suddenly realized why Alva Hadryn Thomas remembered things. "They couldn't unwind you. Because you weren't even in the same dimension."

"By the time I came out, the Eldritch were gone. No one remembered they were ever there. Everyone thought I was a crazy person, talking about lights coming out of the sky. I'm not sure who decided it was a tornado that destroyed Summerland, but everyone agreed that's what had happened. It was the most logical explanation, I suppose. No one remembered you, either. But I did. There was a boy named Finch who could do impossible things.

"I decided that day that I was going to do impossible things, too."

While Hadryn was talking, Arlo felt the vines around his wrists and ankles loosen slightly. Did Hadryn have to keep concentrating on them? Arlo tried to wiggle more slack without being too obvious.

Hadryn continued: "I stuck with Rangers. I earned my Owl, and my Wolf, and my Ram and my Bear. I took the Vigil. I learned everything. But I didn't learn the things you could do. I couldn't control spirits. I couldn't see hidden things. Because I wasn't like you, Finch. I wasn't born like you. I wasn't a tooble."

He said that word deliberately, looking for Arlo's reaction.

"Yeah, Arlo Finch, I know what you are. I know why the Eldritch need you." He held up the wrapped knife. "It's not because of this—they want it, sure, but it's *you* they really want. They've been looking for you almost as long as I have."

"Why?"

"Because that spirit in you makes you good at finding things. Better than anyone, maybe. Certainly better than me." Arlo wondered if Hadryn knew about Rielle. If she was a tooble, maybe she had the same skills.

"The Eldritch and me, we've had a few run-ins. I've stolen some things. They keep trying to catch me, but this"—he held out the yellow crystal on his necklace—"makes me difficult to find. Almost as hard as you."

Hadryn paced as he talked. "After that night on the lake, I looked everywhere for you. But there was no Finch on the camp roster. How was I to know you'd traveled through time? Very sneaky, by the way."

"It was an accident."

"There are no accidents, Arlo Finch!"

"It was the moon! It was in just the right place, and we were on the lake . . ."

"And somehow you ended up at exactly that moment? That place, that time? You still don't understand, do you, Finch? You find ways into things that no one else can. Even when you're not looking for them, you find them."

Instinct, thought Arlo. Those moments when he calmed his mind and let his inner spirit guide him.

"I looked everywhere for you," said Hadryn. "But all I had was your name: Finch. And there were no Finches that matched you anywhere. Because you hadn't been born yet, it turns out. So I did the next best thing. I learned everything else there was to learn, especially the things they don't teach Rangers. And if someone didn't want to teach me, I'd find a way to make them.

"Those vows you make as a Ranger? Those principles? I used to think they were noble. But I came to see them for what they really are. They're chains holding us back. We were put here to blaze trails, not follow theirs."

Arlo had nearly worked his left wrist free. He just needed to keep Hadryn busy talking.

"How did you find me?"

"Google, of all things. A couple of years ago, I set up a news alert for any mention of *Finch* and *Ranger*. Then this winter, your patrol placed second in the Alpine Derby. There was a story in the *Pine Valley Gazette* online, with all the Rangers' names. I read it and there was a photo. Click! There you were. The boy I'd met thirty years ago. Only now I was older and you were still twelve."

Hadryn smiled to himself. "Do you know how pathetic it is to be jealous of a twelve-year-old boy? It's pretty sad. But I'm not jealous anymore. This was a long time coming, but I've gotten what I want."

He began unwrapping the knife.

"I'm sorry. I didn't mean to leave you behind on Giant's Fist. I just . . . I thought you were . . ."

"A monster? A villain? That's just it, Finch. You were right. You were just early."

Hadryn unveiled the knife handle, shaking off thirty years of dust and dirt. He wiped it clean on his shirttails, then grasped it tight. He smiled as he suddenly was able to see the translucent blade.

He kneeled down in front of Arlo. "After all this, it would be very fitting if I just slit your throat. If I took your life for what you've done to mine." He held the translucent blade to Arlo's neck. "But it would go right through you. And the truth is, you're still more useful alive than dead. This knife is not the only artifact out there. There are treasures you cannot imagine. And together, we'll find them."

"I won't help you," said Arlo.

"You won't have a choice," said Hadryn. "I know where you live, Arlo Finch. I know your family, your friends, your school, your patrol. And I'm guessing you'd rather they be alive than dead. So you'll do exactly as I tell you."

Arlo didn't answer. He willed himself not to cry, but he felt the edges of his eyes getting wet.

"Let's start with an easy one. I need you to choose between Indra and Wu. Who should I kill first?"

Arlo refused to answer, or even look him in the eye.

"You have to pick a best friend, Arlo. You can only have one.

The other one dies." Hadryn shrugged when Arlo again didn't answer. "Well, we'll do eeny meeny, then. Or you can just give me what I want."

Arlo looked up, sniffling. "Okay."

"Okay, what?"

"I'll help you! What are you looking for?" Arlo hoped the tears would convince Hadryn he had given up, that he was willing to cooperate.

Hadryn smiled. "I know what the Eldritch want more than anything. And if we can find it first, we could live like gods."

Then, a sound. A rustle. It was coming from the trees. Hadryn looked up, confused. "What is that?"

As if to answer, an ear-piercing wail rang out. Then another. Then dozens.

"Howlers," said Arlo. "They're attracted by peanut butter."

It took Hadryn a moment to understand what Arlo was implying. "Where would you get peanut butter?"

The caterwaul kept growing louder. The trees began shaking. How many howlers were there? Hundreds? More?

"I got it from Wade. Remember? He had it in his pack."

At the Broken Bridge, just before he hid the flashlight under the stone, Arlo had had an idea. He rubbed the knife with peanut butter and rewrapped it in the neckerchief before putting it back in the flashlight. He suspected the peanut butter would dry out over the next thirty years, but he hoped just enough would remain.

That was the dust Hadryn had shaken off. But it was on him. His hands. His clothes. He was covered in it.

Suddenly, the howlers erupted from the trees in a wave of teeth and fur and claws. Arlo couldn't even make them out clearly at first, not until Hadryn had thrown one off. Just larger than a squirrel, the howler was apparently blind—it had no eye sockets. It sniffed the air and leaped back into the swarm. Arlo had never seen anything so ferocious.

He felt the vines loosen around his wrists and ankles. He fought his way to his feet.

Hadryn was screaming, completely covered with howlers. They were like a vicious fur coat.

Arlo started kicking over the wards. He felt a ripple of energy as they fell.

Trying to break free of the howlers, Hadryn kept changing forms, growing larger and smaller. His necklace broke, and the yellow crystal was stomped into the dirt.

Finally, Hadryn dropped the knife. Arlo dove for it. But once the knife was in his hands, a few of the howlers suddenly became interested in him. There was still enough peanut butter on it to be attractive.

He had to get out of there. But where could he go that the howlers couldn't reach him? The forest surrounded them on three sides, and the fourth was a cliff.

Arlo chose the cliff. Psyching himself up, Arlo Finch ran full speed and jumped.

In cartoons, when a character falls off a cliff, they hang for a second in midair. Arlo didn't. He immediately began plunging towards the bottom of the canyon.

He grabbed the knife as tightly as he could, hoping to spot a shimmering cloud coming to catch him. But there didn't seem to be any hope. There wasn't time. He was going to smash against the jagged rocks in three, two . . .

The air suddenly swept up from below, lifting him. His ankles dragged along the tops of pine trees.

Breezy had caught him. He was alive.

Arlo looked back up to the top of the mountain, where the sky was cracking open.

"Up!" shouted Arlo, pointing. The wind carried him higher so he could see.

A smoky tendril reached down and enveloped Hadryn. Arlo could see him writhing and fighting it, but to no avail. He was stuck.

Hadryn locked eyes with Arlo, shouting something Arlo couldn't hear. It seemed like a warning, or a threat.

The tentacle pulled Hadryn up into the heavens. The crack sealed over.

Hadryn was gone.

48
FIREBIRD

CARRIED BY THE WIND, Arlo slowly descended to the gravel road near the Trading Post. Ten feet. Five feet. He reached with his toes, hoping to make a perfect superhero landing.

But he hadn't anticipated how hard it would be to find his balance. He teetered, slipped, then fell back on his butt. Dust swirled as Big Breezy departed.

It was embarrassing. At least no one had seen it.

"Finch?!"

Arlo looked back to see Darnell and Trix. Both were wearing shorts and running shoes, evidently out for a morning jog.

"Hey, Darnell. Hey, Trix." Arlo got to his feet, wiping off the dust and dirt.

"Was that Big Breezy?" asked Darnell.

Arlo shrugged. "Yeah."

"Look at you, trying to sound humble." Darnell looked at Trix. "This kid's just a Squirrel, you believe that?"

"I know! I have him for Canoeing."

"You all right, Finch? You good?"

Arlo smiled. "I'm good."

"See you in class, then." With that, Darnell and Trix jogged past him. Arlo saw Trix playfully poke Darnell in the ribs, then sprint ahead.

Indra and Julie are right, thought Arlo. *They're definitely dating.*

Arlo was surprised to find himself the first back at Firebird. The campsite was deserted, tent flaps still open from the night before.

He wasn't sure how long he'd been on the mountaintop with Hadryn, but he'd figured Fox would have been able to lead the rest of the patrol back faster than this. Arlo retrieved his Ranger's compass and was ready to go out to search for his friends, when he heard familiar voices.

Indra, Wu, Jonas and Julie emerged from the aspen grove. Like Arlo, they were exhausted, but still managed to run the last few steps. What started as a series of individual hugs became a group huddle.

"Wait," said Julie, pulling away. "How do we know it's really him?"

"She's right," said Indra. "Say something only you would know."

Arlo racked his brain to come up with a new detail to convince them of his identity. He ended up reaching back to a moment nine months earlier. "The night of my first Ranger meeting, you were waterproofing the seams in the tent. I didn't even know that was something you had to do. I remember looking at the other patrols and being sure that Blue Patrol was the best one. I couldn't explain why. I just knew. I knew right from the start."

They pulled him in for another hug. In the distance, a bugle sounded reveille.

"Guys, it's time to get up!" said Wu.

They laughed. They'd been awake all night.

Over a big breakfast, Blue Patrol tried to sort out what had happened and what their next steps should be.

"I knew Thomas was bad from the start," said Julie. "He was too nice. No one's that nice all the time."

As they went over the events of the previous ten days, it became clear that Thomas-slash-Hadryn had impersonated each of them at different times. He had asked probing questions and stirred discord whenever possible. And he'd seemed convinced that the patrol already had the knife.

"I wondered why Arlo was always searching his own backpack," said Jonas. "Every time I came back to camp, you were digging around in your tent."

Arlo turned to Indra. "Were you really planning to transfer to Green Patrol, or was that him?"

This was news to the rest of the patrol.

"I mean, I considered it," said Indra. "I talked to Diana about it."

"You can't leave!" insisted Julie.

Jonas agreed: "It would be so weird without you."

"Green Patrol doesn't need you," said Wu. "We do. We'd be dead without you."

"I know," said Indra. "But that's not the only reason I'm staying. I can't imagine being in Rangers without you guys."

Indra, Wu and Arlo apologized to the twins for keeping them in the dark about the Broken Bridge. And since it was impossible to know exactly who had said what to whom, the patrol decided to enact a blanket policy of forgiveness.

Jonas proposed the wording: "Anything that was said before this moment is hereby forgiven." They all put in their hands to swear on it.

Next they had to figure out what to say to others about Thomas. "People are going to notice we're one patrol member short," said Indra.

Ultimately, they decided to tell Diana what had happened. They left out certain details about Fox, the knife and the Broken Bridge, but made it clear that Thomas was an impostor who had been taken by the Eldritch. Diana went with them to tell Warden Mpasu, who seemed intrigued by the whole thing.

"And through all this, you didn't think to come to me for help?" she asked.

"We thought about it," said Wu, looking at Arlo and Indra. "But we didn't know if we could trust you. You could have been the impostor."

Indra agreed, adding: "And on the first night, you said you wanted us to solve our own problems. So we did."

Warden Mpasu shook her head. Arlo couldn't tell if she was impressed or annoyed. "The fact is, you could have been killed."

Arlo stepped forward. "Honestly, Warden, things have been trying to kill me for a while. I wouldn't be alive without my patrol. So if you're going to blame anybody, blame me. I'm the one who caused all this."

She looked at each of them closely, as if judging their souls. Then she rendered her verdict. "This camp always finds a way to teach its lessons, and never in ways we expect. It seems you've learned something at least." With a nod, she dismissed them.

"I have one more thing," said Wu. He took his phone from his pocket. Indra was aghast to see it. "I should have handed this in the first night. It's my fault. I'll take the demerits, or punishment, or whatever."

Mpasu took the phone. "Why reveal this now?" she asked. "The camp is nearly over. You could have easily kept it secret."

"It's the principle, I guess," said Wu. "It wouldn't have been true."

Arlo spent the last few days of camp simply being a Ranger. He went hiking. He tried out archery and rock-climbing. One blazingly hot afternoon, he went swimming by choice.

At Wu's suggestion, they came up with a new duty roster. Arlo got to cook for the first time: chili dogs and green beans. The chili got a little burned on the bottom, but that added texture and a smoky flavor.

Pine Mountain Company won their game of Capture the Flag against Cheyenne Company. With the rest of Blue Patrol running as decoys, Jonas carried the flag across the line.

In Canoeing, Arlo and Indra placed first in the tandem race. The secret was to pretend there was a giant mystical serpent chasing you. Arlo earned that skill patch along with one for Elementary Spirits, which put him on track to get his Owl rank by fall.

It rained on the final afternoon of camp. Arlo found himself in his tent playing spades with Indra and Wu. They were simply hanging out. They hadn't done that in a long time.

As she was shuffling the cards, Indra asked Arlo whether he was ever aware of the second spirit inside him.

He wasn't. "It's like how you don't feel your blood. It's just part of you."

"I wonder why the spirit picked you?" asked Wu.

"It didn't," said Indra. "It picked Arlo's mom." She dealt the next hand.

As Arlo sorted through his cards, he considered the random chance that had led to his holding three sevens in his hand. *Why not three sixes? Or four fives?* "I don't think the spirit picked anyone," he said. "I think it just happened."

"But your mom wouldn't have been in the Long Woods if you hadn't taken her there," said Wu.

Indra agreed. "He's right. It was fate."

"After all, you're the mystical-destiny guy."

"But what if I'm not?" asked Arlo. "This whole time, I thought it was some kind of prophecy. Like I was special, unique, and the universe had picked me for some reason. But that's not really true. It's like these cards. You get what you're dealt, but it's how you play them that matters."

Wu objected. "What about the stuff Indra found in Pinereading? The forest had already picked you."

"Not really," said Indra. "Pinereading is history, not prophecy."

Arlo agreed. "That wasn't about what I was *going* to do. It was about what I'd *already done*. And that's the thing: I could have said no to all of it. Big Breezy, Summerland, crossing the lake—I could have decided to just stay put. But I went for it. And I don't think I would have before Rangers, not before I met you."

Wu and Indra exchanged a look, surprised to find themselves singled out.

"It's not about my eyes or my mom. Who I am isn't fate or destiny, really. But it's not an accident, either. It's like . . ." *Like what?* he wondered. *Like these cards. Like paths in a forest. Like life.*

"I wasn't *chosen*." he said. "I *chose*."

49
EXTRACTION

"IS IT GONNA HURT?"

"I don't know," said Arlo. "It might."

Russell shrugged. "It's fine. Just do it." He pulled his T-shirt up over his head. The fabric passed right through the spectral grisp, whose fangs were latched deep into the boy's meaty shoulder. But Arlo suspected the real connection was ethereal: a thread of light extending from the creature's thorax into Russell's shoulder. It looked very much like the silver cord that had ensnared Big Breezy. The spirit knife had cut that binding. It should be able to cut this one.

It was the last morning of camp. Tents had been swept out, dining canopies folded. At the flag ceremony that morning, Diana had told all patrols to be ready to hike down to the parking lot at nine A.M. sharp.

As the Rangers were dispersing, Arlo had pulled Russell aside and asked if he wanted him to try to remove the grisp. Now, with ten minutes left before leaving camp, Arlo and Russell were standing in the middle of the aspen grove, just out of sight of the rest of the company.

Arlo raised the spirit knife. With it, he could see the grisp, and the grisp could evidently see him. Its eyes swiveled, reacting to the threat.

As the smoky blade poked against the creature's scales, all ten legs skittered across Russell's back. Yet its mandibles remained firmly locked.

Russell craned his neck to look. "What's happening?"

"Just hold still," Arlo warned.

Arlo could now see the silver thread clearly. He turned the blade, and with one quick flick sliced through it.

The grisp spasmed so violently that Arlo jumped back. Russell was understandably alarmed: "What is it? What did you do?"

Without the cord to connect it to Russell's body, the grisp began slipping to the ground. As it fell, it pulled something with it: thick spectral tentacles that writhed and convulsed, twisting themselves into pretzel-like knots. They spilled out in a wriggling heap.

What Arlo had thought of as the grisp was actually just the creature's head. Most of it had been growing inside Russell's body like a nightmare squid.

Russell fell to his knees, woozy and shaking. He couldn't see the wriggling mass beside him. That was probably for the best.

"Did you get it?" asked Russell.

Arlo nodded.

Like an octopus on land, the grisp tumbled over itself to move. It was desperately trying to get away.

Arlo debated pursuing it. He suspected he could kill it with the knife. But he also saw the grisp for what it was: a simple creature of the spirit world. It wasn't evil, not any more than a spider or a shark. It was simply surviving as best it could.

He watched as it disappeared into the brush, then looked back at Russell. "How do you feel?"

"Different," said Russell, slowly rising to his feet. "Better. Like when you're sick and you throw up and you're better after that." He pulled his shirt down, then wiped the last bit of blood off his neck. His color was already improving.

"You're not going to tell anyone about this, right?" It was a question, not a threat.

"No," said Arlo.

Russell looked him in the eye. "Thanks."

With that, Russell Stokes turned and walked back to camp.

Arlo stood alone in the aspen grove for another minute, watching the floating fields of light around him. Each one was a spirit. None of them were as intelligent as Fox, but they were definitely alive.

He felt the wind in his hair. The leaves shook. Arlo smiled.

Big Breezy didn't have words, but she was conscious. She had recognized Arlo after waiting for him for thirty years. Her mind was completely alien, but there was clearly a mind. The notion that the Eldritch could shackle her to use her power was repugnant. It was like kidnapping a person to be a slave. A civilization that would do that wasn't civilized.

The spirit knife could cut those bindings. Maybe that's why the Eldritch had wanted it so badly. They were afraid of the spirits getting loose.

They were right to be afraid.

Arlo put the spirit knife back in his pocket. The moment his fingers left the handle, the fields of light faded. He was back fully in the normal world.

It was time to leave Camp Redfeather.

50
THE RETURN

AS THE BUS PULLED into the church parking lot, Blue Patrol rushed to the windows to look at who had come to meet them.

Connor was standing with his father. He was wearing a face mask like a surgeon, but he was alive and upright. He waved as the bus pulled in.

The patrol crowded around him. "I'll be okay," he said. "They had to take out my spleen, but I can live without it. I just have to be more careful to not get infections." The mask was just a precaution for a few days, and only when he was out of the house.

Connor said he couldn't do anything strenuous while his stitches healed, but he assured them he'd be back up to full speed by the Alpine Derby.

Wu proposed they elect Connor patrol leader again. The vote was unanimous.

While everyone was talking, Arlo spotted his mom waiting on the sidewalk.

He began walking towards her without consciously realizing it, pulled by a kind of gravity. In his mother's face, he could see the outline of nine-year-old Celeste's. He dropped his pack and hugged her tight. "I missed you," she said, ruffling his hair. "I was worried about you."

"I was worried about you, too."

Uncle Wade had returned from Jackson Hole late the night before. Arlo found him in his workshop, smashing apart a salvaged newspaper vending machine.

Arlo asked him how his art installation had gone.

"Can't imagine it could have gone any worse," said Wade, tossing the hammer on his workbench. "These resort owners, the buyers, they throw this big party. An unveiling. Fine. It's your money, I'm thinking. I'll eat some appetizers. Some canapés. But then they go and invite the worst kind of people. Fancy New York and California types—you know, the ones who read *Artforum*."

Arlo didn't know those people.

"So they're looking at it all, and I can hear them murmuring. That's what these people do; they never actually speak, they just murmur." Wade imitated the sound. "And then one of them, this bald guy with little glasses that pinch on his nose, he says to me, 'Your work is an indictment of the American caste system.' Can you believe that?"

Arlo couldn't, mostly because he didn't understand what it meant.

"Who's this guy to tell me what my art means? Then he goes and reviews it online. Online, for anyone to see! My buddy Nacho, he gets an alert and reads it aloud to me on the phone."

"Was it bad?"

"It was awful! This guy calls me a 'genius provocateur.' A 'once-in-a-decade-talent.' The biggest discovery since Ferdinand Cheval."

All of these sounded like compliments to Arlo.

"The phone hasn't stopped ringing. Not just from people wanting to commission me, but agents and galleries. How am I supposed to get any work done when people keep trying to fly me to New York or Paris?"

Wade went back to his work, taking a screwdriver to the newspaper machine door.

Arlo paused for a moment, considering his next words. "I found something I think you might want." Arlo pulled the photo from his back pocket, unfolding it. "It's Yellow Patrol. You're at the Summerland campsite."

Wade took the photo. Studied it. Exhaled loudly.

"That's me, obviously. Mitch, Chuck, Jason. Except who is that?" He pointed at the one kid mostly obscured by the others.

"Thomas from Texas."

"That's right! The new kid. Wonder whatever happened to him."

"His name's Hadryn now," said Arlo. "He's pretty much evil."

"Well. Never really liked him anyway." Wade handed Arlo back the photo. "There's something I've been meaning to ask you for a while, Arlo. This is going to sound crazy, but we are both familiar with some very unlikely ideas, so I want you to tell me honestly . . ."

From a nearby drawer, Wade pulled out an old photograph. It was glossy, faded on the edges.

"Is that you?"

The photo showed Arlo, Thomas and Mitch. They were in the raft, looking back at Wade, blinded by the flash.

"It's me," said Arlo, taking the photo. He remembered the precise moment it was taken during the raft trip to Giant's Fist.

"Found it a couple of months ago. Held off showing it to you until you got back, just in case it created a paradox or temporal loop."

"I don't think it works like that," said Arlo. "What happened, happened."

Wade nodded, *Fair enough.*

"Tell me what you remember," said Arlo.

Wade sat down on his stool, balancing the handle of the screwdriver on the workbench. "Well, I know we'd caught us a little water spirit. Me and Mitch mostly, but the whole Yellow Patrol was in on it. We had it in this big pot in the center of camp. Not like we were going to hurt it or anything. We were just screwing around.

"Then Mitch, he had a raft. A small one. He and I got to talking that we should row out to Giant's Fist. I guess you and the other kid were with us."

"We were," said Arlo.

"This part gets hazy, but we're out at Giant's Fist, and we're looking back at Summerland. Suddenly, this storm kicks up out of nowhere. Clouds and thunder. This crazy light."

The Eldritch, thought Arlo. *Wade remembers them as a storm.*

"And I guess it was a tornado, but it felt more like an explosion. Right in the center of camp. Knocked down trees. Blew them apart. Some kids got hurt—one boy broke his arm—but it's a miracle no one got killed. That cyclone, whatever it was, it destroyed Summerland. Looked like a bomb had gone off.

"Next morning, they're investigating what happened, and it all comes back to that water spirit we'd been keeping. Wardens say that some Yellow Patrollers must have been tormenting it or something. Like maybe they put the pot on the fire to boil. Everyone swears they didn't, but who knows. Kids do stupid stuff. The Wardens figure that the other spirits got so angry that they brought the storm. Smashed the camp to get it back."

"What happened to Yellow Patrol?" asked Arlo.

"They sent us home. Our parents had to come pick us up. Believe me, that's an unpleasant four-hour car ride. My dad—your granddad—he was not pleased and told me quite plainly what a disappointment I was. Not the last time he said that, incidentally. The next week, they disbanded Yellow Patrol. Some of the kids went to other patrols, but me, I just quit. I couldn't see myself ever going back to Rangers. Not after that."

Wade took a big swig from his energy drink. "You and that girl friend of yours, you keep digging around about Yellow Patrol like it's some big secret. It's not, really. It's just something I don't care to revisit. There'll be things in your life you'll regret. Dumb mistakes, bad choices. They're like these awful tattoos you can't get rid of. So you wear something over them. Keep them out of sight. That's all I've been doing. Just trying not to look at it."

Now that Wade was finished, Arlo was ready to explain about the Eldritch, the spirit knife and their midnight visit to Pine Mountain. He could tell Wade that the destruction of Summerland had had nothing to do with the water spirit. That he and Yellow Patrol had been wrongly blamed.

"Do you want to know what really happened that night?" asked Arlo with a smile.

Wade drummed his fingers on the workbench as he considered. Finally, he shook his head. "It was thirty years ago. If I got the details wrong, if it didn't all go down quite the way I remember, then knowing the truth's not going to change anything. Like you said, 'What happened, happened.' Best leave the past to the past and get started on what's next."

He picked up his screwdriver and went back to work disassembling the newspaper machine. Wade had decided the conversation was over.

Arlo set the photo facedown on the workbench. That's when he noticed three names written on the back in pencil:

MITCH
THOMAS
FINCH?

They were simple box letters, but Arlo immediately recognized the handwriting. He'd seen it before in the margin of Pine Mountain Elementary's copy of *Culman's Bestiary*, next to the entry for *Troll*. Someone had written *FINCH*.

"Wade, did you . . ." Arlo stopped to consider what his uncle had just said about wanting to leave the past in the past. Arlo didn't need to know every answer. It wouldn't help anything. It would just take Wade back to a place where he didn't want to be.

"Did I what?" asked Wade.

Arlo changed the question: "Did you always love Black Flag?"

"Heck, yeah. It's true punk. That's never gonna change."

51
UNBOUND

SUNSET IN THE SUMMER wasn't a distinct moment, but rather a gradual transition from blue to pink to orange. You barely noticed it was happening until suddenly everything took on a golden glow.

It was Arlo's favorite time of day. Even with his eyes closed, he could hear the change as crickets began chirping and new birds took over from the daytime shift.

Arlo was on the front porch, stirring his dirty camp socks in a bucket of soapy water with a stick. He wasn't sure how much bleach to add, so he kept pouring until it smelled like the public swimming pool in Chicago. Then he added a splash more for good measure.

He had just screwed the cap back on the bottle when he saw Rielle waving from the edge of the woods. Arlo had been wondering when she'd come.

Rielle seemed less nervous than the last time they'd spoken.

She wasn't checking over her shoulder or trying to stay hidden. *They know she's here,* Arlo thought. *They probably sent her.*

"They want the knife, don't they?" he asked.

Rielle nodded. "They're worried it could fall into the wrong hands."

Whose hands? Arlo thought. "You already have Hadryn. It's safe."

"What if someone else tries to take it from you, though—or threatens your family and your friends? You want to keep them safe, don't you?" Her words sounded practiced. Coached. Arlo wondered if the Eldritch were listening.

In case they were, he spoke slowly and clearly: "If anyone tries to take it, or comes after my family, or my friends, they'll regret it." He had been practicing, too.

For half a second, Rielle gave a glimmer of a smile. Arlo wondered if it was real.

"What is it like there, where the Eldritch live?" asked Arlo.

Rielle seemed surprised by the question. "The Realm? It's incredible."

"Incredible how?"

"For starters, it's beautiful. Not like the Long Woods, but more like Paris or Rome, I guess."

"The Realm is a city?"

"In a way. There are buildings, things we'd call palaces, but everyone has them. Everyone's equal. Everyone's an artist. There's no war, or poverty, or suffering. No one gets sick, or old, or dies. It's basically paradise. You'll see."

"When?" asked Arlo.

"Soon, I think. That's probably why they're letting you keep the knife."

She wasn't supposed to say that, thought Arlo.

Rielle seemed to catch her mistake, adding, "They told me to tell you that what happened at the lake was a misunderstanding. They didn't know who you were back then. What you were. You're very important to them."

"So are you, right?"

A shrug. "I don't know. Maybe they only need one of us. You seem to be the one who's good at finding things."

Is she jealous or relieved? Arlo wondered.

Rielle shooed away an oddly persistent fly. It was moments like these that reminded Arlo that Rielle was just a kid like him. He joined her in waving it off. Rielle smiled, then suddenly took a step forward, whispering into Arlo's ear: "Do you remember what we saw at the bonfire?"

Arlo did.

Months earlier, at the Alpine Derby, Arlo had found himself standing next to Rielle. It was just the two of them. Everyone else had vanished. A flaming dragon had floated above the bonfire. It didn't move. It simply burned.

It's sleeping, Rielle had said. *It's been sleeping for centuries. This is its dream.*

Back in the present, Arlo whispered to Rielle, "They want to find the dragon, don't they?" Rielle nodded. "Why? What do they need it for?"

"I'm not sure," said Rielle. "I just know it's important."

Just then, a blue jay landed on a nearby branch. Was it simply a bird, or an eavesdropper? A tiny breeze stirred the grass. Was that just the wind, or a spirit? Every moment—every sound—felt heightened. Loaded with portent. Rielle and Arlo each took a step back.

"That's all I needed to tell you," said Rielle. "Enjoy your summer, Arlo Finch."

"You too."

She smiled. "It's autumn there. It's always autumn." With that, she headed back into the forest.

Arlo hesitated, then called out after her, "You're wrong, though!" Rielle turned, but he was speaking to the Eldritch as much as to her. "You said the Realm was paradise, but it's not. Not for the spirits they've captured."

She gave him an odd look, a cross between pity and disappointment. "You don't understand."

"Sure I do. The Eldritch are keeping them as prisoners."

"Look around, Arlo. So are you." Rielle turned and kept walking. A few steps later, she circled behind a tree and vanished.

Arlo puzzled over what Rielle could have meant. He was nothing like the Eldritch. In fact, he was the opposite of them. He had freed Big Breezy and stopped other spirits from being taken. He had vowed to protect them. To say he was imprisoning spirits was a flat-out lie.

Walking back to the porch, Arlo spotted Cooper making his rounds. Dawn and twilight were the most reliable times to see the ghostly dog. Perhaps the borders between the worlds were thinnest then.

Arlo kneeled down on the driveway and waited for Cooper to approach. As always, the dog clawed at the dirt by the tree stump. Arlo skritched the space behind the dog's translucent ear, knowing that in exactly seven seconds Cooper would cock his head, hearing a distant noise. He would begin silently barking at something on the road.

Arlo suddenly knew what it was. *It was the Eldritch.* The dog took off running, pursuing this nonexistent threat. Arlo stood up and watched, a sinking feeling in his stomach. Cooper's endless loop had begun thirty years earlier, on the night the Eldritch arrived. This event was forever imprinted on the dog, a memory of pure supernatural terror. Even after death, Cooper had been stuck repeating it forever.

Arlo slipped his hand into his pocket. As his fingers grasped the spirit knife's handle, he closed his eyes. He was nervous about what he would see.

Three. Two. One. Arlo opened his eyes.

A glowing silver cord stretched from the ground where Cooper had been scratching to the road. It was like a leash. A chain. This was what was keeping the dog tethered there.

Cooper started trotting back, the loop repeating. Reaching the stump, the spectral dog pawed at the ground. This time, Arlo saw it differently. Cooper wasn't just idly sniffing. He was clawing at the silver cord. He was trying to dig it out. Break it. He was trying to get free.

After seven long seconds, Cooper looked up, hearing the sound by the road. He barked silently at the threat that would never actually come. Then he took off running.

With his free hand, Arlo wiped the edges of his eyes. He kneeled down and waited.

Cooper returned, and began digging futilely at the dirt. Arlo petted behind the dog's ear. "I'm so sorry," he said. "I didn't know."

Arlo took the spirit knife and cut cleanly through the silver cord. It dissolved.

Cooper looked up. This time, he didn't stare at the road. He looked Arlo directly in the eyes. He seemed to recognize him. Cooper leaned his muzzle against Arlo's hand, his phantom tongue licking.

"You're free, okay, boy?" Arlo's voice trembled. "You don't have to stay here any longer."

Arlo knew that Cooper didn't really understand, but the dog's natural curiosity eventually kicked in. Tail wagging, Cooper began exploring the area, venturing off the path he'd been walking for decades. He sniffed and scratched, leaping over rocks.

There were other spirits in the field—floating swaths of light that seemed to fascinate Cooper. He silently barked, chasing them.

Arlo sat on the gravel, smiling through tears.

As Cooper reached the edge of the forest, the dog turned and looked back at Arlo.

"It's okay!" shouted Arlo, his voice cracking. "You can go."

Cooper bobbed his head, then disappeared into the woods.

52
REUNION

JAYCEE RETURNED FROM CHINA one week later. Arlo went with his mom to pick her up.

The Denver airport had a roof that looked like a massive tent, with endless fields of white canvas stretched across giant poles, secured with steel cables wider than his arm. Arlo wondered how much fabric it took, and if it ever got torn, and why anyone had thought to build it that way.

He stood by his mom, scanning the crowd as a new batch of passengers emerged from the escalators.

Arlo spotted his sister before she saw him. Jaycee was carrying her pillow and a small backpack, headphones in her ears. She looked much older than Arlo had expected. Not just mature, but *old*, like a teenager who had suddenly turned sixty.

"Jaycee!" their mom shouted, waving. His sister smiled wanly. She consented to a hug across the stanchion lines.

"How was your flight?" their mom asked. "Did you have any trouble at Immigration?"

"It was all fine," Jaycee said.

"Bet you're glad to be back."

"Yeah," she said.

Arlo knew she was lying.

Back at the house, Jaycee ate a bowl of cereal and went to her room. She shut the door. Arlo heard the lock click.

"Jet lag is rough," said their mom. "Especially at this age. Your body doesn't know whether it's day or night."

"The airplane is essentially a form of time travel," agreed Wade. "Half of you is one place, the other half of you is still back where you left it. That's why I refuse to fly. If I'm going someplace, I want all of me together." He shook the milk carton to see how much was left, then put it to his lips and drank from it.

"Wade!" protested Arlo's mom.

"I'm finishing it!"

"It's still a bad example."

Wade wiped the remaining milk from his lips. "C'mon, Celeste. These kids don't look up to me. At best, I'm a cautionary tale." He gently knuckled her head as he walked out.

Arlo watched his mom's reaction. She shut her eyes and shook her head, but with the tiniest smile. Maybe it had always been there, but Arlo was noticing it for the first time.

Jaycee picked at her dinner, then headed outside. She was carrying her phone. Arlo knew where she was headed.

He found her sitting on Signal Rock, feet dangling over the edge, looking out over the valley in the pink light of dusk. She wiped her eyes as he approached.

He stopped, not sure whether to come any closer. Then she waved a hand. It was fine.

"Do you have photos of Dad?" he asked, sitting down beside her.

She handed him her phone. As he scrolled through her photos, he scarcely recognized his sister. In the photos, she was smiling, laughing, silly. She looked giddy. He hadn't seen her that happy in years.

It was easy to see why: their dad. Whenever he was in the shot, Jaycee was leaning against him. When he was taking the photo, Jaycee was looking directly into the lens, beaming.

Most of the shots were from Guangzhou, the city where their father lived. Arlo flipped through trains and restaurants and tiny stores packed with trinkets. But there was one batch of photos from a forest, where Jaycee and their dad had evidently hiked.

"Where was this?" he asked.

"It's right in the city. This huge park with temples and a lake. But it wasn't crowded at all. There were parts of it that reminded me a lot of here. You're just out in nature."

The final shot in the roll was one of their father at the airport in Guangzhou. Dad was smiling, but Arlo could see a glisten in his eyes, tears he was fighting back.

"That's a good photo," he said.

"Thanks."

"I wish Dad could be here with us."

Jaycee shook her head. "It's not going to happen. They're never going to let him back in the country."

"You don't know that."

"I do. He told me. He said even if he went to another country, they would arrest him." Her voice quavered. "He's stuck there forever."

Arlo scrolled back a few photos, looking at the Chinese forest. The next idea came to him so quickly it startled him, like a ghost whispering in his ear.

That forest in China was really no different from the forest in Pine Mountain. It had to connect to the Long Woods. After all, *the Long Woods go everywhere.* They must even go to China.

Arlo looked at his sister. "Let's go get him."

This book is dedicated to three locations that helped inspire it.

The first is Ben Delatour Scout Ranch in Colorado, and the nearby Red Feather Lakes. I'm grateful for the years I spent walking these trails and scrambling over these boulders.

The second is Traunsee, a lake in central Austria. I gasped the first time I saw it, and marveled every time after that.

The third is Pont d'Avignon, an unfinished bridge across the Rhône river in the south of France. Like the best fiction, the mind fills in what's missing.

—J.A.

DON'T MISS

ARLO FINCH
IN THE KINGDOM OF SHADOWS

COMING IN 2020

DISCUSSION QUESTIONS

1. Most of the action in *Lake of the Moon* takes place away from Pine Mountain. In what ways does leaving home affect how you act?

2. Arlo finds himself caught in a power struggle between Indra and Wu, but doesn't want to pick sides. What are some challenges of being friends with people who don't get along? Have you found yourself in that situation?

3. A major theme in *Lake of the Moon* is trust. How does Arlo decide who he can trust? How do you decide who to trust in your own life?

4. Darnell warns Arlo that Ranger skills (like shifting) can be used for evil. Can knowledge be dangerous? Who should decide what can be taught?

5. Is Arlo to blame for Thomas becoming Hadryn?

6. Arlo meets his mother and uncle as kids. In what ways are young Celeste and Wade like their adult forms? How are they different?

7. As part of the Ranger's Vow, Arlo promises to "guard the wild" and "defend the weak." Does he do that in *Lake of the Moon*? Do you do that in your own life?

8. Big Breezy has no body and no voice. Is she still a character? If so, what are her most important traits?

9. Arlo declares he wasn't destined to be a hero. "I wasn't *chosen*," he said. "I *chose*." How does that compare with heroes in other stories you've read?

10. The Eldritch rely on bound spirits to power their devices. Can you think of other societies that used captured beings to do their work?

11. Why does Arlo decide to cut Cooper's silver cord? Would you do it if you were in the same situation?

THE RANGER'S VOW

LOYAL, BRAVE, KIND AND TRUE—
KEEPER OF THE OLD AND NEW—
I GUARD THE WILD,
DEFEND THE WEAK,
MARK THE PATH,
AND VIRTUE SEEK.
FOREST SPIRITS HEAR ME NOW
AS I SPEAK MY RANGER'S VOW.